The Highwayman

A Novel Inspired by
Alfred Noyes' Poem

by Deborah Ballou

**Cover designed by
Dean Lundstrom**

ISBN: 1-4033-0593-5 (Softcover)
ISBN: 1-4033-0592-7 (Electronic)

This book is printed on acid free paper.

1stBooks - rev. 05/20/02

Dedicated with love and gratitude to my husband—*my* highwayman,
though he never stole anything except my heart
and rides an iron horse instead of a real one—
for his constant love, support, and tolerance.

My thanks, too, to all my family and friends who helped bring this
book to production, especially Judith, Elaine, Peggy, Chris, and Joan
for their honest critiques,
and my brother, Dean, for his lovely cover design
since some people *do* judge a book by its cover.

And last, but definitely not least, I thank God for lending me His
enthusiasm and His endless strength throughout my life.
I know I am in Good Hands.

The Legend[1]

The wind was a torrent of darkness among the gusty trees,
The moon was a ghostly galleon tossed upon cloudy seas,
The road was a ribbon of moonlight over the purple moor,
And the highwayman came riding—riding, riding—
The highwayman came riding, up to the old inn-door.

He'd a French cocked-hat on his forehead, a bunch of lace at his
*   chin,*
A coat of claret velvet, and breeches of brown doe-skin;
They fitted with never a wrinkle; his boots were up to the thigh!
And he rode with a jeweled twinkle—his pistol butts a-twinkle,
His rapier hilt a-twinkle—under the jeweled sky.

Over the cobbles he clattered and clashed in the dark inn-yard,
And he tapped with his whip on the shutters, but all was locked and
*   barred:*
He whistled a tune to the window, and who should be waiting there
But the landlord's black-eyed daughter—Bess, the landlord's
*   daughter—*
Plaiting a dark red love-knot into her long black hair.

And dark in the dark old inn-yard a stable-wicket creaked
Where Tim the ostler listened, his face was white and peaked;
His eyes were hollows of madness, his hair like moldy hay,
But he loved the landlord's daughter—the landlord's red-lipped
*   daughter.*
Dumb as a dog he listened, and he heard the robber say:

"One kiss, my bonny sweetheart, I'm after a prize tonight,
But I shall be back with the yellow gold before the morning light;
Yet, if they press me sharply and harry me through the day,
Then look for me by moonlight, watch for me by moonlight,
I'll come to thee by moonlight, though hell should bar the way."

---

[1] See last page

He rose upright in the stirrups. He scarce could reach her hand,
But she loosened her hair i' the casement! His face burned like a
*   brand*
As a black cascade of perfume came tumbling over his breast;
And he kissed its waves in the moonlight, (Oh, sweet black waves in
*   the moonlight!)*
Then he tugged at his rein in the moonlight, and galloped away to the
*   West.*

He did not come in the dawning. He did not come at noon;
And out o' the tawny sunset, before the rise o' the moon,
When the road was a gypsy's ribbon, looping the purple moor,
A red-coat troop came marching—marching, marching—
King George's men came marching up to the old inn-door.

They said no word to the landlord, they drank his ale instead,
But they gagged his daughter and bound her to the foot of her narrow
*   bed;*
Two of them knelt at her casement with muskets at their side!
There was death at every window—and hell at one dark window,
For Bess could see through her casement the road that he would ride.

They had tied her up to attention with many a sniggering jest;
They had bound a musket beside her with the barrel beneath her
*   breast!*
"Now keep good watch!" and they kissed her. She heard the dead
*   man say—*
"Look for me by moonlight. Watch for me by moonlight.
I'll come to thee by moonlight though hell should bar the way!"

She twisted her hands behind her, but all the knots held good!
She writhed her hands till her fingers were wet with sweat or blood!
They stretched and strained in the darkness, and the hours crawled by
*   like years,*
Till now, on the stroke of midnight—cold, on the stroke of midnight—
The tip of one finger touched it! The trigger at least was hers!

The tip of one finger touched it; she strove no more for the rest.
Up, she stood at attention, with the barrel beneath her breast.
She would not risk their hearing. She would not strive again,
For the road lay bare in the moonlight—blank and bare in the
moonlight—
And the blood of her veins in the moonlight throbbed to her love's
refrain.

Tlot-tlot, tlot-tlot! Had they heard it? The horse-hoofs ringing clear.
Tlot-tlot, tlot-tlot, in the distance? Were they deaf that they did not
hear?
Down the ribbon of moonlight, over the brow of the hill,
The highwayman came riding—riding, riding!
The red-coats looked to their priming! She stood up, straight and
still!

Tlot-tlot, in the frosty silence! Tlot-tlot, in the echoing night!
Nearer he came and nearer! Her face was like a light!
Her eyes grew wide for a moment. She drew one last deep breath,
Then her finger moved in the moonlight, her musket shattered the
moonlight,
Shattered her breast in the moonlight and warned him—with her
death.

He turned; he spurred to the westward. He did not know she stood
Bowed with her head o'er the musket, drenched with her own red
blood!
Not till the dawn he heard it. His face grew gray to hear
How Bess, the landlord's daughter—the landlord's black-eyed
daughter—
Had watched for her love in the moonlight, and died in the darkness
there.

Back he spurred like a madman, shrieking a curse to the sky,
With the white road smoking behind him and his rapier brandished
high!
Blood-red were his spurs in the golden noon. Wine-red was his velvet
coat,
When they shot him down on the highway—down like a dog on the
highway—
And he lay in his blood on the highway with a bunch of lace at his
throat...

Chapter One

Bloody hell, he hurt. Everywhere. His head, his shoulders, his legs. Even breathing hurt. He forced himself to take shallow breaths to fend off the worst of the pain beneath his right ribs. He didn't dare move either. He'd tried that when he'd first regained consciousness and nearly screamed from the jolt that had swept through his body. And he didn't want to scream. Not here. The others would be on him like rats on a carcass if they thought him incapacitated. In fact, now that he considered it, he wondered why they'd let him alone for so long. Perhaps they knew who he was. Perhaps his notoriety was keeping them away.

He tried to look around in the darkness to appraise his surroundings, but even turning his head a little made him suck in air between his teeth, and then he regretted breathing in at all. Oh, Christ, why was he still alive? He shouldn't be. *Maybe I'll die soon,* he thought desperately. *Anything is better than this bloody pain.*

He'd heard she'd die instantly. He hoped so, for he would not wish on her the agony he now felt. He hoped she had not felt even a momentary pang but knew he probably hoped in vain. *He* had felt each musket ball quite distinctly, all three of them, the fire of their paths burning through his flesh and knocking him from his horse. But perhaps, at close range, she had died so quickly that she hadn't felt it.

Stupid, stupid girl! He silently cursed her for having more beauty than brains, then stopped himself. That wasn't fair. She'd had more *heart* than brains perhaps. She'd said she loved him, and he'd loved her, too, but they had not meant the same thing by it. Bess was pretty and fun and he loved how she thought him important and treated him special. But he would not have done what she had done. Never. He knew himself well enough to know that. His love was not the self-sacrificing kind. He had never loved *anyone* enough for that. Well, perhaps Eleanor.

1

Foolish girl! He wouldn't have faulted her for not warning him. He knew the way life worked, especially for a thief. It was simple. If you're caught, you hang. He accepted that, had *always* accepted that.

He had said as much to her once, boasting, he supposed, and trying to impress her with how bravely he faced the dangers of his 'trade.' She had hushed him, told him not to worry her so, begged him to be careful, for she could not bear it if he were harmed. He remembered taking her hand to his lips and vowing as he kissed it to always come back to her. He was too clever, he'd told her, to be caught by a bunch of oafish soldiers. But he had lied to please her. Was she more naive than he'd supposed? Had she really thought him immune to misfortune? Jesus, no one was! If they had taken him last night, even *killed* him, then it was only to be expected. She'd be alive now if she had only understood that. At this very moment she'd be tearfully worrying about him or mourning him, thinking she'd never find another man to love as she'd loved him…but at least she would be alive. Time would have cured her sorrow. He knew. He hardly ever thought of his sister anymore, and he had once been so inconsolable, he had thought of hanging himself.

Well, he mused wryly, *I'll get my wish now.* If he didn't die here on this cold, shit-covered floor, they'd hang him for sure. He'd never liked the thought of hanging. He'd hoped he'd be shot down, nice and quick. He smiled in the dark. *Nothing nice or quick about it.*

He rolled his eyes around again and made out a small, barred window. It was night beyond. He'd been taken near midday. Was it just dusk or near morning…or somewhere in between. How long would he have to linger until death came?

Perhaps if I take a few deep breaths, the pain will kill me, he thought. *Worth a try.* He steeled himself for the effort, then sucked in a huge gulp of air. He heard himself cry out against his will and then the dark world disappeared.

Someone was pawing at his clothes, jostling him about, and pain still shot through his gut and thigh with every movement, though not as keenly as before. It was strangely comforting, this half-understood human contact. He thought maybe his wounds were being tended, then dismissed that notion as a fool's optimism. He felt his boots tugged down his legs. *Ah, my finest pair,* he lamented as his feet grew cold, then colder as his stockings followed his boots. *Will they strip me naked?* he wondered disinterestedly. Maybe he'd freeze to death. He'd heard that wasn't a bad way to die, though how in Christ's name would anyone know? Dead men weren't forthcoming with such useful information. He chuckled to himself.

"He's coming 'round," someone hissed.

The scrambling hands grew more frantic, and he groaned as someone grabbed him beneath his armpits and hoisted him to a sitting position.

"Get the coat! Get the coat!" a harsh voice ordered.

"It wouldna fit you! 'Twas my idea to take his things."

"Stop yer whinin', you little prick. You can have the damn coat, and most of the rest, too, if you give 'em *your* clothes. The turnkey'll search us out otherwise, if he's left stitchless."

"*My* things? But his shirt's all bloody, *and* his pants."

"Just button the coat," another voice advised. "They're too fine to leave. You can wash and mend 'em after you're out."

"Two weeks in a bloody shirt?"

"Shut up," the harsh voice ordered again. "Strip off your things. And be quick."

"You should consider yourself lucky to be able to fit this fancy gear," came another looter's voice. "You know who this is?"

"Course I do. I ain't stupid."

"Then you know he'd only buy the finest. These here is probably from France, or at least London. Jeremy Knox wouldna have no less."

"Well, he's about to have a whole lot less," snickered the whiney, would-be recipient of his clothes. Jeremy tried to rouse himself, but he couldn't quite manage it against so many rough hands. He could not even seem to voice a complaint. *Probably blood loss,* he decided ruefully. *How humiliating to be at the mercy of this low-class mob.* Ah, well, maybe they'd inadvertently help him along to his Maker. He could feel them shove a rough shirt over his arms, then drop him back to the floor. His head hit the stone with a thud.

"Watch it, watch it. Jesus, his pants are tight. I can't get 'em down."

Jeremy felt fingernails clawing at his waist. *The buttons*, he wanted to say. *Undo the fuckin' buttons, you simpletons*, but no words came. He felt his breeches finally slip down his thighs and his heels hit the floor with a whack as they were tugged free. Then he was being dressed, he supposed, for he felt thick wool on his legs and some sort of lumpy cloth around his waist.

And then it was quiet again. He listened hard but couldn't even hear anyone breathing. Had he passed out again or were they still there, hiding in the shadows of the big cell? They must be. Sitting silently. Watching. Triumphant. *I must look a sight.* He had always prided himself on his appearance. Pride, he suddenly realized, had been his ruination. Would the authorities have been so anxious to pinch him if he'd been a less conspicuous thief? If he hadn't flaunted their ineptitude at apprehending him? He'd thrived on the notoriety for years. Jeremy Knox, highwayman extraordinaire. *Catch me if you can. Better than Turpin. Better than Duvall. And I need no partner. A partner is a weakness. I work alone.* Women had been the only partners he'd ever had, and never on the road. Bess' black, loving eyes suddenly flashed into his mind and he shivered.

The fools hadn't even bothered to button the shirt and his chest felt cold. He tried to move his stiff arms and found that he could manage better than he'd supposed, though two buttons later, he dropped his arms to his side again in exhaustion. Better. He wouldn't think of Bess anymore. She was dead and gone and he was helpless to help her, or himself for that matter. He would just lie here and, God willing, die.

Jeremy opened his eyes slowly. Something was different. He wasn't where he'd been before. A cold, stone wall pressed against his side and there was straw beneath him, poking into his back.

And someone was sitting next to him on his other side, a back against his hip. He tried to move a bit, but was pinned by his own weakness and a sudden hand on his shoulder.

"Keep still," a young voice whispered. "Keep still or you'll hang."

Jeremy wanted to inform the boy, for so he now saw his protector to be, that he was bound to hang whether he moved or not, but he kept still anyway. There was a commotion at the far end of the cell.

"Come along, you," a voice boomed angrily.

"But I ain't him!" complained the whiny voice of the man who'd taken his clothes.

Jeremy smiled to himself. *Now he's fixed himself,* he mused. *If he admits he snagged my clothes, then he's a thief, highwayman or not, and he hangs.* The sound of wood against bone and flesh told him the guard had probably subdued the uncooperative thief with his rifle butt.

"Take 'im out," came the bellowed order, then the screeching of the hinges as the door banged shut.

"Now we'll both hang," Jeremy said quietly.

"Not if you listen to me," the boy said, turning to look at him. "That there was Philip Twigg. Me, I'm Benjamin Twigg."

"Your brother?"

"Half-brother."

"Well, I'm sorry then," he said insincerely. "But as soon as he straightens out the mix-up, he'll be hanged for a thief right along with me."

"Not if he can't straighten it out."

"Others know him. Helped him rob me." He had to pant out the words. Breathing still hurt like hell.

"Think they'll say so?" the boy laughed quietly.

"What about you? You know he's not me."

"I may know, but I ain't sayin'. No love's lost 'tween us, as they say. I hate his black heart and he don't give a shit about whether I live or die either. He'd already cut me loose 'fore ya arrived, blamed me fer landin' us here."

"What'd you do?"

"I didn't do nothin' really. Stood lookout while he had his way with this tavern girl's all. I've done it before...lots a times, but this time he hit her and I didn't like that." He bowed his head in seeming embarrassment. "Guess I shouldna have shouted at him, though, 'cuz the keeper heard me an' charged out the door like a bull, draggin' some other blokes with 'im, and before ya knows it, we're in here for brawlin'."

5

"Brawling?" Jeremy asked in disbelief. "Not rape?"

"That sort a got overlooked in the hurry. The judge was movin' ta the next district that day, so he weren't overly thorough. Innkeeper said he'd kill us when we was sprung, and Philip said he'd kill me afore that fer gettin' him in this mess, so I been stayin' clear."

Jeremy considered the boy for a minute, sizing him up. Twelve, maybe thirteen. Hardened by life. Good. He'd have a better chance at surviving if he were tough.

"So when are you getting out?"

"*We* are getting out in two weeks."

Jeremy saw the boy smile smugly. "We? How do you figure that?"

"Cause I'm gonna say you're my brother. You're Philip Twigg. I'll swear ta it. Who's gonna think I'd trade me own brother in for a highwayman?"

Jeremy looked at the boy through squinted eyes. A momentary thrill of hope had quickened his heart, but now he resented that unkind hoax. "Who indeed?" he said coldly. "I'm not so great a fool as you take me for, boy. Go play your pranks elsewhere."

Benjamin looked at him with no apparent offense and nodded. "God's truth, Mister Knox. May I turn blue and die if I'm scammin' ya. I hate Philip good and proper. If I could a done it, I'd a killed him meself years ago. He killed our pa, ya see. He ain't right in the head, that's what I think. I think he'd a really killed me when we was sprung."

"How do you know I won't?"

The boy hesitated only a moment. "You ain't even killed on the road, have ya? What'd cause ya ta kill me? I ain't done nothin' to ya, and maybe I even saved your life. That's worth somethin', ain't it?"

Jeremy was silent, looking at the boy's earnest face. "Well, don't get your hopes up, boy. Your brother's not shot. They know they shot *me*."

Benjamin laughed again. "You think these horse's arses care about that, even if they remembers it? King's soldiers dropped ya here, then marched on. Left orders to try ya and hang ya. As long as someone gets hanged as Jeremy Knox, all legal and properlike, everyone's happy."

6

That thrill of hope was back, stronger than before. It might work. Maybe he'd make it out of this scrape after all. In his growing excitement, he breathed more deeply and groaned with the pain. *If I don't die first.* It suddenly seemed important to try to live.

"Can you get water and a cloth, boy? We need to clean me up if we're to pull this off."

"Water I can manage. We'll have ta tear some a your shirt or somethin' for a cloth. But we best wait 'til it's darker. The others don't know you're over here with me. I dragged ya here after they was sleepin'. They might even think ya died and was dragged out by the coffin maker in the night. Lots o' people disappears that way in here. Nearly one a week in the last six months."

"Where is here?" Jeremy wondered, more to himself than to Benjamin. "Not Goole surely?"

"A ways south o' there. Thorne."

Jeremy nodded and closed his eyes. He needed to rest. "You keep watch, boy. Wake me if you need to." And then he drifted off into a dream-plagued sleep where Bess' teasing smile and adoring eyes met him at every turning.

"Ya gotta eat somethin'" came Benjamin's whispered voice, and Jeremy stirred himself. Somehow he was sitting propped against the wall. *The boy is stronger than he looks.* He could breathe more normally, though his thigh still throbbed with immediate intensity. He nodded as he focused on the crust of bread Benjamin offered him, then slowly raised his hand and took it. It tasted moldy. *Of course it would be*, he thought. *No use wasting good bread on criminals.* They'd all have bellyaches soon, but it *did* ease the gnawing in his stomach. There was still a little light coming in one of the windows.

"I slept the afternoon?" he asked.

"More like the night," Benjamin grinned. "That's mornin' light and this here's breakfast."

Jeremy shook his head. He was losing track of everything. Time. Direction. He felt a little feverish. He touched his brow but it was cool enough, then pulled up his shirt to examine the lump he felt there. A strip of cloth around his chest held on a folded wad of cloth where the bullet had ripped into him. It looked incredibly filthy.

7

"I think I did a proper job of it," Benjamin whispered proudly. "It was hard ta see in the dark, but I couldn't feel anymore crusted blood when I'd done. How do it feel?"

"Better," Jeremy admitted. He reached down to touch his thigh. Beneath the baggy trousers he felt another, larger lump of cloth where the other two balls had torn through his leg. "Maybe I'll live after all."

"Ya got to do better than that," Benjamin said sternly. "Ya have to be in the pink before we walks out o' here so's ya don't make the jailer all curiouslike."

"Any news about your brother?"

The boy was quiet a moment, then shook his head. "I reckon he's hanged by now. The magistrate's here again, from what I can tell. Lots o' people in and out, ya know. Unlucky fer Philip, I suppose, cuz usually the circuit's longer—nine months, sometimes even a year. He probably figured he'd be long gone 'fore you and your fancy clothes were tried." He smiled ruefully. "But lucky fer us."

Jeremy nodded. A strange kind of luck. He leaned his head back against the wall, feeling lightheaded again.

"Have some more bread," Benjamin ordered.

"That's yours."

"I'm not so hungry. And I'm in fine health, too, not nearly bled out. Take it."

Jeremy opened his eyes again. He looked at the boy's anxious face, then took the hunk of bread. "Thanks," he said, trying not to sound too grateful. One of the first rules of survival: Take no favors, owe no allegiance. But he knew he already owed Benjamin plenty. He only hoped it wouldn't make him do something idiotic someday out of misplaced loyalty, nor make Benjamin do something as foolish as Bess had done out of some sort of hero worship. For an even more important rule of survival was surely, "Every man for himself."

"You don't talk much," Benjamin said with a sigh a week later. "I thought ya was just sick at first, but now you're better, ya still keeps quiet."

"I've nothing to say," Jeremy told him dismissively.

"I'd like hearin' 'bout your times on the road. How ya do it, what ya say, like that."

"I'll especially not tell you that," Jeremy said flatly. "First, it would be stupid of me to chronicle my misdeeds to anyone, and secondly, I've no desire to play teacher to a future felon. I'll not have *that* on my head as well."

"You've not told anyone 'bout your robbin'?"

Jeremy looked him in the eye. "No one."

"Not even the ladies?"

Bess' face, anxious and tearful, flashed before his eyes, and he closed them. "Not even the ladies."

Benjamin seemed to hesitate before speaking again, but he finally took a deep breath and pressed on. "I heard the chatter round here, after they took off Philip. Said your lady was killed by them Redcoats. That true?"

Jeremy kept his eyes closed. "True enough," he whispered. "I wasn't there."

"I knew some o' them was low, but I didn't think they'd do a thing like that. Not to a lady."

"She wasn't a lady. She was just a girl."

"Why'd they kill her though?"

Jeremy opened his eyes and stared straight ahead of him. "They say *she* pulled the trigger. It was the only way she could think to warn me…" His voice trailed off.

"Christ, imagine that."

Jeremy could sense Benjamin wanted to ask more questions, but thankfully, he didn't. Jeremy felt close to tears lately and damn it, he didn't want to bawl in front of the boy.

"Philip and Benjamin Twigg?"

For the first time in two weeks, Jeremy left the darkened corner of the prison room and followed Benjamin to the cell door. He forced himself to walk without limping, though the effort had him sweating in just a few steps. His side still ached, too, but he held himself as upright as he felt a man of Twigg's nature would, not proudly tall, but not beaten down either. A sort of defiant and defensive hunch.

"Philip and Benjamin Twigg?" the jailer asked again.

9

"That's us," Benjamin piped up.

"You're free to go. And I'd keep goin', too, if I were you two. No one wants ya round here after what ya done to Sara." The big man stood back to let Benjamin pass, then stepped in front of Jeremy and planted a meaty fist in his stomach. The unexpected blow sent Jeremy stumbling forward. He braced himself on his assailant's shoulders for a breathless moment, then pushed away in case there was another blow to follow.

"Somethin' ta remember us by," said the guard, his foul breath spitting into Jeremy's face, then he stepped aside once more.

Jeremy hesitated. He could feel warm blood trickling down his stomach and pooling at the waist of his pants. He had to get out now. He squared his shoulders, looked the jailer in the eye with a murderous glare, then dashed through the door and down the hall after Benjamin. His leg was throbbing with renewed vigor, but he didn't care. Getting outside was the only consideration now.

Benjamin had stopped at the prison door to wait for him, frowning in dismay.

"That innkeeper's waitin' outside," he hissed. "It'd be a pity if ya was shot now."

"He won't shoot me here," Jeremy said matter-of-factly. "He values his neck too much. He just wants me to see him and be afraid."

"But you ain't?"

"Not really," Jeremy forced a smile. "But I'd better look it. It'll give him some satisfaction to think he's cowed me and maybe that'll keep him from coming after us out of spite."

"Well, ya look like hell," Benjamin said honestly, "so's it won't be hard to look afeard as well. Ready?"

Jeremy nodded. He wanted to press his hand into the slowly trickling wound, but knew it would only soak into his shirt and make his injury more apparent. Like wolves, men were attracted to blood, he knew. Looking afraid was one thing. Looking vulnerable was another.

"Which one?" he whispered in Benjamin's ear as they scurried along the prison wall away from the jeering spectators that greeted all the prisoners being released that day.

"The big man with the blue coat," Benjamin told him without looking that way. "He ain't followin' us, but he sure looks aggrieved."

"Why such a grudge over a barmaid?"

Benjamin kept walking, and Jeremy thought he hadn't heard him.

"Why—"

"Weren't just any chit. I heard later that girl Sara be his daughter. Philip sure'd pick the wrong'un that night."

"Christ!" Jeremy swore under his breath. "Why didn't you tell me?"

"What good it'd do? Ya did na want ta stay in that hole, did ya, just to be safe from her pa."

Jeremy had to admit he'd have been less enthusiastic about stepping out the door if he'd known, but the boy was right. They'd have to get out of town, and fast, but his damn leg felt like it would buckle any minute, and the further they went, the hotter and more lightheaded he felt.

"Where are you going?" he managed to pant out.

"See those trees," Benjamin pointed. "There for now."

So far? Jeremy wanted to protest, but knew that even that distant shelter might prove too close for safety. They had to get horses. They had to get further away. They had to get as far from Thorne as they could. Hide out. Get well. Get money. And above all, get revenge. For Jeremy had had a chance to dwell on that bitter justice for nearly two weeks. He knew who'd sung to the authorities about him and he was going to make the weasel pay for it.

Anger made him breathe more heavily than even the exertion of running. He was close to collapsing but willed himself onward.

Hide. Rest. Get a horse. Get money. Kill Mott.

Suddenly the distant trees seemed wonderfully near. They would be more easily gained than all else that was needed.

11

Chapter Two

The wind across the moors was unusually warm and Jeremy smiled. He'd had a good morning on the Goole Road, as he'd expected he would. The coach and four had left the inn bound for London with only a driver, an elderly guard, and a wet-eared lad to see to the persons and belongings of Sir Anthony Bisquet and his spinster daughter. At least, that's who they claimed to be. Jeremy had noted them the night before as they'd dined, and they'd seemed more besotted with one another than was proper for a man and his daughter. It was his guess that the middle-aged squire was traveling with his children's governess-turned-mistress, or some other such illicit association, and that the man would therefore prefer to remain inconspicuous. If robbed, he would be less inclined to alert anyone. London's Bow Street Runners, those self-proclaimed protectors of the roads, kept themselves well to the south of Yorkshire. No worry from that quarter, at least for the present. And Jeremy had found the local magistrates and landlords to be an unconcerned lot. As long as they weren't personally affected and no one was hurt in the matter, they left him alone.

He'd even gotten the distinct impression that it was nearly a matter of local pride that so gallant a fellow as himself roamed *their* roads. *Jeremy Knox. Surely a gentleman down on his luck and no run-of-the-mill thief. Well-spoken and polite in the extreme. Showed mercy upon occasion, leaving the ladies their lockets, or at least the likenesses within. And as to appearances, he excelled on all points. Dark and lean, his victims reported. Not a pretty boy, though he'd often heard himself called Pretty Jeremy. Not soft looking but possessing a face with the cut of a nobleman. His bearing was proud and hinted at concealed strength. And his clothes could only be admired. The best that money could buy, if one didn't begrudge him the fact that it was **stolen** money that purchased them. High-grade* *velvet coats, French-laced shirts of the finest linen, well-fitting breeches and Spanish-made boots. He favored dark colors—wines, forest greens, midnight blues. No foppish yellows or sky blues for him.*

Jeremy had followed the coach at a discreet distance when it had departed the next morning, then cut through the woods, forded a little steam, and was waiting just around a turn, at the narrowest point of the road, when the coach appeared. There was no place for the driver to go, no avenue of escape, no chance of turning around and no pushing through at a high-speed, for the road took a sharp dip into the valley beyond. And so, as he'd known it would, the coach jangled to a stop.

"Good morning, sir," he'd greeted the squire as he'd poked his head out the window. "No need to be alarmed. I'll just bear your purse for you if you don't mind, and relieve you of the little cache beneath the lady's seat, then be on my way."

The squire had sighed and turned over the items requested with gentlemanly disdain. With a tip of his tricorn hat and a, "Good day to you, sir. And to you, pretty lady," Jeremy had returned down the road the carriage had just come. *An easy piece of work*, he'd mused as he'd enjoyed the brisk morning air on his face and the reassuring clop of his horse's hooves in the dirt. Only when he'd entered the inn yard and dismounted had his merry mood changed, for coming out of the stable to tend his horse was Tim Mott.

"No cold water this time," Jeremy said gruffly. "And I'll be out in half an hour to see he's been rubbed down properly." He met Mott's eyes with composure but the man's hate-filled glare made him reconsider his inclination to turn away in contempt. The half-wit was certainly capable of hurting Satin out of spite if not incompetence. *Christ, why does Hobbs keep such a poor excuse for a hostler,* he fumed to himself, then forced what he hoped looked like a friendly smile to his lips. "And if all's fit and proper, with a extra measure of grain for my lad, then there's an extra copper in it for you, right Tim?"

"Yes, sir, Mister Knox, sir," Tim replied, but there was no deference in his manner. Jeremy could almost hear the "someday you'll get yours" in the man's mocking tone.

13

Never show concern or fear, that was Jeremy's motto, and he followed that maxim now, giving Mott an acknowledging nod of his head before turning confidently away.

He thought he heard spittle hit the dust behind him, but he didn't turn to find out.

He quickly scanned the large main room of the inn as he entered and found the person for whom he looked wiping down the casks behind a high counter.

"A drink, Mister Hobbs," he called, "though it's not yet noon."

"Good hunting?" inquired the landlord, pouring out a measure of ale and handing it to Jeremy with a questioning, hopeful look.

"Indeed," Jeremy smiled, shaking the little casket he held under one arm. The metallic chinking, though muffled through the wood, left no doubt as to its contents. "Are you at leisure to work on the books, or shall I come back later?"

"Now suits me fine," the innkeeper said with a gleeful gleam in his eye. "Bessie!" he shouted. "Get out here, girl, and tend the front."

As Jeremy followed the innkeeper to a back room, he saw the man's daughter scurry out of the kitchen, wiping her hands on her apron then smoothing her black hair away from her face. Her dark eyes sought his, then she flushed a lovely shade of pink and lowered those same eyes so that her father wouldn't see. *I'd best tread carefully,* he thought, not for the first time. He had a sweet thing going out of this inn. The business literally came through the door to him. Though he was not so foolish as to always scout out his marks from this same inn every time, it was his favorite base. For one thing, it was cleaner than most of the other inns he frequented, especially the beds. And Mister Hobbs, for a collaborator in crime, was an honest man to deal with, or had been so far. Still, he wasn't at all certain how Mister Hobbs would react to the information that his daughter was also an attraction for the young highwayman. Oh, there were willing lasses to be had at the other establishments, it was true, and he had not spurned their advances. But Bess was different. She was ten years younger than him for one thing, just sixteen, though her saucy behavior when they were alone often drove that fact from his mind. She was smarter than most women he knew, or at least most women of her social class. She actually helped her father with the tallies each day and entered them into the ledgers in her neat hand, especially when Mister Hobbs had imbibed a bit too much of his own wares. But it was the way she looked at him that most separated her from the other women with whom he slept. Unlike their simple, lustful entreaties, Bess' eyes were filled with adoration. He hoped it was no more than that, for he certainly had no place for a lasting dalliance in his line of work. But it *did* make him feel especially eager to stay at the Running Lion Inn as often as was prudent, for the good stew, the clean bed, and Bess' worshipful eyes.

He brought his mind back to the business before him. First the counting out, then the proper split, all fair and square, for silence came at a price. Mister Hobbs and the other landlords were willing to turn a blind eye to robbers *if* they were kept clear of blame and *if* they got their share of the booty. It was a satisfying arrangement all around and one that Jeremy saw as Providential. Providential, too, was the presence of the lovely girl with the black hair and black eyes that he knew would come knocking at his door that night, eager to let him taste the red fullness of her soft lips.

Red lips. The brush of hair on his cheek. Oh, sweet Bess. Her small, work-hardened hand took hold of his chin and he waited for her kiss. But instead she shook his head back and forth. And he hurt, couldn't take a breath without pain radiating through his chest and belly. Stop. Stop.

"Stop," he gasped out, and his eyes flew open. He sucked in another breath, prepared to scold her—for what, he wasn't quite sure—when his dream-clogged brain finally identified the face looking over him. There was no cloak of black hair surrounding him as he'd expected, nor a teasing smile to sway him from his anger. Only the gnomish face of Benjamin Twigg.

"We should be movin' on," the boy said matter-of-factly.

Jeremy squinted around him. It was barely sunrise.

"Yes," he said, managing to sit himself up. "We need to find some food. Maybe some horses—"

"Horses?" the boy asked with an amused laugh. "We'd stick out like whores at mass. 'Sides, horse thievin's worsen murder if you're caught. No, I'll walk, thank ya. But food, that we need."

And so they started through the predawn woods, skirting by a farm or two until a likely hen house presented itself. *Raw eggs aren't the best meal,* Jeremy thought as he broke the fifth one into his mouth, *but they'll do in a pinch,* and they eased the gnawing for a while, at least the gnawing in his stomach.

The remembered image of Bess' red lips and black hair, however, gnawed on his mind throughout the day. No, it was *more* than her image, for surely he had *felt* her presence in his dreams. He imagined, even as he trod wearily behind Benjamin in his ill-fitting shoes, that he felt her fingers resting upon his arm. He was sure he smelled the rosy scent that used to waft from her hair filling his nostrils as he struggled against the pain for each breath and every step. And with each tormented step he swore not only at the pain but at the man he knew to be the cause of both it and Bess' ghostly companionship. The man's presence haunted him, too, though it was a self-conjured image that brought no sad pleasure, only disgust and rage. Tim Mott, that ill-begotten whoreson, would pay for his treachery as Jeremy gladly squeezed his hands around the man's scrawny neck until he begged for mercy...and got none.

"Where ya think we be?" Benjamin asked, looking out from their cover in the forest to the rolling landscape beyond.

Jeremy smiled. "Near Hemsworth. I know this area well." He straightened and took a deep breath, something that had gotten easier with each day. They'd walked and pilfered their way west, away from Thorne and all the trouble there for almost five days. His injured leg had made the going excruciatingly slow and even though he felt stronger each day—his side and thigh hurting less and less—he knew he would never make the Scottish border at this rate. It galled him when he thought of how he could have covered the same distance by horseback in a day, maybe two. A horse, any horse, would be his first priority, despite Benjamin's misgivings. With a horse beneath him, he'd be almost whole again.

He *did* feel nearly himself again during the long days. If only he didn't have to sleep each night. It was in his dreams the troubled ghosts of days now past haunted him just as surely as if they were real. Awakening from a dream in which he rode tall and proud upon Satin or in which he lay entwined in Bess' arms to find himself, instead, a wounded man sleeping ignobly beneath a pile of leaves in the dirt was such a shock, it tore through his body with a violent shiver, almost as if he'd been shot again. Yes, if only he did not need to sleep, and dream, he would be his old self again.

And thinking like his old self suddenly made him frown. "I'll be recognized here," he said, almost to himself. "We'll have to avoid the road."

Benjamin laughed. Jeremy had noticed the boy did that a lot. "Recognize a scarecrow walkin' down tha road? Not likely," he jeered. "Ya ain't seed yourself. Ya ain't a Jeremy Knox *anybody'd* recognize. Why, ya could claim ta be old King George hisself an have better luck o' convincin' folks it were true."

"That bad, eh?"

"Full beard, dirt everywhere's, and let's just say me brother weren't no fine dressin' gent. I'm thinkin' your own ma'd pass ya by without a second glance."

The mention of his mother deepened Jeremy's scowl. He wondered momentarily where she was these days, then dismissed the thought as one he couldn't afford to entertain. Wherever she was, he hoped it was far from him.

"Well, then," he said, forcing a smile at Benjamin's assessment of his looks. "Let's see how good this disguise of mine is. I know a little place where we might get some food and lodgings if we muck out a stall or two," and he started out of the trees toward the wheel-rutted road.

Benjamin and Jeremy sat cross-legged in the hall beside the kitchen eating eagerly from the hot bowls of stew they cradled in their hands. Jeremy realized when his share was nearly gone that he had not had anything decent to eat in nearly a month, since the day of his capture, and that, he now recalled, had been a meal only half-eaten. News of Bess' death, brought by an excited crofter to the inn at Barmby had stopped him in mid-bite, banishing all appetite—

"Did he say we could have another?" Benjamin whispered, his own bowl empty.

How could the boy eat so quickly? "Aye, but we'd be wiser to wait a bit. Our stomachs might not appreciate this feast after so long a holiday from food."

17

Benjamin nodded with resigned agreement and wiped his sleeve across his mouth. "That sure were good, though, eh? Think we could stay on here a bit? Keep mucking the stables?"

Jeremy wondered at the boy's lack of aspiration. It had nettled his pride to be reduced to shoveling out the stalls behind the inn when he had once stabled Satin there with the toss of a coin. What a fall from grace. He would do whatever he must out of bitter necessity, but he did not plan to make such tasks his new life's work.

And he did have a new life. With every spoonful of the thick stew, that realization had become more clear to him. He wasn't dead. His wounds were healing, if slowly. He wasn't even a wanted man, for Philip Twigg had conveniently, if unwillingly, hanged in his place.

Conversation from the tavern drifted down the dirty hall and brought his musings to an abrupt, gut-wrenching halt.

"Jesus, Billings, where'd you find the blunt to afford that gear? You look as good as ol' Knox."

Jeremy's head shot up at the mention of his name and his body tensed to bolt out the back door. Had someone recognized him despite his filthy appearance? The next words slowed his racing pulse.

"I should think I look better than 'im, seein's as he's rottin' on the gibbet, or so's I hear," the man, who must have been Billings, replied with a sneering chuckle.

"That's right. I saw him last week," came a new voice, one that sounded vaguely familiar to Jeremy, though he couldn't quite—

"He looked wors'n I ever seen him, and I know'd him well. Unrecognizable. Fact, I think it weren't him at all."

"Course it is. Who else'd be?" someone asked, but they sounded intrigued by the man's suggestion.

"Don't know," he replied. "But somethin' about that corpse weren't right. The hair was reddish-brown, and you know Knox had dark hair, almost black. His face, what was left of it, were too long, too, but the main thing was the nose o' that corpse. It were hooked real sharp like."

Speculative murmurs arose among the bar patrons and Jeremy inadvertently ran a finger down his nose. It was one of his finer features, straight and strong with no hint of a hook. Who was the man talking? And where, he wondered morbidly, was Philip Twigg's

18

gibbet? At the Thorne crossroads a day's ride back? Hung there to warn off other would-be robbers?

"Death makes great alterations," the innkeeper said sagely as he tapped out another pint of ale, "and that's a fact. Maybe they broke his nose afore they hanged him."

"Maybe. But I'd bet a pound on a pony, that fancy-dressed corpse ain't Jeremy Knox."

Hearing that familiar expression, Jeremy knew who was speaking and he wished he could strangle the little bastard before he convinced everyone of his doubts. Nelson! Damned little pinchpocket. That'd teach him to get too cozy with street thieves. Next time—

"You might be right," the innkeeper said with a nod. "I heard they shot Knox on the Drax road. Could be they tossed him in a ditch near there to save themselves the trouble 'o haulin' him to Thorne, then hung up some other poor bastard just to make sure we all got the message like."

"Aye, that's what *I* think," Nelson said. "Course either way, he's dead, and I for one will miss him. He was as fine a fellow as any I've ever known and always treated this worthless sod right. Broke bread with him for a time 'round Carlisle. Say what you will, he were a fine, fine highwayman."

"That he were," came Billings' voice. "A toast to Pretty Jeremy, may he rest in peace."

"Here, here."

Jeremy felt strangely pleased at this post-mortem tribute and more kindly toward Nimble Nelson, though he worried about the young man's presence. Nelson had a quick eye. That's why he was so good at what he did. If he spotted Jeremy here, would he be able to see through the beard and the grime to the real man beneath?

"We're leaving tonight," Jeremy whispered to Benjamin. "Go get your other bowl of stew."

"What about you?"

"I can't chance it. You heard them talking. Now go."

Without asking, Benjamin grabbed Jeremy's bowl and scurried away. *Damn the boy.* He might miss out on his own portion if he appeared too greedy to the landlord. But in no time at all, Benjamin was back with the two bowls of stew.

19

"I just told 'im ya sent me ta fetch your grub," the boy smiled. "Don't know why ya couldn't figure that out."

Jeremy took the bowl gratefully and smiled. "Because I'm not accustom to giving orders to lackeys. I've always done for myself, and if I couldn't, I did without."

Benjamin nodded as he attacked the fresh bowl of stew. "Well, now ya got me. You're my big brother, remember, to do with as ya please."

Jeremy looked at the smiling boy dubiously. "And what do you get out of this arrangement?"

"Protection mostly."

Jeremy chuckled dryly. "I'm no good to anyone for that. If anything, you've been *my* protector."

"Just for now," Benjamin said lightly. "And ya'd still be able to best most blackguards I'm thinking, better'n me leastwise."

Jeremy sighed and went back to eating. He didn't like the way things were shaping up. If he weren't careful, he'd be stuck with the boy for good. He'd have to think of a way out of this "partnership" eventually. His new life did not include being the protector of a young scamp.

Jeremy awoke with a start. He'd been dreaming of riding across the twilight-purple moors, toward what he didn't know, when a question had startled him awake.

Where was Satin? He hesitated only a moment before jostling Benjamin awake with the toe of his shoe.

"Time to get going," he said stonily.

Benjamin groaned but sat up. "Ya sure we need ta be leavin' here so soon? Where we goin'?"

"I thought north at first, but now I'm thinking we should go back to the east."

Benjamin frowned.

"I need a horse," Jeremy spat in frustration. "I can't endure this leaden-paced life any longer, and I won't!" His voice was low but resolute. "Did you ever hear what may have happened to my horse?"

"Your horse?"

"The one I was riding when I was captured. What would they do with a man's horse?"

Benjamin scratched his shaggy head. "Don't know. Take it with 'em maybe. Or give it over to a local bloke for a price."

Jeremy considered the situation. Satin was a fine piece of horseflesh, a temptation, surely, for some captain of the guard. If he'd been commandeered, then he was gone for good, part of the king's army. But if he'd been sold to someone, a farmer, say, or a local squire, then perhaps he could get him back. Satin was his horse after all. It wouldn't be exactly like stealing.

For he'd made that resolution—somewhere between the time he'd regained his senses on the Thorne prison floor and this chilly morning sitting on a stable floor in Hemsworth—that he was through with robbing. No use tempting fate. He'd escaped his due by the smallest bit of chance. Bess had paid for his folly with her life. It had been a grand way to live for the most part, and thrilling, too, but he knew that if he went back to it, nothing would be the same. When he considered his former lifestyle, he felt only dread now, not excitement. And fear was a killer on the roads. If he'd been successful before it was because he'd been confident and brash. He'd approached each job with an arrogance about his cleverness than now made him wonder. How could he have been so cocky? He'd seen many a thief die in many a manner and acknowledged that the same fate awaited him…but not in his heart. In his heart he had been invincible. They wouldn't be getting him until he got all the blunt he needed to…

To what? That had always been a question. He had no specific plans for his future, only knew that whatever he decided upon meant having plenty of money. A farm in the Midlands? A house in London? An estate in the colonies? Life abroad? He couldn't decide and had never taken the time to work it all out, just kept on doing what he was good at and waiting for a day of clarity or divine intervention.

Perhaps a few musket balls in his leg and chest had been that divine intrusion, perhaps not, but it had certainly led to a change of perspective about what he could expect from life. Nothing. Bess had loved him and what had it gotten her? An early grave. He had robbed with impunity for so many years, but in the end, one short day and a series of bad circumstances had literally stripped him of everything—

No, he reminded himself, and his face brightened into a joyful grin.

"What's a matter, Mister Knox? Ya look like ya just been struck daft."

"No, just suddenly more hopeful," he smiled. "We'll be all right if we can get to Kirkpatrick."

"To Scotland? Why? What's there?"

"The key to my future…and yours, too, I suppose."

"Then why we goin' east stead'o northlike?"

"To see about my horse. Did you gather up those leavings from the dust bin?"

"And bundled 'em, too," the boy said, holding up the burlap sack. "The keeper won't miss it."

Jeremy frowned. It looked as if the sack was bulging enough to burst. "Can't be very good food, I guess, if all that was tossed out."

A guilty look swept through Benjamin's eyes. *Not all trashed food then*, Jeremy realized. A petty theft. Well, it was too late now. They had to be off, first to Asselby or Knedlington or even to Howden, to the Running Lion, to see about his horse. And then to Kirkpatrick…for his stash.

The walk northeast was not nearly as troublesome as their prior trip, though Jeremy cursed himself every chilly night for wasting his time and not heading north from the start. Cold fear had driven him; that's all he could find as an excuse. Like a hunted, wounded animal, he had fled away from the vicinity of his capture and imprisonment out of sheer panic. *Get away, get away*, had driven him as he'd struggled for every breath and step. Now, with the return of his reasoning and the renewed vigor of his shattered body, other instincts began to take over, ones that had been honed during his years on the road. *Do what is the most expedient to survival. Get your horse, or any horse. Then get to Scotland and your money.*

He had not told the boy about the money. He had never been a trusting man and he couldn't see a reason to change that particular trait. Trust could be betrayed, and betrayal could be deadly. He actually had a bank account in Kirkpatrick under the name of Jeremy Harwood. He grinned to himself at the irony of that alias. Wouldn't "Papa" be astounded that his bastard son had assumed that fine family name for the business end of his nefarious dealings, especially as the Harwood lands were just a day's ride from Kirkpatrick. Maybe he'd drop in for a visit on his way through…or better yet on his way back. He'd always wondered how his sire would greet him now that he could look him square in the eye. He had also wondered whether his father had put two and two together and realized that his unacknowledged son was the same Jeremy Knox known throughout the northern shires for his thievery. Jeremy savored the notion of telling him someday, but for now, Daniel Harwood could rest in blessed ignorance. He had more pressing business.

Jeremy knew he couldn't use his real name, that dubious gift from his mother, ever again. He had made it infamous with his flamboyant style of robbing. By now news of his death must have gotten around, maybe even to London. So he couldn't be Jeremy Knox anymore. It was only fair that his father should contribute something useful to his bastard son, and a name, at the end of a day, was just another word.

"You'd better not call me Mister Knox anymore," he told Benjamin solemnly as they neared a little village just over the hill from Knottingly. "That name died with your brother. I'll miss it, there's no denying that, but I've another I use sometimes that'll do just as well. From now on, I'm Jeremy Harwood."

"Can I use it, too? Might look funny if I'm a Twigg and we're s'pose ta be brothers."

"For now," he nodded, put on the spot by the boy for yet another time. Why would he begrudge Benjamin the use of a family name that he himself had never legally owned? He forced a smile. "Benjamin Harwood. It sounds well."

"It sure do," the boy grinned. "How'd you think of it?"

Jeremy shrugged and let the matter drop.

Jeremy longed for a bath, a shave, and fresh clothes, but he couldn't afford to clean up, not this close to his old robbing grounds. His only protection was his anonymity, for his fine pistols and sword had disappeared along with his horse. With a sharp eye he had scanned the meadows since they'd left Asselby to see if Satin was pastured anywhere along the way. It was too much to hope for, he knew, but he looked anyway.

What he found he did not expect and for the first time since his capture, he felt his stomach retch.

A horse's carcass lay feet up off the road as they neared the crossroads at Knedlington. It was badly decomposed, but Jeremy was almost certain it was Satin as he scrambled down the shallow embankment for a closer look, willing his stomach to stop lurching at the sight.

"That your horse?" Benjamin asked sadly.

"I think so."

"How ya know?"

The bridle and saddle were gone, of course, but… He nudged the horse's right flank with the toe of his shoe. No doubt now. He gazed with sickening acceptance at the jagged scar through the dark hair, the one the saddle usually hid, from Satin's run-in with a stable nail in Huddersfield. And he saw, too, the reason for Satin's death—two neat holes high on the shoulder surrounded by congealed blood. The miniballs that had torn through his leg had continued a killing path into his horse. How close had they been, those soldiers who had dispensed the King's harsh justice on the open road? How could he have ridden so blindly to within practically arms length of their muskets?

Hot fury. The worst kind of anger. He deserved to be dead for succumbing to that sort of spleen quite apart from any of his crimes. It was a matter of pure survival that a man never lose his composure even in a moment of rage, for with loss of reason came loss of perception, and a man needed every scrap of discernment to survive in this dangerous world.

He could add Satin, that fine and generous beast that had been a better companion than any man he'd ever known, to the list of useless destruction he'd caused. *Christ, let that be all*, he mused darkly, but even as he half-prayed the plea, he thought of Tim Mott. Mott was a different matter. His destruction would not be useless. His death would bring Jeremy the satisfaction of doing something righteous in a corrupt world. Bess' blood cried out for retribution. Jeremy was as certain as he'd ever been of anything that Mott had played informant to set a trap for him. Unfortunately it had been Bess who had been caught. His own wounding and capture, and now Satin's death, could only be attributed to his own stupidity and carelessness, yet Mott's betrayal had instigated Jeremy's foolishness as well. Well, the stableman would pay with his life. *No great loss,* Jeremy thought darkly, *but necessary.*

"We gonna go on ta Howden?" Benjamin asked quietly.

Jeremy looked up from his murderous musings and saw Benjamin's young face showing uncertainty for the first time since their meeting. Had Jeremy's rekindled rage shown so clearly that it had unnerved the plucky boy? He forced a grim smile to his face.

"No need to now. We'll head to Selby, maybe borrow some food from some places I know along the way. We can make Leeds in a couple of days, I think, though I'm no judge of foot travel, that's certain," he chuckled, and the boy smiled, both remembering several nights they had not made a town and ended up sleeping in a hollow off the road. "In Leeds we'll get some work or something, make ourselves more presentable, buy a horse—any nag will do at this point—and head for Scotland as soon as we've the scratch not to starve on the way. That is, if you still want to throw in with me. I've not been blessed with luck lately, boy. I'll not take it unkindly if you cut loose a bad load. I owe you more than I can repay already."

Benjamin frowned. "I'll stick with ya fer awhile yet, leastwise till we gets ta Leeds. Then I'll see."

Jeremy was surprised by the boy's answer, but even more surprised by his own reaction to it. He'd expected the boy to persist in his unreasonable devotion and had expected himself to be annoyed by that persistence. Instead, the boy was actually willing to consider parting company and Jeremy was left feeling unaccountably hurt. Hadn't he wanted to be rid of the burden of his young traveling companion? Hadn't he often wished they'd parted company at the jail house door? In fact, hadn't he even wished he didn't feel so obligated to the boy, that their partnership hadn't been necessary at all? And now he was hurt by the boy's willingness to go their separate ways? It didn't make sense.

"Good enough," he nodded, turning his eyes back to gaze at Satin's carcass one more time. "We'd best be walking then." He nodded to the horse in parting. "Sorry, boy," he said quietly, then climbed back up the bank to the road they'd so often traveled together.

Chapter Three

"I know who you are," the girl whispered as she handed him the tray with his daily portion of soup and bread.

Jeremy met her gaze with apparent disinterest, but her words had startled him. He and Benjamin had hired on at a furniture maker's shop when they'd finally reached Leeds. Benjamin swept up the sawdust from beneath the work benches in the evenings and made himself generally useful to Mister Tolver's apprentice, Sam, and his three daughters. At first Jeremy had only carried in wood for the elderly craftsman or gone to fetch it from the local mill. Lately, though, he'd found he had some talent with the plane, for Mister Tolver had let him smooth down the planks for a travel chest and been pleased with the outcome. "You've got hands for the wood," he'd said with a nod as his own gnarled hands swept over Jeremy's work. "Thanks for lending them to me while Sam was gone out."

Jeremy had found the compliment unexpectedly gratifying.

It was one of the old man's three daughters, Lillie, who spoke to him now. Her blue eyes, though oft times averted in what he had supposed was maidenly bashfulness, met his with surprising boldness and unwavering confidence now.

"I should hope you'd know me, Miss Tolver, after nearly a month's acquaintance," he replied with a friendly smile.

"'Twas before. Then you were dressed in a gentleman's gear and riding a beautiful horse, not wearing homespun and lookin' to buy Allan Ludlow's swayed mare," she said, her voice warm and low. "But I'm not about to tell anyone, so don't be afeared on that score." Her assurances seemed sincere and Jeremy nodded.

"Can you sit then, Miss Tolver, and tell me who you think I am?"

She glanced back at the kitchen door. "I suppose so as I've served up Papa and Sam already." She settled down on the stool opposite his near the workshop fire. Her original boldness seemed to fade a bit as her eyes met his again and she lowered her eyes from his gaze.

"It's all right, Miss Tolver. I'm not going to bite you, not within shouting distance of that hulking protector of yours."

Lillie laughed nervously. "Oh, Sam's a dear, for all he looks so fierce. He'd only toss you out the door, I think. 'Sides, he's sweet on Rose, not me." She sighed, then gave him a wary smile, some of her easiness returning. Of Tolver's three daughters, Lillie was the one he'd most enjoyed being around in the last four weeks, both to talk to and to look at. Though she'd been sparing in her conversation, what she *had* said was often teasingly witty or spoken with honest sincerity. She had finer features than her sisters, too, and a slighter figure. What he could see of her hair beneath the concealment of her ever-present lace cap appeared to be the color of flax, while her sisters had pale brown locks. And her eyes, which fixed him now with a challenging stare, were so pale as to be almost colorless.

"It's not Jeremy Harwood, is it, though the Jeremy's right enough? I worked for a time at my uncle's inn in Castleford," she said, as if that explained everything, then continued when he pretended puzzlement. "It was nearly five years ago. I was just fourteen then, but I remember you well enough. You used to visit there quite often. My cousin Marian was sweet on you, 'til she got married that is." She lowered her voice. "You were Jeremy Knox then, that highwayman they say was hanged a couple of months back. Lord, I cried when I heard, for I remembered you being such a fine young man and it didn't seem right you were dead and all, and your lady killed, too. Not right at all. I was so glad when I saw you weren't hanged, though I didn't know it was you 'til after you'd cleaned up a bit," she admitted with a smile.

Jeremy knew from her tone of voice that she was thoroughly convinced of his identity and he thought quickly about whether to attempt a denial or trust her apparent good intentions to keep quiet.

"And you've been keeping this mighty secret for nearly a month, have you?" he asked with a smile of indifference. "Oh, my dear Miss Tolver, I'm glad of that, for I must tell you I'm *not* that unfortunate man, nor would I have wanted the authorities to catch me up on your mistaken testimony."

Lillie looked at him with such a look of hurt on her face that he almost relented and admitted she was right. Almost. But he could not afford that anyone, not even the good-hearted daughter of his employer, know with certainty who he was. Jeremy Knox must stay dead if Jeremy Harwood were to live.

"I'm sorry, Mister *Harwood*," she said, standing to go. "I thought only to offer consolation, an ear for your troubles, you know. Sometimes you look so sad—"

"As I am *not* the late, unlamented man of whom you spoke, I am in no need of consolation, Miss Tolver. An understanding ear, of course, is always a welcome offer."

She nodded, her face a mixture of hurt, anger, embarrassment, and, he could not mistake it, affection. She bobbed a curtsey and hurried back to the main part of the house.

Surely the chit hadn't been entertaining romantic notions of him! He sighed. He would have to be leaving, the sooner the better. He wanted no entanglements of that sort again, not for a good, long time.

Jeremy had thought he would have to avoid the enamored Miss Tolver, but she seemed bent on avoiding him instead, which made the next week proceed more tolerably than he had anticipated. Rose or Martha usually brought out his and Benjamin's supper, and on the one occasion when Lillie brought it, she was carefully friendly, as if he were only a customer at the shop. Benjamin noticed.

"That were odd," he commented through a mouthful of bread. "She use ta stop and visit a bit. You do somethin' ta grieve her?"

Jeremy shook his head and swallowed. "Not that I recall."

"Maybe she's gone sweet on ya," Benjamin teased.

"Doubt it," he said sullenly.

And so he worked and saved. He'd bought a new shirt and breeches for himself and Benjamin first thing, though Mister Tolver had been understanding about their ragged clothing, suggesting only that they were welcome to use the laundry tub next wash day. He'd gotten used to the rough feel of his clothes long since, but there was no joy in the wearing of them as with his former apparel. "Someday," he promised himself as he'd set down the money at the dry goods store. "And soon." Benjamin, on the other hand, had never had such

29

fine clothes the whole of his life, or so he claimed. "Always wore others' leavins," he grinned. "Always had stains and mending patches twice over. Ah, I'll take good care of these, Mister Harwood."

Another week, he thought, *and I'll have enough put by for Ludlow's nag and food along the way. Then it's Kirkpatrick.* Never had he thought when he'd stashed part of his money in Scotland that it would be so hard to retrieve. He'd always taken for granted that he'd be on horseback, not afoot, and that he'd be fleeing capture with coin in his pocket, not recovering from gun shot wounds and penniless to boot.

"Jeremy my lad," came Mister Tolver's voice above the grating of Sam's plane. "Give me a hand here, will you?"

Jeremy hurried over and helped the old man lift an oak leaf onto a worktable. It amazed him that so old a man could have three such young daughters. Rose was twenty, Lillie almost nineteen, and Martha only fifteen. By his observation, Mister Tolver was seventy if he were a day, which meant he'd begun siring his offspring when he was at least fifty. And where was Missus Tolver? That information had not been offered by any of the Tolver family and he was not about to ask. The less known, the better when it came to getting mixed up with other peoples' lives.

"Thanks lad," the old man smiled. "And I'll be needing those others from the store room if you'd fetch them please."

Jeremy nodded and left. He found he enjoyed some parts of his current life, and, surprisingly, taking orders from Mister Tolver was one of them. The work was sometimes strenuous but not oppressive, and it was pleasant not to have to think about what one had to do next. There was a routine to the day dictated by necessity, and then there was doing what Mister Tolver said with no need to wonder about the wisdom or folly of it. Worthy labor for honest wages. He had once chafed at the idea of making ones way in the world by such menial methods, which is why thieving had appealed to him. Now he realized it was not so bad, though he knew that Mister Tolver was probably a more agreeable taskmaster than most.

"Oh," came a squeak as he bumped open the storeroom door. "Oh, it's just you," Lillie laughed, her hand on her chest.

"Sorry to give you a start. You need help with those?"

She had taken two small barrels down from a shelf—kitchen supplies he supposed—and had been bending to pick one of them up when he'd surprised her.

"No, no, I move them all the time."

"But one trip instead of two," he pointed out. "Surely that would serve."

Lillie smiled and looked at the two barrels. "Very well, Mister… Mister Harwood, if it won't inconvenience Papa."

"He seemed in no hurry," he said amiably and slung one barrel onto his shoulder while she cradled the other. He realized that the effort had cost him little discomfort to either his leg or midsection, a realization that made him smile to himself with satisfaction. Perhaps he'd be less plagued by the phantom pains that awakened him at night, jolting him from his sleep with a such a start that he felt as if he had been shot again. The notion came as a great relief—

"You're merry today," Lillie commented shyly as he began to follow her from the storeroom.

"'Tis a fine day," he answered. "It has enticed me from my usual melancholy."

"I'm glad to see it. You're face improves with cheerfulness."

"You cannot know, Miss Tolver, how gratified I am to have brightened your day by not being my usual grumpy, ugly self."

She turned to face him again, a worried look on her face. "I surely didn't mean to imply any such thing," she protested. "I only meant—Oh, you're teasing," she said, stammering to a halt, a blush brightening her cheeks. "Shame on you, Mister Harwood, and shame on me for being such a ninny." She gave him a scolding little glance, and turned back toward the kitchen again. Then—so suddenly that he almost trod on her toe—she turned around again to face him.

"I have to say it now, Mister Harwood. It's been bearing on my mind this last week. I'm so sorry to have intruded upon your privacy as I did, truly I am. I do understand why you must pretend as you do. And I promise to *never* bring my suspicions before you again. I just want you to know that your secret is safe with me. I'd *die* before I'd tell anyone."

Her words summoned the oft-dreamt, nightmarish image of Bess, her chest a gaping mass of crimson, and the suddenness of it shook his usual composure.

31

"Don't be a damn fool," he scolded and saw Lillie take a step back from the unexpected harshness of his voice. He took a deep breath to calm himself. "Go ahead and tell them," he commanded quietly but earnestly. "Scream it from the roof if it means you'll live. I'll have no more silly, lovesick girls dying out of a false sense of honor. Do you understand me?" he asked when she remained silent and wide-eyed before him.

She nodded, then turned around resolutely. Their companionable interlude of a few moments before had vanished into bitterness and, curse him, it was his fault. He could have been less stern. He could have laughed it off. But, damn, he couldn't bear to think of Lillie harmed—

"Thank you, Mister Harwood," she said stonily when they reached the kitchen. "You can put it down here."

He did as he was told, then left without looking at her. Thank goodness he was leaving in a week, he reminded himself. He'd make Ilkley the first day if the old mare would accommodate him, and leave Leeds and the troublesome Miss Tolver far behind.

"Now's the time to decide," Jeremy told Benjamin one evening as they straightened the shop. He'd bought the mare that morning, paid Ludlow a day's stabling, then bought two warm coats, one for himself and one for Benjamin, though it was yards too big for him, he knew. The boy would grow. All was ready.

"Ain't ya goin' to give Mister Tolver notice then? Nor even a fare thee well? He's been more'n kind."

"That he has, but I'm not one for farewells, Benjamin. They're a waste of time when all's said, and no one the happier for them."

Benjamin had stopped sweeping and stared down at the floor. Then he muttered something.

"What?" Jeremy asked.

He was surprised when Benjamin turned up a tear-streaked face. "I want ta stay," he said earnestly. "But I want us *both* ta stay. It's been right good here, hasn't it? Got food, a bed, a roof, no complaints..." His tears ran faster as he recited these virtues. "I ain't never had..." He stopped, his face darkening with a sudden thought. "Think they'd turn me out if ya goes without me?"

32

Jeremy shook his head. "No. But I'm leaving a bit of blunt with you to mind 'til I come back through here," he said, the resolution coming to him as he spoke, for surely he'd had no such plans mere moments ago. "You'll be able to live all right on your own if they do. So, what's it to be?"

Benjamin looked at him with such uncertainty, Jeremy was tempted to spare the boy his inner battle and order him one way or the other. The problem was, he wasn't sure which to choose himself. The idea of being alone again was both appealing and appalling. Benjamin was a pleasant companion, but was it selfish to drag the boy away from the only stability he'd ever known—

"I'll stay," came the boy's strangled words. "But what'll I say when they ask me why ya up an' left so sudden like?"

"Tell them I've gone to collect an inheritance we've come into," Jeremy said matter-of-factly. He'd already worked out that much of an explanation at least. "Tell them I just got word our old auntie died and I've gone to fetch our share."

Benjamin nodded. "Good story," he said sadly. He took the coins Jeremy handed him and stared at them without really seeming to see them for a few moments.

"That's to see you through," Jeremy explained again.

"Till ya come back," Benjamin said flatly.

"I'll not forget you," Jeremy said. "Shall we say our good-byes now? I'll be leaving before the sun's up."

Benjamin nodded, slipped the coins into his pocket, then set aside his broom. "Good-bye, Mister Knox, for that's who ya'll always be ta me. It were an honor throwin' in with ya for a time." He straightened his shoulders and extended a hand in almost as good a manner as any gentleman could have managed. Jeremy returned the gesture.

"Take good care of the Tolvers," he told him, fighting an unexpected urge to throw his arms around the boy. His throat felt unaccountably tight. "And always know I hold it to be an act of God and one Benjamin Twigg that I'm still in this world at all. You saved me from the noose, boy, and that's a mighty accomplishment." He paused. "Thank you, Benjamin."

The boy nodded, his face still wet. "Night, Mister Knox."

* * *

33

"So you're going," a soft voice stated as he lifted the latch to the back door.

He turned to face her. "Aye, I must. Benjamin'll explain things in the morning."

"It *is* the morning," she said. "You didn't know I did the morning baking, did you, or you'd have been gone before I'd a chance to discover you."

Jeremy nodded. "Aye. I'm not one for good-byes."

"Or for thank yous either."

He frowned, realizing the justice of her words. "I'm coming back, Miss Tolver. Benjamin will explain—"

"No you're not," she said simply. "We'll never see you again."

Jeremy scowled more deeply. "You're wrong, Miss Tolver. I'll be back. But if you insist on believing I won't, then here I offer my thanks for your father's kindness and trust. Will you convey my gratitude to him for me?"

"Of course," she said.

The pause between them lengthened into awkwardness. Jeremy wanted to turn and go, but he could not seem to take his eyes from hers. He noticed, not for the first time, what a pale shade of blue they were, like two pieces of a summer sky.

"Come here," he said quietly, speaking before he'd fully considered his words. It was only when she began moving slowly but willingly toward him that he knew why he'd called to her. He wanted to see those eyes more closely before he left, to really look at them and not just try to remember them from the brief glimpses he'd gotten in the past six weeks. And then, when she was at last standing before him, he knew he also wanted to kiss her and that he should not. He held his sack of belongings over one shoulder and his other hand was on the door. He was safe as long as he didn't move.

"You're a good person, Lillie," he said sadly, drinking in the watery blueness of her gaze. "Don't throw away your heart on some undeserving fellow who hasn't an ounce of honor to repay common kindnesses."

Sure as he could read the contents of a purse to within a shilling, he read the sudden look of pity in her eyes and he frowned again. She felt sorry for him, this naive girl safe in her family and with her tidy view of the world. His hand clenched on the door to pull it open.

"No," she commanded with a whisper. "Don't go away angry. Please. May I give you a common kindness, Jeremy?" And without waiting for a reply she put her hands on either side of his face and tiptoed up for a kiss.

Jeremy's eyes shut involuntarily. He found himself savoring the warmth of a human touch even more than the intimacy of her kiss. He had not known himself capable of missing such a simple thing as the caress of fingers on his face or the yielding softness of lips pressed to his. And when she withdrew, he felt suddenly adrift, like a boat cut from its moorings in a swift river. He opened his eyes to see her figure disappearing down the corridor that led to the main house.

She had said she offered him a common kindness, but Christ, it didn't feel like a kindness. Rather a curse, for he now knew the sad truth of his life and the reason for her pity. He'd chosen a path unencumbered with emotional ties, not even to the boy who had saved him or the old man who had trusted a dirty beggar to do an honest day's work. And certainly not to the young woman who knew who he was and offered her understanding anyway. "An unencumbered life" he'd thought it. "A life alone and lonely" he now knew it to be.

He tugged open the door and pulled his coat tighter against the pre-dawn chill.

Chapter Four

He well knew the figure he cut along the road skirting the Dales was not the figure he had once cut just a few months ago. Here was not the straight-backed, impeccably-dressed, well-armed gentleman on a fine, spirited steed dancing along the road with a smile of assurance on his lips. Far from it. He could not see himself at a distance, of course, but he imagined how he must appear to passersby. The mare—what had Ludlow called her? Nellie? Nibbly? Some such unworthy appellation for an unworthy beast—plodded at best, even when he managed to compel her into a trot. He'd brooded on their slow progress the first day, knowing he'd be lucky if he made shelter by nightfall. The next morning she'd begun making a kind of wheezing sound, and he worried instead that she might not even make it to Scotland at all. He'd let her keep her own pace from then on. Any horse was better than no horse, he'd learned that much, but could God have created a more pitiful animal? Jeremy almost felt guilty burdening her with his weight and wondered if others silently reproached him for being a heartless scoundrel for riding the poor creature.

And as to *his* appearance that, too, was a great alteration. After buying the nag, a broken saddle and crumbling tack, and clothing and coats for himself and Benjamin, he had not had the money to spare on better shoes, so Philip Twigg's boxy half-boots hung loosely on his feet. The stirrups were all that held them on when he rode, as he'd discovered when his foot had slipped from the worn stirrup one afternoon and his boot had promptly fallen with a thud onto the dusty road. His stockings were knobby wool to the knee, there to be met by bulky woolen breeches that a man twice his width could have worn. Indeed, for the lower classes, unless one made ones own clothing or had a wife to do it for him, the dry goods store sold only three sizes— small for the boys, large for most men, as he now wore, and extremely large for the more portly. It was no advantage to keep ones figure if one were poor, he mused, for what did a fine figure matter when it was concealed beneath massive folds of fabric? The sack-like shirt was no better but was hidden most of the time by his coat, which, despite its ugly cut, was a welcomed bit of warmth on the November road.

As to his posture, though that was certainly within his power to control, he had discovered within a few days of dragging along the road that he could not force himself to assume his former haughtiness of bearing. He did not feel proud, either of his horse or himself, so to ride as if he were seemed a terrible sham. Worse than a sham, it appeared idiotic! And dangerous, too, for he did not have the means to defend himself if someone took umbrage at his stately manners. Better to make oneself look like so much baggage atop a miserable nag, a down-on-his-luck crofter, perhaps, seeking better luck elsewhere. That image, at least, was nearer the truth.

Although he had purchased only one meal a day, and a scant one at that, and never a bed for the night, he found his money running low well before he reached Penrith. His slow pace had lengthened his journey by many days and he cursed himself for having been soft in the head and giving Benjamin part of his wages. The Tolvers wouldn't turn the boy out, or at least he doubted they would, so it had been an empty gesture and one he was now regretting every time his stomach growled. He briefly considered copping some food from a farmhouse, but he'd never been one to steal from those who could ill-afford to replace what he'd taken. He had enough for some bread and a bit of cheese when he reached the next village. Maybe he'd see about working a few days there, any job would do, then pushing for Penrith where there was bound to be more opportunity for work—

Penrith. It was the last place he'd seen his mother nine years ago when he'd lit out with a purse of her money and a tossed back curse. She wasn't one to stay in one place for long, and now that she didn't have either himself or his sister to concern her—not that they ever much had—she could be anyplace.

What would he say to her if by chance they met? The same murderous inclinations that warmed his blood when he thought of Tim Mott quickened his pulse as he thought of the circumstances that had sent him fleeing from her in disgust and which had nearly

37

prompted him to suicide at seventeen. But one mustn't kill one's mother, he thought, no matter how foul a creature she was. There was something soul-deep, perhaps from having inhabited her body before one was even a conscious being, that kept most people reluctant to make a strike against the woman who had held the power of life and death over their infant selves. And his mother had wielded that power over his hapless young sister, too.

To say Lydia Knox was a whore was to not quite describe her adequately, though in the beginning, perhaps, she had been merely a foolish woman who enjoyed the heady feeling of being sought after by powerful men. She had been the daughter of a well-to-do gentleman farmer and that, perhaps, had been her greatest misfortune, for although her family moved in society upon occasion, it was on the lowest fringes. This placed her and her stunning beauty in the way of men who might yearn for her favors but would never consider extending her the honor of a marriage proposal. Once, when he was just a lad, she had told him of her first affair with such a tone of bitterness that he had wanted to find the man and challenge him for his mother's sake. After that initial heartbreak, she said, she had learned the way of things. She didn't want to marry the sullen gentlemen of her own rank who applied for her hand before her scandalous behavior became generally known. She wanted what wealthy men could give her and gladly exchanged her body and attentions with one after another.

Early on, Daniel Harwood, the arrogant young heir to the barony of Carlisle, had become enamored of the beautiful Lydia Knox, who, according to Jeremy's mother, had noticed her as they'd both attended a traveling theater performance in Carlisle. He had pursued her to her father's home outside of Brampton, for she was still under that worthy gentleman's roof at the time, and convinced her that she would forever be his love if not ever his wife. Lovely apartments in Carlisle were rented and Lydia, who doubted his vow of constancy but had seen an opportunity for more merriment than the country offered, agreed to the affair.

It was to be short-lived, as it turned out, and Jeremy was often upbraided for his part in its premature ending, for he had had the audacity to be conceived within the year, which cooled the future Lord Harwood's ardor significantly.

Despite the birth of her first bastard, Lydia Knox managed to coax Daniel Harwood into paying her way a while longer and even escorting her to various outings where she might find his replacement. He was willing to comply, it seemed, not just because of her beauty. Even in illicit activities there was a code of honor among the high born. Not that his father really cared about Lydia, Jeremy now understood, but the opinion of his fellow peerage, that was another matter. It was a gentleman's duty to see that his former mistress found another protector.

It didn't take long, according to his mother. Of course, she had told the story as a way of bragging about her great beauty and eliciting a compliment from her impressionable son, but the upshot had been that she had moved with her new lover, a Sir Percy Southey, to Manchester. Jeremy remembered liking Manchester, for when he was hardly a toddler, its streets had been his playground. There was much bustle to keep him occupied and he actually attended school (one of the "requests" his mother had been granted by Sir Southey) for nearly ten years. Of course by the time his formal education was terminated, Sir Southey was a distant memory, having been replaced by a string of lovers he found too tiresome to bother remembering. One of them, though, had fathered dear little Eleanor, and Jeremy had become an adoring big brother at the age of six. He watched her in the evenings while their mother was "entertaining" her latest conquest. Whenever he thought of Eleanor, Jeremy found his inclinations toward her were more fatherly than brotherly, for he had never felt the urge to tease or tattle on the little girl, but only to protect her and offer tenderness.

They had moved again, and then again, and each time Jeremy made it a point to know the city or town as best he could, partly to glean those advantages that familiarity invariable brought—like when the big houses cleaned their larders of perfectly grand foodstuffs and set it out for the rag and bone men, or who was willing to give a boy a cup of gin just for cleaning up a bit of puke from the pothouse floor— and partly because he'd realized early in life that the better one knew one's surroundings, the safer one was. And it was his job to keep Eleanor, and, to a certain degree, his mother, safe.

Lydia's "admirers" became more numerous and less exalted, but then she was in her mid-thirties and had lost the blush of youth if not any of her stunning looks. The family had been installed in Penrith by an ancient gentleman of commerce when Jeremy was nearly seventeen and Eleanor a pretty eleven-year-old. The year was 1751— a year he would never forget—and just as Jeremy was beginning his reconnoiter of Penrith, the ancient lover had died...in his mother's bed! It was a dilemma, for who should be contacted to dispose of the remains? The man's family? Hardly. And surely not the constable. Jeremy had carried the thin gentleman a ways down the street in the middle of the night and leaned him as kindly as he could against a wall.

Although Jeremy hired on at the smithy, times grew hard. They had to move to smaller quarters, but not so small that there wasn't always a room where Lydia could do her entertaining. Her admirers, if they could still be called that, visited mainly in the afternoons when he was gone at work, but Eleanor had no such escape from the sordidness of her mother's "means of support." She grew somber and withdrawn, and Jeremy ached to make her smile again but did not know how to go about it. He put by any extra he could manage, though that was just pennies a week, and planned to take Eleanor and himself away to "someplace better," wherever that might be.

But his plans never reached fruition, at least not for Eleanor. He came home one afternoon to find his mother curled up in a corner and weeping uncontrollably.

"Oh, Jeremy," she'd sobbed over and over. "Oh, Jeremy, what shall I do now? I didn't know he was that sort or I'd have never agreed. Oh, poor little Ellie. Poor child. Poor child..."

Eleanor? His chest had frozen with dread, for he had never seen his mother cry in his entire life and if something to do with Eleanor had moved her to such grief, it must be terrible indeed.

"What of Eleanor?" he'd asked, then shaken her shoulders to gain her attention. "Mother, where's Eleanor?"

"I didn't mean her any harm, and we needed the money. He promised to pay well, and we need the money, don't we? It's a simple thing, usually, and often pleasant—"

He hadn't bothered to question her further but had dashed toward the back room, praying as he ran that his apprehensions were groundless, that Eleanor's dear face would greet him as ever, with love and patience.

He had lost the contents of his stomach against the wall upon seeing her partially-clad body atop the bedclothes, and sank like a rag doll to his knees, his head in his arms to hide the reality lying before him. He thought his heart might stop, it was pounding so wildly, and his whole body trembled. Not dead! Not dead! He refused to believe what his own eyes had told him in just a glance. She *was* dead. The open vacancy of her eyes above her twisted, bruised neck left no room for denial, yet still he would not believe it. Not Eleanor! Oh, God, not my dear little Eleanor.

He had come out of his paralysis in just a few moments, though in that short stretch of time his entire life had shifted and dissolved. Still breathing heavily, he had risen from his knees and gone to the bed, seating himself upon it and gazing in cold fascination at his sister's body. He mechanically pulled her blouse down to cover her chest, which had just the beginnings of breasts on its childish expanse, then did the same with her bloodied lower torso. Had this been her first time or had the encounter merely been so brutal it had wounded her? He wasn't sure that he wanted to know, and yet he did. He wanted to know just how badly he had failed as her protector. Had her growing unhappiness been only because she'd had to endure an unwholesome home life as he'd presumed, or had she been forced to become a child whore and there had been the cause of her despair?

The man had strangled her while they'd coupled. His thumbs had left their grim marks in nearly-black bruises across her thin neck. Such a small neck, it had probably not taken long, he thought numbly. It looked broken besides, so perhaps she had not suffered long...

He heard footsteps behind him and stood to face his mother.

"How long have you been selling your own daughter?!" he'd demanded.

Lydia Knox had not answered, only shaken her head in what seemed to Jeremy like self-pity. "What will I do?" she'd asked him. "She brought in good coin. I'm not young anymore, Jeremy. What will I do now?"

"Go to hell, I hope," he'd hissed and then pushed past her as if he no longer knew she was there. He had taken up his traveling satchel, stuffed it speedily with his belongings, then kicked his boot through the secret panel beside the bed.

"What are you doing!?" his mother had demanded as he'd grabbed out a purse of coin. "You can't leave me with nothing."

He'd wrenched open the purse and tossed a handful of coins at her feet. "Enough to bury your daughter," he'd said coldly. "You deserve no more."

"Go hang yourself, you little bastard," she had responded with surprising vehemence, and made a grab for the purse, but he had sidestepped her and sent her to the floor with a quick shove.

"Maybe I will," he'd answered.

And that was the last he'd seen of Lydia Knox.

He had heard of her, of course, and wondered at the vagaries of this world. For it had been *his* reputation as a highwayman that had led to his mother's renewed favor among some of the older roués in England. She was now the mother of an infamous thief, a titillating attraction evidently, for he had heard her mentioned in fairly high circles.

He had not fallen to thievery immediately, of course. At first he had continued smithing in Penrith, but the proximity to Eleanor's place of murder and the occasional mention of his mother about town, especially in connection with some coarse chap or other, had driven him to near self-destruction. He had utterly failed his sister and could not forgive himself for having been so blind to her peril. He found he enjoyed the easy dullness of drinking and spent more than he could afford at the pothouses each evening.

One night he had tried to forget his sorrow in the arms of a tavern girl, but had found to his embarrassment that he could not perform, for Eleanor's young, blank-eyed face rose up to remind him of where one man's lust had led. That night—drunk and humiliated and utterly without a notion of why he should have even been born let alone why he should keep living—he had tied a rope around the crossbeam of the smithy and prepared to hang himself. He'd passed out before he'd managed to tie the loop, and in the cold light of morning had known he had to leave Penrith if he were to retain his sanity and his life.

He had gone to Huddleston and smithed there for a time, but although it was honest work, it had barely kept him clothed and fed. For most of his life, his mother's gentlemen friends had kept them all in fine style and he missed the ease of that time. In short, he wanted more. Much more. In the back of his mind was a desire to show the world, and his cursed parents especially, that he was not just a common laborer, a nobody. He wanted them to know he was exceptional and to regret that they had failed to appreciate that fact. Yet he did not want to give them the satisfaction of feeling proud of his greatness. He must not become a clever businessman or a man of medicine or even a successful farmer. The theater might do, but even that was gaining some respectability.

His first hold-up had been on a dare; a stupid affair, really, but one that had set him on his illicit course.

He'd left Huddleston for York a year after Eleanor's murder and had fallen in with a band of burglars quite by accident. They thieved from houses in the dark of night, especially houses where the owners were absent and only a few servants remained. Jeremy was quick to see the disadvantages, for city houses were often hard to breach, were surrounded by helpful neighbors, and even the most ancient steward had ample time to produce a firearm to protect his master's possessions. He'd pointed these things out to his three "friends."

"'Spose you got a better idea?" Charlie Flinch had taunted. "You young fellas always think ya know best."

"'Tis less hazard on the road," Jeremy had offered, "if it's done well."

That had led to a chorus of laughter. "Just ride up pretty as you please, eh? 'Scuse me, sir. 'and over your booty.' 'ow's that less 'azardous, might I ask?"

"If you pick your mark and the place well enough," he'd said with a shrug.

"We dare's ya," said John Boole. "We'll keep ta thievin' our way, you goes your way. We'll meet up again, what? In a month? Compares our takes."

"He'll be dead in a month," Rupert Boole had laughed. "'S'been nice knowin' ya, lad."

But he hadn't died. He'd prospered. He'd taken his cut and bought himself a fairly able horse, then had his best clothes laundered and pressed so his horse didn't look better than he did. He bought a pawned sword and an old pistol, both more gaudy than fine, for he thought that might have some emotional advantage, both for himself and his victims, during a robbery. And then he started riding the countryside south of York, searching out places where it would be easy to secret himself or where a coach or wagon wouldn't be able to make a run or turn. It took him nearly three weeks to set himself up, but finally he had done the thing…and it had been wonderfully easy.

He'd seen a likely mark at an inn in one of York's finer districts. The portly man was traveling alone with only a driver. The carriage was small, the two horses past their prime, but Jeremy had spotted the man's elegant waistcoat, a golden watch fob hanging on his round belly, and then noted the excellence of the man's shoes. He would learn in the years to come what true indicators of wealth shoes often were, even for a man traveling in less that dashing attire. He had heard the man tell his driver to make sure the horses had an extra measure of feed for their journey the next day.

Wandering into the courtyard the next morning, a pipe between his teeth, Jeremy had leaned against the stable wall in seeming boredom and watched the driver bring out a small lock box and put it in the boot of the carriage. Then, while the portly gentleman was still breakfasting within, Jeremy saddled his horse, took an extra length of rope to secure the box to his saddle if needed, primed his pistol, and set out on the most likely road the carriage would take in its journey south.

And he'd been right. Along came the carriage at a modest clip. He scanned the road to make sure there were no travelers near enough to interfere, then nudged his horse forward just in time to startle the driver into pulling up the pair so tightly that they nearly stepped back through their traces. He saw the man reach for thc pistol in his waistband.

"Kindly put up your hands, there's a good man," he'd said, trying to cover his youth with elegance. His mother's lovers had at least taught him how to speak like a gentleman.

"And good day to you, sir," he then greeted the head that popped out the window. "I've already cocked my piece, so you'd best throw down if you value your head."

The man begrudgingly tossed his unprepared weapon out the window and Jeremy whistled in admiration. "That's a fine weapon, sir. Too bad you missed the opportunity to demonstrate its superiority to my own poor pistol, though mine's sufficient to the day."

"What do you want, you blackguard? As you can see by my personal effects, you've made a poor choice of victims."

"Your pair of pistols is enough to tempt me."

"I've no pair—"

"Surely that has a mate," he said with a nod toward the pistol in the road. "I'll ask you to throw down the other, please, butt first."

The man scowled but complied. "Now let me pass," he ordered.

"Of course," Jeremy said obligingly. He found he quite liked the banter of his new trade. "But first have your man step down and retrieve that rather heavy looking chest from the boot. These old horses of yours will never make it to your destination with all that weight."

"Not on your life!" the man had said, red-faced with anger.

Jeremy had extended his arm and taken careful aim at the man's head. "I beg you to reconsider, sir, for t'will not be my life forfeit this day, but yours."

"You bastard."

"How perceptive of you. Now do it," he'd ordered, his eyes never leaving the gentleman but keeping track of the driver in the corner of his eye as he'd hurried to fetch the box from the back.

"Leave it in the road and drive on," he'd commanded, "oh, and *your* pistol, too, my good man. Can't have you shooting me when I go to fetch my prize."

"I'll see you hang," the fat man had yelled as his carriage had jumped forward.

"And a good journey to you, sir," Jeremy had called, tipping the point of his tricorn hat up with the barrel of his gun.

When he'd met Charlie, John, and Rupert the following week, he was wearing a new and costly velvet coat and vest, a linen shirt tied with a lace cravat, form-fitting breeches, and the finest pair of boots that could be gotten in York, most all of it done to order for himself alone. It was amazing how the sight of several gold sovereigns could speed the pace of most working men. His friends were visibly impressed.

"You win, lad," Charlie agreed. "We'll throw in with you from now on. Make a pretty penny, we will."

Jeremy had taken a swig of his ale, then shaken his head. "I work alone, my friends."

"You was just lucky this time," Rupert countered. "Even ol' Dick had Matt King at 'is side."

"And ended up at the end of a rope with him not far from here," Jeremy had replied matter-of-factly. "I'd like to avoid that eventuality for as long as possible, and partners seem more a liability than an asset."

"What's that you say? Speak plain, man."

"I work alone," he'd repeated.

"Then we'll do our own hold-ups, us three tagether," Rupert had threatened.

Jeremy had nodded and finished his ale. "Then good luck to you. I wish you well. And may we never see one another on the gibbet."

He'd headed further south, then, so as not to collide or compete with his old comrades, though that had turned out to be unnecessary. All three were dead, one shot and the others hanged, by the end of the year.

Chapter Five

Penrith was as cluttered a town as ever, or maybe it was just the ghosts of near-forgotten nightmares that made it seem so. Jeremy had been through its environs many a time, of course, to make "deposits" in Scotland, but he had never lingered long. Eleanor's murder would be enough of a strike against the place, he supposed, but here was also the birthplace of his hatred for his mother and the place, too, that had seen him close to self-slaughter. But this time, his money gone, he would have to stay awhile.

It continued to amaze him that his inclination for thievery had so abandoned him that he was willing to stay even here. After all, he was traveling to retrieve his ill-gotten wealth in Scotland, and planning to put it to good use again. Why not steal a bit more to speed his journey along?

Because, came the answer, *that was then*. Then it had been a different Jeremy, a Jeremy who had never considered that his actions would affect anyone other than himself. He had not thought a lovely, dark-haired girl would lose her life on his account, nor that if he were ever shot it would be his horse and not himself who would die. He suddenly realized that in this he was very like his mother. She, too, had led an ill-considered life. She had not thought of the children she might bear to face the taint of illegitimacy. She had not thought how her immorality would then poison their young years, for certainly he and Eleanor could never be proud of anything about their lives or their mother except, perhaps, her beauty. And worst of all, she had not considered how the more perverted of her admirers might victimize those children. He had often wondered since Eleanor's death how he himself had escaped being buggered all those years, attributing it finally to luck and his penchant to be gone from home whenever possible. His mother's self-serving thoughtlessness had seen her daughter slain and yet, from all he had heard about her in the last nine years, she had recovered her balance quite nicely and gone on to more infamy. He wondered how she was faring now that he had supposedly been dispatched, either by gun shot or noose depending on the preference of the pothouse storyteller.

He would be like her no longer! That was part of his vow to reform. His years of thieving with impunity had at last had a terrible consequence, just as his lack of foresight had been partially to blame for Eleanor's fate. If it took him days, or even weeks, to earn the money that he'd need to eat until he reached Kirkpatrick, so be it. It was only a day and half ride to the border usually, but more like three or four at old Nellie's pace. He might do without food for a day or two, but not three or four, not willingly. No, it was work or go hungry. And it was Penrith or no place.

"What ya starin' at, lad?"

The old man's voice startled Jeremy from his contemplation and he forced a smile to his face.

"I used to live there," he said, nodding to the building across the street from the tailor shop before which he stood. By his appearance, the old gentleman was the proprietor of that establishment and must have become concerned by the less-than-dashing stranger loitering before his door, his gaze fixed upward. "I just wondered... It looks better than I recall."

"Changed hands and been fixed up. 'Bout time, it was. Descent folks livin' there now, not like before—" He stopped, suddenly aware of how his words might be taken. "Beg pardon, lad. No slight intended."

"None taken," Jeremy assured him, turning his gaze back to the second story window that had once been his mother's. "I'm glad, believe me, for my memories are not fond ones, I assure you."

"Evil doin's, and a-plenty. Tosspots brawlin' in the middle of the night, doxies plying their trade...even a few murders. Was you here then?"

Jeremy nodded. "I was. A little girl was murdered—"

"Oh, aye, I remember!" the man said with a vigorous nod of his head. "Poor little thing. Her mother was a whore, you know, but the lass was a sweet child. Made the Missus and I weep to hear of it."

"Did they ever catch the man?" Jeremy asked with as much disinterest as he could manage over his thundering heart. He wished he hadn't come, and then he was glad that he had.

"No, but not 'cuz he weren't known," the tailor said with a snort. "I knowed the minute I heard of it that that villain, Bramhearst, must a been in town, and right I was."

"Bramhearst?"

"Earl of Varnley, down Dorset way. Comes visitin' his kin up here, treats himself to a night or two on the town, then leaves. Usually a whore or two dead or missin' after he goes."

"Why—" Jeremy stopped, taking a deep breath to control the fury he'd heard spring into his voice. He exhaled, smoothing his features into what he hoped looked like idle curiosity. "Why, then, hasn't this Bramhearst fellow been apprehended?"

The tailor shrugged. "No proof for one. And two, he's got the blunt to pay his way clear, I'd expect. There's no other explanation I can see, and I can't think he'd just single out our poor girls. Like as not he does the same wherever he goes."

"So he lives in Dorset? Whereabouts?"

"Don't know."

"What's his first name?"

"Don't know that either. Why ya want ta know?"

Jeremy forced yet another false smile to his lips. "Avoidance," he said simply. "It doesn't pay to cross paths with such an animal."

The tailor nodded and turned back into his shop, obviously satisfied that Jeremy wasn't there to do any mischief. Jeremy watched him go with an odd feeling of gratitude and anxiety. The man had given him a piece of information that, if true, answered a question he had long held in his mind.

Who had killed Eleanor?

But now, with a bit of money in his pocket and his course set for Scotland, he had to decide whether or not to act upon that information.

The sheets felt good on his skin. The pillow, though not of the best feathering, was far superior to the leaves and dirt that he'd endured for so long, or even the straw bedding in the Tolver's little workshop room. He'd just stripped off his new clothes, but their feeling stayed on his skin. The soft linen shirt with the ruffled cuff and neck. The lined, woolen breeches that actually had a waistband and fit him well. The thin leggings that hugged his calf. And best of all, the boots that let him walk with a normal stride rather than a shuffling clomp. He had not purchased the best that money could buy, though not for lack of desire. He had wanted the finer things from the Kirkpatrick clothier, had even let his hand wander over the more valuable materials before selecting the lesser quality fabrics. Common sense, and a healthy portion of fear, had determined his choices. He must not appear as he once had. He did not want to jeopardize his anonymity, and dressing to the nines would perhaps raise unwanted suspicions. Also, now that he was set to travel the roads again, he did not want to appear too tempting a mark. Odd, but he had never worried about his fellow thieves robbing from him in the old days. They wouldn't dare, he'd reasoned. Now, as an ordinary fellow, he'd lost his immunity, or so he supposed. In fact, although he was taking a good amount of money with him, secreted in various locations on his new horse's gear, he was also leaving a good portion of his stash behind...just in case. As difficult as it had been to get to Scotland this time, at least the money had been there for him. If he ran into more bad luck, he might need that security again.

And it was more likely, he mused, putting his hands behind his head and staring at the beamed ceiling, that he would run into bad luck than good, especially if he were to follow the course he had determined upon.

He was armed again, and in a mood to use those weapons. He sought the blood of two men now instead of one, and at first he'd been uncertain of who to dispatch first. Both were well deserving of death, both pieces of human refuse the world would be well rid of. But finally he had decided to head south to London first, and then to Dorset if need be. Find the Earl of Varnley, this Bramhearst villain, and see that he laid his hands on no more innocent girls for his sick pleasure. Although he planned to kill the man with no fanfare, he felt he'd hear cheering even in heaven when the deed was done. Yes, south first, to search out Bramhearst. Tim Mott, that treacherous knave, wouldn't be hard to find when it was his turn. He was probably still mistreating the horses at the Running Lion. Jeremy thought a quick piercing of Mott's black heart with a silent blade would be fitting, much as one would dispose of a rat.

Then there was the matter of his father. By mid-day tomorrow he could be standing on the man's doorstep, for the Harwood estate was just outside of Carlisle. But would he go as himself, or as some anonymous gentleman on some vague errand? The former was a risk, for what if his father had realized his illegitimate son was the notorious robber. Would he alert the King's men? Or if a row ensued and brought attention to his visit, would some servant report him even if his father did not? It was foolish to go out of mere curiosity, but damn if he didn't feel compelled to see his own father just once in his miserable life.

He couldn't go as Jeremy Knox *or* Jeremy Harwood, he finally realized. Neither were prudent monikers. What then? Something ordinary. Smith? Too ordinary. He'd most likely be turned away. Williams? That was plain enough, but with a hint of respectability. Jeremy Williams.

And what would be his excuse for visiting? The son of an old acquaintance? That was true enough even if his father had never known a Mister Williams, for surely Lydia Knox was an "old acquaintance" if his father pressed for specifics.

Jeremy sighed and turned on his side. Tomorrow he would see his father, if only briefly. He knew he shouldn't go, but he was going anyway. He shook his head at himself. What kind of soft-headed fool had he become? The old Jeremy wouldn't have given a rat's ass about meeting his father.

Now it seemed essential to his survival.

He saw the bit of odd coloration in the copse of trees near the next bend in the road and casually reached for the gun at his waist, sliding it out behind the horn of his saddle and cocking it. His new horse, a finer beast than Nellie by a mile but still unfamiliar to him, seemed to sense his sudden tension and pranced a bit in his stride.

"Easy, boy," he said softly, then thought to use the horse's antics to his own benefit. He pulled him up and dismounted, patting his neck soothingly and bending to pretend an examination of the horse's front leg. Out of the corner of his eye he studied the trees again. He didn't see anything now, but he was sure... Yes, there it was. A movement of pale blue well beneath the horizon. And while such a shade might be a bit of flower patch in the spring, in the cold of November it could be nothing else but a scrap of fabric. A woman's dress or a man's coat? He'd bet on the latter, and not a traveler like himself or why the concealment. Jeremy smiled, remounted, and turned his horse back down the road, as if he meant to return the way he had come. He kept his horse to an easy walk, as if it were nursing an injury, and listened. The thief would either pursue him or wait for another mark.

Once around the hill, Jeremy urged his horse up the far side and circled south again, keeping the copse of trees off to his right. If the man had moved to a new location, he would have to be careful... But no, there he still was, waiting for another victim. Jeremy frowned. Another victim. Was this thief interested only in a purse, or did he accost his victims as well?

Christ, why should I care? he scolded himself. What kind of half-witted notion is that, to worry about the next traveler? But he found himself reining in his horse and staring at the man in indecision.

The robber made the decision for him. As if sensing that he was being observed, he pivoted slowly in the saddle and looked directly at Jeremy. He could not entirely hide the surprise on his face, but he covered it quickly enough, Jeremy gave him credit for that. They were too distant from one another to consider firing their readied pistols, so they just contemplated each other for a moment or two. Jeremy tried to think of what he would have done if he had ever been confronted as he was now confronting this highwayman. *Ride on, and hope to gain another day*, he thought. And then he saw the man nod his head, tip up his hat with his gun barrel, and nudge his horse out onto the road and back toward Gretna. Jeremy sat and watched him until he was past the same hill he had just circled, then hurried his mount down the incline, keeping him in a canter for over a mile. He did not want to be surprised twice in one day by the same thief.

Consequently he reached his father's estate long before he'd supposed, or was it merely because he wasn't used to riding a horse that actually covered the ground at a decent pace? He hesitated only a moment at the gates, then straightened his back and proceeded up the neat drive. The main house was visible in the distance. Not as grand as some he'd seen, but grand enough to suit. He realized suddenly that his heart was pounding uncomfortably and he willed it to slow down. It was not wholly cooperative.

A groom hurried from the stables as he approached.

"Good afternoon," Jeremy greeted, then dismounted with as much ease as his still-tender leg allowed. He swept his hat from his head and smoothed his hair back into place. "I've come to call on Daniel Harwood. Is he in residence?"

"Indeed, sir," the man said wide-eyed.

Jeremy handed the man a coin and smiled. "I've been on the road since early morning. Could you manage a bit of a dressing for him?"

"My pleasure, sir. I'm sure Lord Harwood would have it no other way for a visitor such as yourself, sir."

The man's adulation mystified Jeremy as he watched him lead his horse away, only mildly concerned about the coins he had hidden in the saddle stitching. The man looked harmless enough, if a bit daft. Then he turned toward the front steps and forced himself to go up them.

"Good afternoon," he greeted the footman who answered to door. He did not miss the look of surprise on the man's face, nor the quick frown. "I beg his lordship's pardon for not sending word of my coming, but it was an impetuous decision on my part. I am the son of an acquaintance of his. Jeremy Williams is the name. Would you see if Lord Harwood will receive me?"

He was readily ushered into the entry and offered a seat, which he declined. Standing seemed safer somehow. Easier to make a run for it.

"His lordship will see you in the library," the footman said when he returned, then led him down a corridor of gilded-framed portraits. It struck him like a blow that the people pictured there were *his* kinsmen just as much as they were Lord Harwood's, and he wanted to do more than sneak chance glimpses of the faces he was passing. But he could not stop to stare, not with the efficient little footman scurrying ahead of him.

At last a pair of doors were swung open and Jeremy stepped inside. He let out a pent up breath when he realized the room was empty.

"His lordship will join you in a moment. Would you care for a drink, sir?"

Why not? "Is it too early for brandy do you think?" he asked congenially.

"Not at all, sir," the footman nodded. "Would you like me to pour you one, or will you help yourself?" He pointed with the flat of his hand toward a server against one wall, atop which were glasses and bottles at the ready.

"Don't trouble yourself," Jeremy answered, and started across the room. He hoped the man would leave quickly, for he wasn't too sure how steady his hands were for pouring, and was relieved to hear the door click shut behind him.

He let the burning comfort of the brandy slide down his throat, relishing the quality of the liquor with an involuntary closing of his eyes.

"A fine brandy, is it not?" came a voice.

Jeremy quickly opened his eyes, then found himself unable to inhale. Indeed, he wasn't entirely sure he wouldn't swoon like some silly female. He forced himself to take a steadying breath, and then another. The two men eyed each other from across the room, much as he and the highwayman had summed up each other only hours before.

No wonder the groom and the butler looked at me so queerly, he thought. No one with two eyes could deny the kinship that existed, for he and his father were of a kind, almost as alike as twin brothers, for the older man had kept himself well-figured and showed little sign of indulgent living.

"Indeed," said Jeremy, bobbing his glass. "The finest I've ever tasted."

"What now?" asked Lord Harwood stiffly. "Shall we avoid the obvious with polite conversation or shall I just ask why you have come?"

Jeremy sighed and shook his head. "Neither. The first would be useless, and I've no answer to that question other than 'to satisfy my curiosity.'"

"Curiosity? Not money? Demand for recognition? Maybe even retribution?" his father asked, nodding toward the pistol handle showing beneath Jeremy's coat. "Just curiosity?"

54

"A curiosity that has been amply rewarded. I've no need to wonder again what my father looks like. I've only to look in a mirror."

"And that's all you want?"

"I find the notion…comforting. Yes, that's all I want. May I finish my brandy, your lordship, or would you prefer that I left immediately."

His father seemed unsure for a moment, then raised his chin slightly and indicated two sofas before the fireplace. "Let's sit, shall we? You can finish your brandy and I, I can ask a few questions myself. I've my own curiosity to satisfy."

We even walk alike, Jeremy noted as they made their way toward the sofas, each sitting a careful distance away from each other.

"You call yourself Jeremy Williams?"

"For today only. You'll think it unseemly, I suppose, but I am also known as Jeremy Harwood." Now that they were closer, Jeremy saw that his father was not so young as he had appeared at a distance. Fine lines crinkled the corners of his eyes and mouth, as if he were use to smiling. He was not smiling now.

"That is a presumption, indeed," he said. "But as you've never made a claim against me, it can be overlooked. But that is not the name I had heard… I had supposed you went by another."

"Aye, sir. A name best left unsaid and forgotten."

"Indeed. I'd heard you'd been killed, months ago. Which makes your appearance here today a double surprise."

"You hid it well."

The older man looked away for a moment, then fixed him with a steady gaze. "May I inquire after your mother?"

"You may inquire, sir, but I've no first-hand knowledge to offer. I've not seen her these nine years or more and I pray I'll not lay eyes on her again until one of us is dead."

The baron raised his eyebrows. "So bitter a parting?"

"More than bitter, sir, and a sordid tale that I'd rather not relate."

"She did not treat you well?"

The question surprised Jeremy as much by its being asked as by the seeming concern in his father's voice.

"As well as she was able, sir, but she had a careless nature, as you may yourself recall, for I cannot think she changed much in essentials

55

since your acquaintance with her. The consequence of her carelessness fell upon my sister, not I, and for that, I cannot forgive her."

"A sister?" he asked. "Not my daughter, surely. Lydia would have told me—"

"No, not yours." Jeremy shrugged. "I'm not sure even Mother knew at whose door to lay Eleanor. Eleanor was more mine than anyone's, so it didn't matter anyway." The sting of tears threatened, and he squinted. "I hate my mother for her carelessness, and make no excuse for doing so."

His father looked suddenly embarrassed. "Yes, she was careless, though so was I in my youth." He shook his head. "I will not go down that road with *you*," he said sternly. "You have had your own wild days from what I've heard, wilder than mine by an ocean."

"Different certainly."

There was an awkward pause and Jeremy drank down the last of his brandy. It was time to go. He stood and his father followed his lead.

"Where are you bound, may I ask? Are you still under judgment?"

"Not if I keep the world thinking I'm dead. Some idiot got himself hanged in my place."

"I'd heard you'd been shot on the road near Howden."

"Aye, I was, and still feel the ache of those musket balls most nights."

Lord Harwood shook his head. "I won't ask you to explain, Jeremy, for I think it may be better not to know."

Jeremy nodded. "Have I brothers and sisters?" he suddenly asked.

Lord Harwood grimaced. "Curiosity again? Yes, you've two sisters and a brother, all younger than yourself, of course. You were my first child...that I know of, that is. I'm glad they are not home this afternoon. Our likeness would not go unnoticed."

"By your wife either."

"Most certainly not by her, though she knows of you, I think. A slip of the tongue while in my cups one night." He shrugged. "Still, it would be awkward."

"I won't come again," Jeremy said simply. "I just had to look you in the eye, to know what that felt like."

"And?"

"I'd expected to be angry with you. I'd expected I might shout at you for carelessly creating me and then casting me off. All foolishness, of course. I've no idea how many bastards I may have fathered with as little regard. God willing, none, but not from any chastity on my part." He smiled ruefully. "But now I find you're just a man. A man who resembles me, or should I say, whom I resemble. 'Tis too late for any recompense anyway. I've made my own way."

Again his father raised his eyebrows and Jeremy felt an odd feeling of chagrin, like a shamed son feels before a disapproving father, for he immediately recognized the irony of his words. "His own way" had been as a notorious highwayman who had been a hair's breadth from hanging. Then his father took in a breath and audibly exhaled.

"If you need to come again," he said, "then come as Jeremy Harwood. Not as my son, you understand, but as a young cousin of sorts. I had a cousin who went off to the Caribbean. Quite the disgrace at the time. Died of a fever, or so I heard. A lost limb on the family tree, but what's the harm of a bud or two."

Jeremy nodded, then stared at the hand his father had extended to him. He took it as manfully as he might, but lost all thought of contested strength when he felt the warmth of his father's palm on his own. *I'm shaking my father's hand*, he thought in a kind of wonderment. Never had he thought...

"Thank you for receiving me," he heard himself saying. "And with more consideration than I deserve."

"We could all stand a little forgiveness," Lord Harwood said matter-of-factly, "I hope your road will be a smoother one than you've had thus far."

Jeremy didn't answer, just nodded and left the grand room, his boots sounding down the portrait-lined hall to where the footman waited to open the front door.

Chapter Six

They were both here, the two responsible for Eleanor's murder!

Philip Bramhearst—for that was the Earl of Varnley's full name—Jeremy had not yet seen, but inquiries had assured him that the earl was in residence and not planning to leave anytime soon. The winter season had struck with an early vengeance, leaving London's streets choked with snow and the countryside nearly impassable. It had been a stroke of luck that Jeremy'd been able to continue on from Birmingham, following in the ruts of several ale wagons whose drivers hoped to take advantage of the increased consumption of their product during the approaching Christmas season and the cold months to follow.

He sat in the Lamb and Flag nursing a pint of ale and brooding. He pictured a brutish man of middle years tightening his meaty hands around a young girl's neck. Each night Jeremy wondered if his inaction had cost another young girl her life, yet he could not bring himself to act now that he was so near. For one thing, with the wind raging outside, gathering information and making observations about his quarry had become impossible. He had discovered the location of Varnley's London home, had even stood for a time before it, pretending to fix his horse's tack. But he couldn't just walk up the earl's front steps, murder him, and then walk casually away, not if he wanted to escape hanging.

And something else, something bone deep, stayed his hand as well. Robbery was one thing, and he had always been prepared to use defensive force if a job went bad. But outright murder—the deliberate ending of another's life—was quite another crime indeed, especially planning it from afar. It struck him as unfair to plot Bramhearst's death while the man knew nothing of his peril. Unsporting somehow, even against an animal like the earl. Yet stealth was an obvious component of murder, wasn't it? Murder

58

wasn't sporting, had no rules, and flew in the face of all that was holy, or at least all that was human. He was not sure, now that he was nearly face-to-face with the deed if not the man, if he was capable of killing him.

He tried to feed his hatred, calling to mind Eleanor's death scene again and again. Such machinations, apart from saddening him for hours afterward, brought no angry resolve, however, only frustrated tears. He wanted Philip Bramhearst dead, but he wasn't sure he could kill him.

And then, just yesterday, his already bad mood had been blackened further.

He had seen his mother.

At least he was almost sure it was her. He'd been coming out of a tavern frequented by the upper crust gentry. There, as elsewhere, he'd discovered the Earl of Varnley wasn't a popular topic of conversation. Besides the most basic of information, men were unable or unwilling to divulge more. Worse, it seemed that simply asking about the man was enough to earn you suspicion and eventual censure. Were the man's perversions so well-known that even lecherous types were revolted? Did they think that Jeremy shared the earl's proclivities and sought an association with him? These questions filled his mind as he stepped from the tavern and glanced across the street at the clock tower of another establishment.

A woman exiting that building was wearing a luminous, purple satin cloak that caught his eye. He suspected from its bulk that it was lined with fur. She had drawn up the hood against the cold and hung intimately on the arm of an older gentleman, either for support, warmth, or seduction, it was hard to tell. It was when she looked up at the man, her eyes full of amorous promise, that Jeremy nearly missed the last step on the tavern stairs. He looked around to see if his clumsiness had been noticed, then looked again at the couple.

They had turned to walk down the street where a carriage waited at the corner, so Jeremy could not get a clear view of her—just the front bit of the side of her face—but he felt sure the woman was his mother. From what glimpses he could gain, she appeared little older than when he had seen her last, and the hood framed an elaborately-styled pile of chestnut hair. He heard her laugh at something the gentleman said, and the hair on the back of his neck prickled. It was her! She looked happy and unscathed by time or trouble. How dare she! How dare she laugh!

He had been tempted to follow them, to see where they were going, to find out who she was with, to find out if she were under this man's protection for only a night or as his mistress, to ask her... What? What would he ask her? *How can you be happy and healthy and prospering when poor little Eleanor is rotting in the ground near Penrith? How can you live with yourself day after day after what you've done? How is it possible to erase such a stain of culpability and go on as if none of it ever happened? As if Eleanor was no more than a misplaced earring or a lost handkerchief? How?*

And also, *Did you ever miss me? Did you worry about me as most mothers would worry about a wayward son? Did you mourn our alienation from one another? Seek me out? Keep track of my exploits? Feel pride or loathing...or only satisfaction that my infamous doings bolstered your own popularity? What did you feel? Anything? Nothing? What?*

But he had not followed her. He had watched the man help her into the carriage, then enter himself. The frozen looking driver had snapped the horse forward. His grim visage was all that Jeremy saw as the carriage rolled by. The curtains had been fastened against the cold.

"You don't look none too happy if I may say," came a woman's sympathetic voice. "Buy me a drink and I'll listen to your woes, or not, whichever would please you."

Jeremy nodded and tossed a coin on the table. He saw her hand snatch it up as she hurried away to fetch her drink. Whether she returned or not was barely a consideration, though from what he'd seen sashaying away, she might be pleasant company for a time. When she returned, he was sure of it. A world-hardened woman a bit older than himself, but still comely enough, and the look in her eyes was encouraging.

"Thank you, gent," she said, slipping onto the bench next to him. "I'm all ears."

"It's not your ears I've a mind to use," he said with a suggestive smile.

"You're a quick one, eh?" she teased. "All down in the dumps one minute, all fun the next. No need letting good ale go to waste though. And I'll still be here when we've had our fill."

She leaned closer, rubbing a breast against Jeremy's arm and his pulse quickened. He'd bed her, and soon he hoped. No lingering over niceties. It had been too long a drought to go in for flirtation and seduction. Just hard and fast and mind-numbing, that's what he wanted, and she looked like a woman who would understand that.

A thought had come to him during the night. Perhaps there was a way to murder a man without being held accountable. What if the earl were pressed into a rage in front of witnesses and the hapless target of his anger merely defended himself? Would it be considered murder? Would it even be prosecuted? He wondered. Or if one were to catch the wretch in the act of attempting to murder some poor girl, would that testimony be enough for a court to hang Varnley? Jeremy wasn't sure how to find out, and he was afraid that even asking such questions might be hazardous. He might be able to figure out the niceties of the law on his own, but he had no access to law books or papers. Still, his mind turned over random possibilities, searching for one that would mean the end of Philip Bramhearst.

And he knew now that he would have to see the man before he could put any unformed plan into action. Perhaps it was just in his nature to scout out his victims. He had always done so before a robbery, which he believed accounted for his remarkably long, eight-year career of thieving. He always knew the look of his marks, had summed them up and gauged their strengths and weaknesses. Many a full purse had been allowed to pass by untaken if the odds seemed stacked against him. He had to see Varnley for himself. Maybe then a plan would come to him.

"You don't belong at this table, Mister Harwood," laughed the earl. "You're a terrible card player." The other gentlemen at the table chuckled in agreement.

"I agree, sir," Jeremy admitted with a smile. "But then it's to your advantage that I am, is it not?"

"Let him stay, Varnley," urged the drunken Viscount Orser. "We let you stay though you're not nearly so pleasant as young Harwood."

Philip Bramhearst scowled across the table. Was he offended by such a small slight?

"Why thank you, sir," Jeremy said, patting the viscount's arm. "What for?"

"For pleading my cause and complimenting my nature, though I'm not sure his lordship is convinced. See how he frowns."

Jeremy saw the earl force a smile to his lips. "By all means stay, Mister Harwood. Marcus cannot do without you."

Jeremy bowed his head in thanks. He would stay a while longer, but not much. It turned his stomach to sit a bare four feet from the man he suspected had raped and strangled his sister, but he was also glad he had come. It had been an informative if not completely satisfying evening.

The Earl of Varnley was nothing like he'd expected. Here was no middle-aged roué but a man in his prime, surely not past thirty-five. Jeremy had gotten the impression from the tailor in Penrith that the earl had been murdering whores for a long time, though perhaps if he'd started young...? If this man was indeed the man who'd taken Eleanor's life, he would have been about Jeremy's age at the time. Jeremy couldn't imagine wanting sex with a little girl, let alone killing her.

Jeremy looked at the man's hands holding his cards. Certainly not what he'd imagined either. No fleshy paws of rude design. The earl's fingers were long and delicate, almost to the point of being feminine. In fact, much about the earl was decidedly feminine. If Jeremy had met the man without suspecting some foul blemish in his character, he would have passed him off as a harmless fop. It crossed Jeremy's mind that the tailor had been mistaken in his assertions, that the Earl of Varnley was not a debauched murderer after all.

He was not a pleasant man, to be sure. The other gentlemen at the table seemed to tolerate him only. There was an element of fear in the banter, and Jeremy had not missed the look of alarm in the viscount's eyes when he feared he'd offended the earl. Was that only because of their differences in rank, or was there something more sinister involved? Jeremy's doubts about Bramhearst's guilt were increased when the earl unexpectedly reached out and grabbed one of the serving women, pulling her roughly to his side.

"I've almost won all their money, sweetheart," he said, his arm around her hips. He gave her a little squeeze. "Not long, eh, and you and I can get reacquainted."

The woman was no little girl, but the look on her face froze Jeremy's heart. Pure fear. Panic. Terror. Did no one else see the woman's distress?

Jeremy glanced around the table. Most were focusing a bit too intensely on the cards before them, the rest were looking away uncomfortably. He looked back at the woman, who seemed paralyzed with indecision. *Say no*, he willed her.

"I got me another acquaintance, your lordship."

"Tell him you've changed your mind."

"Oh, I can't do that, sir. It wouldn't be right."

"It wouldn't be right," he mimicked her. "Who is this acquaintance, sweetheart? Perhaps I can arrange the matter with him."

The woman looked panicked again. It was obvious she really had no prior engagement.

"Pardon, Bramhearst, but that would be me." It was the viscount speaking, looking much more sober than he had a moment ago.

The earl laughed rudely. "You? You're too drunk, Marcus, to do this lady any good. I'd consider it sporting of you to release her from her commitment to you."

The table was silent, awaiting the viscount's decision. Jeremy saw the struggle in the man's eyes, then a reluctant shrug. His noble but impetuous effort to save the woman from the earl's attentions had failed.

The earl smiled, gave the woman's rump a pat, and propelled her on her way. "See you in a bit, sweetheart," he called. "And make sure that little miss of yours is about, in case I need errands run, eh?"

The woman gave him a look of such fearful loathing, Jeremy thought the earl might seize upon her again and strike her. Instead, he laughed. "None of your cheek, sweetheart, or I'm apt to withhold my always generous gratuity. And I *am* always filled with gratitude, my dear. Always."

The woman hurried away, and the earl turned a pleased face back to the table. "My apologies, gentlemen. That took longer than I'd anticipated. And my thanks again, Orser, for seeing to my best interests...and yours."

The threat was subtly made but struck home. Viscount Orser nodded grimly and looked back to his cards.

"Well, let's play then," said the earl. "Your draw, Mister Harwood."

Jeremy had not thought he'd be compelled to act so hastily, but at the mention of the woman's daughter, all doubts had been erased, or nearly all. So, the woman had a "little miss" at home, did she? *How old?* he wondered. The earl had made a point of ensuring the girl's presence. To run errands? Unlikely. Jeremy could not forget the look of terror and loathing on the woman's face. This was no ordinary assignation between consenting adults. The undercurrents of disapproval had been palpable among the men at the card game. Shortly after the incident, Jeremy had pleaded an empty purse and quit the game. But he had not gone far.

The waiting was cold. He felt sorry for his horse, which stomped against the frigid night air and nuzzled against him in questioning. The wind seemed to have chosen the alley in which they stood to sweep down mercilessly, and Jeremy moved to pull his coat tighter. He froze in mid-movement when the club door opened and Philip Bramhearst appeared. He was alone. Had the woman gone home already to prepare for her after-hours work? Surely she did not live far, then. Jeremy would have to leave his horse and hope the night's surveillance didn't take long.

Bramhearst looked about him, then started across the street and away from where Jeremy watched. *Thank God for small favors*, he mused, then peered around the corner. The inky night seemed to have swallowed the earl whole, but, no, there was the sound of his boots crunching through the layer of snow on the street. Jeremy stuck close to the shadowy walls and followed.

He'd been right. In barely a block, the earl's shadow disappeared into a narrow doorway. Jeremy listened to the sound of his boots on the stairs, waited until they seemed to have turned some corner or gone down some hall, then made his own way into the building.

Now what? Wait? For what? He wasn't even sure why he had followed the man. If this were just the usual sort of carnal exchange, he did not want to be caught peeping or listening at the keyhole. What if there was nothing extraordinary in this night's proceedings, nothing but the age-old exchange of one favor for another.

Yet he could not dismiss his feeling of dread. The woman had been utterly terrified. The viscount, even in his cups, had attempted to come to her aid, though his courage had at last failed him. And then there had been the mention of the woman's daughter. Jeremy might have been able to walk away and leave a grown woman to her unknown fate, but what about the girl? He could not abandon her if she might be in peril. Not when he suspected what he did. He took a deep breath, let it out, then tread as lightly up the stairs as he could.

At the top he paused. There was but a single door, then another flight of stairs. He was certain he had heard the earl walk further than this, which meant he must have proceeded up another flight. Jeremy started up again, more slowly this time. Halfway up, on the darkened landing, he stopped and listened. The hammering of his own heart made him uncertain at first whether he heard what he thought he had. Then it came again.

The sound of flesh against flesh.

Not that more enjoyable joining, but the meeting of a fist against a face. And a female's incomprehensible, mumbled words interspersed with the more coherent demands of her male attacker, "Tell me where she is." A blow. "Tell me now, you ugly whore."

Jeremy started up the remaining stairs as silently as his rage would allow. The door at the top was ajar, a little light flickering through the slit and the sound of the terrible beating just beyond it. He realized he'd pulled his sword from its sheath without thinking. As he toed open the door with his boot, a man's back presented itself, a fist raised above his shoulder. *It would be so easy to run him through,* Jeremy thought, then remembered the woman being held up for a beating. He didn't want to skewer her as well.

"Let her go, Bramhearst," he said quietly.

The earl was quick on his feet, Jeremy had to give him that. In an instant, he had whirled to face his opponent, the sobbing woman pinned like a shield in front of him.

"Harwood?" he said in surprise, then his face hardened into contempt. "This is no business of yours. Get out now." He tightened his hold on the woman, his forearm choking a gasp from her.

"No," Jeremy replied stonily.

The earl smiled, as if an idea had come to him. "You can have her if you've taken a fancy to her. Just convince her to tell me where her girl is and I'll be on my way."

"He choked her the last time," the woman gasp out, her eyes wide with pleading. "Nearly killed her, he did…ahh!" She cried out as her captor's arm tightened again.

Jeremy's last doubt vanished. This was the man who had carelessly snuffed out the light in his little sister's eyes, leaving her broken body like a discarded piece of trash on the bed. How frightened she must have been! Had she called for their mother? For him? Had she wondered why no one came? Or had she felt only pain and panic?

"Let her go," Jeremy said coldly.

"This is outrageous effrontery!" the earl hissed. "I give the orders here! *You* go or I'll kill her first, then put a musket ball between your damn eyes."

"Brave words," Jeremy sneered. "But your pistol is on the table, sir. Besides, she's just a whore. I figure I'd be doing her a favor if I ran her through right along with you. At least her daughter would be safe from your perversions."

Whether his words had frightened her enough to cause a swoon, or whether the earl had finally succeeded in choking off her air, Jeremy wasn't certain, but suddenly the woman was slipping down to the floor in a limp heap. The earl had only a chance to glance at his out-of-reach weapon before Jeremy lunged deftly forward, straightening his arm and burying his rapier as near to the earl's heart as he could manage.

He watched with a kind of curious wonder the strange series of expressions that played across the man's face. Surprise. Disbelief. Anger. Then Bramhearst's gaze seemed to wander, as if searching for something to fix upon. Fear. Confusion. Then finally, a refocusing upon Jeremy, a squinting glare and a slackening of the jaw before his eyes slowly shut and he slid backward off the instrument that had impaled him.

"We mustn't tarry," came a voice behind Jeremy, and he whirled around to find the grim face of the Viscount Orser.

"I—"

"Is the woman alive?"

Jeremy hesitated, but as the viscount seemed to be no immediate threat, he went down on one knee and felt the woman's neck. At the same time he detected a steady pulse, he noted the rise and fall of her chest. "Yes. She's badly beaten, but I think she'll recover."

"Then leave her," the viscount ordered, moving past Jeremy. He picked up the earl's pistol from the table, and Jeremy tensed until he saw the viscount's quick glance around the dimly lit room to see if any other items of the earl's remained. "We'll move him down the street, to the alley of the building behind this one." He rifled into the earl's coat and snatched out his money purse. "I'll leave this, minus the money, of course, a few blocks away." He buttoned the coat over the spreading crimson stain on the earl's shirt, then pulled out a few notes and laid them on the woman's dressing table. "Now, help me with him," he said quietly. He leaned down and grabbed one of the earl's arms draping it over his shoulder. "If anyone asks, we're just helping a friend home after a bit too much drink."

"Why are you doing this?" Jeremy asked as he sheathed his blade and helped the viscount hoist the dead man to his feet.

"Varnley's proclivities are known, or at least suspected. You were justified in your action. I would have done the same if I'd arrived first, or at least I hope I would have. Now let's make sure no suspicion falls upon this woman. She has a child to care for."

They said no more to one another. On the bitterly cold streets outside, no one stirred. They deposited the earl's pale body along the route he would have taken to retrieve his horse from the stables. Even if someone remembered to tell the authorities that he was planning to meet the serving woman, it would appear he'd been robbed after visiting her. Jeremy stared for a few moments at the prone figure of his sister's murderer. His revenge had been accomplished so unexpectedly, he felt no elation, only numbness. The viscount had already begun walking away.

Deborah Ballou

"Best be gone," he whispered back over his shoulder.

Jeremy nodded and turned away, slipping along several side streets and circling around until he was back to where he'd left his horse. The animal moved stiffly but seemed unharmed.

"An extra blanket for you tonight," he promised. "And some oats as well."

Chapter Seven

At first he stayed on because of the weather. He'd procured comfortable apartments near Covent Garden with good stabling for his horse, which he had finally named Pat, short for the too-feminine Patience. Any horse that would stand in the cold so willingly for so long deserved a name. Pat might not be the equal of Satin, but he'd do.

Covent Garden, despite the continued snowfall, was a place of amusements. Theaters and markets, shops and taverns, a mixture of the upper crust and the common man. And he found a sort of perverse satisfaction in living within walking distance of Bow Street, headquarters of the Fielding brothers' brigade of do-gooders who patrolled the roads around London preventing robberies and apprehending criminals. Not content with the job the military was doing to protect law-abiding citizens, the novelist and his brother, John, had organized a private policing force to investigate crimes and seek out law-breakers seven years earlier. Though Henry was now dead, his legacy of lawmen continued. Wouldn't it make their day to discover the likes of Jeremy Knox, alive and well, right in their own neighborhood? Of course Jeremy had no plans to enlighten them about his presence, but it was interesting to speculate.

Though the weather became milder soon after Christmas, Jeremy found himself staying on. He liked London and all its busyness. It reminded him of his happier days in Manchester, though Manchester was small and rural by comparison. There was a comfortable anonymity in London. He found he enjoyed blending in with the crowds and observing people as they went about amusing themselves. It was almost as much fun as participating. It was while watching an impromptu drama on the edge of the market that he overheard three young ladies planning their afternoon outing, and their idea of amusement astounded him. It was his own name that first caught his ear.

"He's no Jeremy Knox, they say," observed one lady, "but I hear he cuts a fine enough figure."

"And Mister Knox went and got himself killed far from London, so we were cheated of visiting him before his hanging," one of her companions, a teenage miss, said petulantly.

"Let's bring him flowers," said the third. She was the prettiest, and, Jeremy thought, the oldest of the young women. He supposed she must be married, for the bulge of a ring showed beneath her glove.

"In winter?"

"Greenhouse blooms. I know a shop, and it's worth the cost. I'd have the eternal satisfaction of giving a condemned man his last glimpse of beauty before he dies."

"His last glimpse of beauty would be of you," Jeremy interrupted. Three startled faces turned his way, then mellowed into sideways glances at one another, the youngest one's cheeks coloring to bright pink. "I'm sorry, ladies. I could not help but overhear."

None of them spoke at first, too flustered it seemed, until the eldest raised her chin and smiled. "Thank you, sir, even if you did speak unbidden." Her words might scold him but her brown eyes held a different message.

"May I venture further?" he asked, returning the lady's flirtatious look with one of his own. She nodded her acquiescence. "Then may I ask how such lovely, obviously well-bred young women are acquainted with a condemned criminal?"

All three laughed at once.

"Oh, we don't *know* Mister Kingsley," the youngest giggled. "It's a bit of sport to visit these wretched men the day before they hang, *especially* the handsome ones."

"Isn't that dangerous?" Jeremy asked. He had recognized the man's name. Elliot Kingsley was a highwayman like himself. He'd never met him, of course, but the man had a hard reputation. He'd done his share of extortion and murder along with thieving.

"The jailers chain their hands and feet, of course," answered the other. "Then they sit them in the warden's office the afternoon before they're to hang so we ladies can pay them a call."

"I brought chocolates when we made a visit last month," said the young one. "I'd heard the man had a fondness for them, and he *did* look appreciative."

They all nodded sadly, though Jeremy had the uneasy feeling that they hadn't an idea in the world what torment it might be for a man to be subjected to such humiliating and frivolous attention while contemplating the stretching of his neck.

"Would you like to accompany us?" the pretty one asked suddenly. "It'll be great fun. You'll see."

It was Jeremy's inclination to say no. The whole idea was repulsive and seemed even to be a kind of betrayal of his fellow thieves. Still, the pretty woman *was* interesting...

He bowed his head and tipped his hat. "Ladies, I'm at your service."

Amazement. That was his overwhelming memory of the afternoon. Jeremy had heard of these "viewings" before, but had passed them off as rumor or exaggeration. He had even once wondered if they would display him before he hanged if he were ever caught. Dick Turpin's hanging had filled the yard to overflowing in York, or so legend had it.

He had anticipated that he and his three new companions would be let into the warden's offices, there to stare at Kingsley, and whoever else might be scheduled to swing the next day, in awkward silence or with perhaps a few giggled niceties by the ladies. Rosalind, Dorothy, and Pamela certainly giggled more than their share, Jeremy discovered, though he had yet to discover their last names. He had pointed out the impropriety of addressing them by their given names, but they had only giggled and insisted upon such familiar anonymity. And they insisted upon calling him Jeremy, too, declaring that "Mister Harwood" sounded much too somber. About all he had been able to discern from closer observation of the trio was that they were related somehow, either sisters or cousins, for their features were of a kind as was the timber of their voices...and giggles.

His astonishment had arisen not so much from their behavior as from the *crowds* of women, and their few escorts, who were waiting around the prison for their chance to see the condemned. Jeremy quit his count at forty and estimated at least that many more. He could see other knots of women strolling toward the prison as well and knew they, too, would soon become part of the "festivities." For it was certainly festive. A little band of musicians had set up at the base of the steps ascending to the prison door. They played little sentimental ditties more appropriate to a lover's tryst, Jeremy thought, than visiting a man hours before his execution. People chattered, women laughed, many held little offerings. Rosalind held her promised posy, tied with a crimson ribbon, and Pamela had decided that chocolates would be a nice treat for Mister Kingsley, too. Dorothy seemed contented to offer only her own presence as a token.

"Hello, my dears," a flamboyantly-dressed woman greeted them as they approached the queue. "Here to see Mister Kingsley?"

"Why else?" asked Pamela in a condescending tone then turned away. Dorothy took her arm and they moved on, obviously disapproving of the woman. Only Rosalind paused to speak.

"Never mind them," she said dismissively. "They're too immature to appreciate the theater as I do."

"Oh, I don't mind them, dearie. Their kind will always be disapproving. Lucky for the world they're in the minority or I'd be out of work. And who's this fine fellow?" she asked, eyeing Jeremy with unconcealed appreciation.

"Oh, of course. Missus Whitcomb, this is Mister Jeremy Harwood. Jeremy, this is Madge Whitcomb, one of the finest actresses I've ever seen."

"Though she's not seen many," the actress laughed. "Daddy doesn't approve of too many trips to the Strand, eh?"

"I know what I like," Rosalind insisted. "Theater is like magic. You can pretend you're back in time living somewhere else for a few hours. I saw Missus Whitcomb in *Antony and Cleopatra*. It was, well, just overwhelming. I wept for days. You really must see her perform, Jeremy."

"I have always enjoyed a good drama," Jeremy said with a smile at both the actress and the young enthusiast. Missus Whitcomb was at least forty, Jeremy could see, but with her ample bosom barely concealed by her gown and her liberal use of makeup, he supposed she would be a more than passable Cleopatra on stage. "I'll plan a theater outing soon, I promise."

"In the meantime, there's this farce to see," Madge Whitcomb laughed ruefully, nodding her head toward the somber prison building. "Hope I never have to play that room."

Rosalind bid her farewell with a half-offered embrace, then took Jeremy's arm again.

"Dorothy and Pamela don't approve of my knowing her," she confided as they strolled away. "But I don't care. I went backstage after her performance and she was so kind to me and grateful for my praise. I cannot snub her when we chance to meet on the street, can I?"

"That *would* seem discourteous," Jeremy agreed.

"Rosalind! Rosalind, look who've we've found!" came Pamela's excited cry as they approached the knot of people where she and Dorothy had stopped. "It's Miss Knatwick. Dear Miss Knatwick and her sister Clara."

"Oh, hello!" Rosalind greeted enthusiastically, dropping Jeremy's arm and hurrying forward to truly embrace the said Miss Knatwick. "Oh, it has been too long. We've missed you terribly."

As it turned out, Miss Knatwick had been the young ladies' governess for a time. *Sisters, then*, Jeremy had concluded. Sisters would more likely share a governess than cousins. There was much news to share, it seemed, and no objection was made by those behind them in the queue when the sisters went no further back but only moved along with Miss Knatwick and her sister, chatting gaily and seriously by turns.

When at last they had made their way up the stairs and into the little office, Jeremy was amazed yet again.

Elliot Kingsley was all smiles and affability. He sat like a king, though the rude wooden chair hardly qualified as a throne and the chains around his wrists and ankles were a far cry from royal adornments. He greeted each visitor with something like mocking exuberance.

"Oh, he *is* handsome," Pamela giggled as they waited for Miss Knatwick and her sister to finish speaking with the man.

"Yes," agreed Dorothy. "Though not so handsome as our Jeremy here, don't you agree, Rosalind."

Rosalind gave him yet another of her many coquettish glances and sighed. "Indeed. But then we mustn't forget that Mister Kingsley

73

will be dead tomorrow. We must enjoy him while we may. Jeremy can wait for our attentions."

All three giggled again.

And then it was their turn to visit with the condemned. Jeremy hung back, as he had seen other men do, and he wondered if he had the same look of mild disapproval on his face. Was Kingsley really as pleased as he appeared with all the fuss, or was he just making the best of the situation? Jeremy tried to put himself in the man's place, for he very well could have been. Would he feel flattered or annoyed? Would he converse graciously or sit sullenly? Would he refuse to give these idle and empty-headed ladies their hoped-for entertainment out of a sense of dignity or damn his pride and take every last bit of fun his worthless life had to offer? Kingsley had obviously decided on the latter, but Jeremy wondered how long he would be able to maintain his geniality. Did he realize how many people still waited outside to see him? It would be a daunting task even at the best of times, and certainly the day before dying was not the best of times. Jeremy was glad when the ladies had satisfied their curiosity and moved away.

"And now we can take tea at Neal's," Rosalind said, her face lit with a bright smile. "Will you join us, Jeremy?"

Jeremy glanced back to where Elliot Kingsley was receiving another bevy of admirers and his stomach felt suddenly leaden. He forced a polite smile to his lips but shook his head. "I'm afraid I'm engaged elsewhere," he lied. "But I'll see you ladies to that establishment if you wish."

"Oh, yes!" Pamela exclaimed, the curls beside her ears bouncing as they started away together. "To be seen in your company will do quite nicely."

"Don't be so bothersome, dear," Rosalind chided gently as she took Jeremy's arm with a gloved hand. "Our new friend will think we are not used to being accompanied by fine gentlemen."

"I could never think so," Jeremy said appeasingly. "For surely your husband must have this honor many a day."

A chorus of giggles from the other two and a frown from Rosalind told him that he had mistaken something.

"And what makes you suppose that I am a married woman?" Rosalind asked with apparent hurt. "Am I so old, do you think? Have I behaved in a matronly way?"

"Certainly not too old to be a maiden," he smiled, "nor too matronly, either. You've been most...encouraging in your solicitations, much as a man might expect from an unattached lady. But there is the appearance of a ring on your finger, though concealed by your glove. I supposed by that observation alone that you were either engaged to be married or were, in fact, married."

Jeremy noted the color rise to Rosalind's cheeks at the mention of the ring, and Pamela let out a squeal of delight.

"I told you someone would guess," she said with a laugh.

"So you *are* married?" Jeremy asked.

"As good as," Dorothy volunteered now, her own delight in Rosalind's discomfort showing. "Rosalind's bound for the altar in two-month's time. And he's no handsome gent like yourself either, but a short, fat fellow for all his money."

Jeremy suddenly felt sorry for Rosalind and the unkindness with which her companions treated her. He felt her hand tighten a little on his arm, and it was trembling.

"I'm sure he must have some redeeming qualities if he's won her heart," Jeremy stated matter-of-factly, but his words were greeted with more laughter.

"None," said Pamela. "And even Rosalind must admit that, won't you Rosalind? It's why we decided to make the most of her days before she must wed. Memories to strengthen her resolve in the bleak years now before her."

Jeremy stopped and placed his hand atop Rosalind's, but his eyes were on the others. "But this is monstrous cruelty," he said simply and saw their silly smiles fade to surprise. "If what you say is true, she deserves your compassion, not your derision. 'Tis gross unkindness, surely."

"Well!" huffed Dorothy, taking Pamela's arm. "You're no gentleman after all, for all your fine looks, Mister Harwood. We'll see you at Neal's," she said primly to Rosalind, then turned with Pamela in tow and flounced down the street.

"Thank you," Rosalind said, her voice uncharacteristically low and meek. All her earlier boldness had vanished. "I apologize, Mister

Harwood, for making you party to this silly adventure. And I'm ashamed of my attempted deception. You must have thought my behavior toward you outrageous if you believed me married."

Jeremy shook his head. "You wouldn't be the first wife who flirted for amusement, Rosalind," he assured her, "though I *did* wonder about your matrimonial happiness, of course. And now," he added, his tone serious, "I wonder even more. Is he as bad as your...who are you to those girls?"

"An older sister."

He nodded. "Do your sisters speak the truth? Is he a horrid, portly man with only money to recommend him as a husband?"

"No, of course not," she said a bit too brightly, and took her hand from his arm. "He is only not as dashing as their youthful imaginings demand. As I said before, Dorothy and Pamela are very immature. I assure you, Mister Harwood, that I am quite happy in the match."

"I'm glad to hear it." He tipped his hat. "They're waiting for you at the corner. Please offer my apologies for offending them."

She nodded. "I hope we have not taken you too far off from your way. Where are you staying?"

"I've taken apartments off Garrick for now. I'm just visiting, you see."

"Ah. Then we probably won't be seeing you again. Well," she said with a sigh—was it one of relief? "Again, my thanks...and my apologies."

"Neither are necessary," he said, taking her hand and bowing over it. "Your company was thanks enough and no harm done, eh? Good day, Rosalind."

He waited until she had joined her sisters at the corner, then turned back toward the Strand.

"Haven't seen much of you," came a vaguely familiar voice.

Jeremy looked up from his newspaper and stifled his surprise with an intake of air. "Good day, Lord Orser," he said, standing and offering his hand. He wondered for a moment whether the viscount would accept it and was pleased when the man's clasp was strong and welcoming.

"How have you been?" Lord Orser asked. "I thought perhaps you might have left London. You haven't been at cards lately."

"I didn't want to take advantage of you and your friends by winning all your money," Jeremy said wryly. "Will you join me?"

"For a moment. I'm meeting some people here. Did you hear about Varnley?" he asked casually as he sat down. Jeremy hesitated, giving the viscount a curious look before sitting himself.

"Some of it," Jeremy replied warily. "A bad business."

"Yes. Killed falling from his horse, they say. The beast slipped on the ice."

Jeremy nodded. He had heard that report, too, and read of it in the *Daily Courant*. Even the location of the incident had been incorrect, somewhere near Mayfair. It had been puzzling at first, and then he had read of Lady Varnley and the two young daughters who had fled in grief from London to their estate in Dorset, and he thought he understood. There were reputations to preserve and respectability to maintain, especially if the earl's daughters were to someday marry advantageously. It was no great shame for one's father to be murdered by a thief, perhaps, but not in Soho, an area known for gaming, drinking, and other less loftier pleasures. The family had put out a fabricated tale of the earl's demise to shield itself from disgrace. Jeremy had had a moment of regret for the earl's widow and her girls, then thought perhaps he had done them a service after all. Given Philip Bramhearst's perversions, he might have turned them on his own daughters someday if he hadn't done so already. It was yet another bit of justification for having planted his sword in the man's chest.

It had been nearly a month since he'd murdered the Earl of Varnley, and Jeremy had expected remorse to overtake him by now. When he had felt nothing at first but relief, he supposed it was shock or some sort of mental oblivion that afflicted his conscious. He had always dreaded being forced to take someone's life on the road and had felt lucky that it had never been necessary. He had suffered so much doubt while contemplating killing Bramhearst that he had wondered whether he would even be able to defend himself should his plan go sour. Now, with the deed done, he wondered instead at his indifference. The Earl of Varnley, age thirty-five, peer of the realm, husband and father, was dead, and all Jeremy felt was that the world was better for it. He did not feel any happiness or satisfaction at having been the instrument of the man's death, but it did not trouble him either.

Now he sat across the table from the one person except God who knew his culpability, and still he felt no fear. Orser hadn't betrayed him the night of the murder, and he did not look as if he were inclined to do so now, despite his grim face.

"Things are a bit unsettled and will be for a few months yet," the viscount began. "I've just heard that Lady Varnley is expecting a child, and if it's a son, well, he will take his father's title. Otherwise, some old cousin is the nearest choice."

Jeremy greeted the news with a silent nod of his head. He felt only a momentary twinge of guilt at depriving the unborn child its father. "Unfortunate. It's an uncertain world to face alone. I never knew my father—" Jeremy stopped and reconsidered his words. "That is, I never knew him well. Left me to Mother's care mostly. I suppose I might have benefited from a greater acquaintance with him, but here I am," he said, spreading his hands half-apologetically, "fairly whole, I think. I don't believe that *any* father is better than no father. Do you?"

Lord Orser shook his head. "I do not. Well, it's good to see you looking so well, young Harwood. I'd...wondered."

Jeremy rose as the viscount stood up to leave. He was surprised when the man turned to him once more.

"I hope you'll not be offended," Lord Orser began hesitantly," but...you bear a remarkable resemblance to my friend, Daniel Harwood."

"I am often told that," Jeremy lied. No one had dared say it to his face yet, but he had seen the curious looks when he'd been searching out Varnley at the various card palaces. "We *are* related, though I'm not exactly sure how. My father was a cousin of his. I suppose that makes me some even more distant cousin, removed and all."

The viscount fixed him with steady gaze and shook his head. "A remarkable resemblance for so distant a connection," he commented. "Have you met?"

"Lord Harwood? Yes, we have. We, too, were quite amazed by the likeness."

The viscount smiled with a mixture of knowing amusement and pity. "I'll bet you were. Well, however you're connected, I'm obliged to extend my services to you as his kin."

"You already have," Jeremy reminded him, and saw the man register understanding. What greater service than helping him cover up a killing to escape a hanging?

"You're a likable fellow, very like your...cousin. Will you join my friends and I tonight?"

Jeremy hesitated. He suspected the viscount had guessed his true relationship to Daniel Harwood. It would be a unique opportunity for a bastard to be introduced into society, of course. Most men would jump at it with both feet. But he and the viscount had an uncomfortable history. More than that, Jeremy was accustomed to staying on the fringes. His life had long depended on it. The viscount's friends were liable to be men of not only substance but influence. The thought of mingling with the very types of men upon whom he once preyed seemed foolhardy. And yet...

"Are you sure it wouldn't be an imposition?" Jeremy asked. It was the usual polite rejoinder when one meant to accept, but he tried to impart the sincerity he felt. He did not want to impose on the viscount's good-nature or sense of duty. He wondered what the man would think if he knew the entire truth of his past.

"None at all," Lord Orser said simply.

"Well, then. I'm at your service, your lordship. You have my thanks and my gratitude."

The older man smiled and placed a fatherly hand on Jeremy's shoulder.

Chapter Eight

Jeremy sighed as he climbed the stairs to his apartments and unlocked the front door.

Another late night. In the fortnight since Viscount Orser had invited him to dine with his party, Jeremy had spent all but three evenings out with either him or one of his other new acquaintances. Some of the affairs had been rather high brow. He'd felt inclined to purchase a new waistcoat and jacket after feeling greatly underdressed at the first such event. But most of the evenings offered only banal, bachelor entertainments—food, cards, drink, or bawdy theater. The viscount was married, of course, as were many of his cronies, but their wives were safely away from town raising their various offspring on various estates.

At first Jeremy had wondered why the wives of such prominent men wouldn't stay with their husbands, if only to discourage their excesses. He knew well that marriages were never the honeyed ideal of love that poets extolled, but he had been disappointed at just how far from the mark that ideal was among these gentlemen. And as for why their wives stayed away? After watching his companions drink to excess nearly every night and then behave more foolishly than they ought, Jeremy thought he understood. What woman, especially if she held any affection for her spouse, could sit helplessly by and watch such self-abuse? It would be likely to kill any affection, and soon.

The less fortunate might envy the high life, Jeremy thought, but it had a heavy price. He had supposed the viscount to be his father's age or perhaps a bit older. In the course of conversation, however, he had discovered the viscount was only ten years older than himself. The man's carousing had obviously aged him beyond his years. It had estranged him from his wife and children. And it had left him open to harm. Jeremy remembered only too well when the viscount had drunkenly attempted to rescue the barmaid from Philip

Bramhearst's unwanted attentions. It could very well have ended badly, with possibly lethal consequences, for the earl had not been beyond homicidal revenge. And Jeremy had on one occasion clamped a staying hand upon a young pickpocket's wrist in the act of lifting the viscount's purse. Lord Orser had been too intoxicated to notice and Jeremy had sent the scamp on his way with only a rough squeeze of his arm and a murderous frown to warn him off any further attempts.

Jeremy kindled the lamp beside the door and carried it into the little front parlor. *This is a lonely bit of living,* he thought. Normally even a merchant bachelor would have engaged a manservant to keep the lights burning until he arrived home each evening. Someone to answer the door, fetch provisions, carry messages. He threw his coat toward a chair and missed. *Someone to hang up my coat,* he thought testily, then lit two other lamps before settling onto the sofa with a groan. He had not wanted to hire anyone until he knew how long he'd be staying, but now he wished there was someone to pour him a drink and turn down the bed.

He was not so drunk as his fellows had been. That had never been his way. One couldn't afford to get careless when one was a wanted man or keeping an eye on a mark. Now he stayed clear-headed to protect the viscount from himself. He had practically carried the man to his carriage on more than one night, tonight being one of them. The viscount seemed a good man, but he was a foolish one, Jeremy had decided. The association was wearing on him.

Tonight had been even more trying than usual. He had met and dined with the fiancé of Rosalind. Rosalind *Pettygrew*, he'd discovered, daughter of a baronet, Sir Thomas Pettygrew. Her sisters' descriptions of the man had not been exaggerated. In fact, they now seemed rather restrained. Stephen Lacey was just thirty but, like Orser, appeared far older, though more from an excess of flesh than hard living. To call him merely fat would be a kindness. Corpulent came to mind. Or rotund. Obese, certainly. Jeremy had seldom seen such weight on a man less than fifty. For Christ's sake, the man's neck had long-since disappeared beneath several rolling chins and his fingers appeared so bloated, Jeremy wondered if he could even close his hand into a fist, though he hoisted a tankard well enough. He flushed bright red the more he drank. He spit when he spoke, and what he said was seldom worth hearing, being mainly vulgar comments concerning the male anatomy and how it might best be used to advantage with the fairer sex. It seemed a subtle form of bragging, and everyone laughed, though more from imagining such an enormous swain in any such amorous circumstances than from the wittiness of the man's remarks.

Stephen Lacey was the second son of the Earl of Derby, however, and so accorded all outward civility from those around him. He might not have a title, but his wealth was as enormous as his person and it made up for personal deficiencies, or so Jeremy suspected. Why else would he be tolerated so willingly by so many? Why else would Rosalind's father consent to marry his daughter to such a worthless mountain of flesh? Mister Lacey was a pathetic, grotesque excuse for a man and the thought of pretty Rosalind lying beneath him and suffering his lovemaking made Jeremy's gorge rise. He was certain that greed alone had motivated Rosalind's father. It was a monstrous betrayal of daughterly affection and Jeremy longed to talk, or if necessary pound, some sense into the man. He closed his eyes and rested his head on the high back of the sofa, and a pair of black eyes came unbidden to mind.

Bess.

He hadn't thought of her for so long that he felt a sudden stab of guilt. It was February. She'd been killed in August. A half a year had gone by since that terrible day. He had forced himself not to think about it time and time again. There had been more important things to do—survival at first, recovering from his injuries, making his way north, revenge. What was his excuse now? There was none. Only a vague fear of remembering. Jeremy might be an expert at trying to avoid unpleasantness, but he did not like to think of himself as a coward.

And so he let his mind wander back to that dreadful day...or rather the day before it—

It had been a stormy week, though nothing too severe. Just the usual spotty showers and a bit of blustery wind across the rolling hills. He'd been in Goole for a week, scouting his next job, and it had been well worth it. The bailiff for a sheep farm was on his way down to Scunthorpe to deposit some of the summer's earnings. It was a goodly sum if Jeremy was any judge of a purse, and he was.

Normally he left such lackeys alone, but this man fairly begged to be robbed. He had not gone immediately south as he should have, but lingered on, evidently enjoying the pleasures of a local doxie more than the idea of a bailiff's job well done. But he had bid many of his drinking chums good-bye that evening before teetering off to his lodgings, saying he was early bound for Scunthorpe in the morning. Jeremy had smiled at the news.

He should not have gone to see Bess that night, he now realized. He shouldn't have let a half-promise dissuade him from his course. But at the time it had seemed harmless enough. He had told Bess he would probably be back by Thursday. She always waited for him, he knew, and worried when he was late. Her concern for him was one of the reasons he enjoyed her company so much. But it had taken longer than he'd expected in Goole. Now the job was set, however, and he reasoned that he had time to ride to Howden and allay Bess' fears before riding to a valley near Eastoft where he'd relieve the bailiff of his money come the morning.

The night road had been well lit, though the clouds had often scuttled across the bright fullness of the moon. It didn't matter. He knew his way well, both on and off the road. He'd had to push his hat well down on his head, he remembered, for the wind had been fierce that night and had threatened to blow it away. His eyes continually scanned his surroundings, as was his habit. Occasionally his gaze had been drawn skyward, for the moonlit clouds seemed to be racing each other through a marvelous, starry sea. He remembered feeling lucky to be one of the few men still awake to enjoy such a grand spectacle.

When he reached Howden some three hours past midnight, the inn was darkened. Satin's hooves striking the stony courtyard rang like bells, but no one stirred. He knew it was a fool's hope that Hobbs would drag himself out of bed to open the doors for him, so he didn't even bother to dismount when he rapped his whip on the man's shuttered window beside the inn door. He waited. The audible snoring within continued unabated. He struck the shutters again. Nothing, not even a curse. He hadn't expected to rouse the man, but it had been worth a try.

He nudged Satin on to the far corner of the broad-faced building and looked up. Did he see the faint glow of a candle through the second-floor shutters, or was it just the reflection of the moon? He wet his lips and whistled a few notes from a song Bess liked, then waited.

It hadn't taken long before he'd heard the lifting of the latch. Then, bright in the moonlight, Bess' eager, beautiful face smiling down at him.

"Shame on you, Jeremy," she'd scolded, still smiling. "I'd given up on you long since."

"Is that why you're still awake?" he'd teased.

"It was a late night," she told him. "Father and I were to bed but an hour ago. I was just braiding my hair."

Jeremy imagined the thick, black tresses and the many times he'd run his hands through their softness or coiled them around his fingers in his passion. When loose, her hair fell to well below her shapely bottom and she had to work it into a braid each night or it was impossible to untangle the next morning. "How I'd love to help with that task," he'd said with a smile, "but I can't stay tonight. I've a purse to fetch, probably before sun-up if the man's liquored head doesn't keep him abed longer. I'll come back in the morning."

His head came about sharply when he heard the creaking of a hinge. Most of the yard lay in the shadows of the stable building, and Jeremy's eyes searched them but found nothing. A gust of wind toppled a leaning pitchfork onto the cobbles and he let out a pent up breath. *Just the wind.*

"You promise me?" Bess was asking, her eyes warm with anticipation.

"If all goes well. If not, then surely by nightfall tomorrow."

"Is there more than the usual danger, Jeremy?"

He had smiled at her worry. "Rather less, I'd say. Count on it, Bess. I'll be back tomorrow night even if I have to get past the Devil himself."

Bess had smiled happily and knelt down beside her window to reach down her hand as far as she might. Jeremy had stood in his stirrups, stretching to take it, but only their fingertips touched. She leaned further forward then, and her untied hair had fallen over her shoulder like a black waterfall. She'd washed it in rose water again, he could tell, for the scent had filled the air as he'd taken a handful of its softness and held it to his face. He'd inhaled deeply, then kissed it tenderly. Bess had giggled.

He'd lowered himself into the saddle again and winked. "I'll be back for more tomorrow," he'd promised one last time, then pulled Satin around and, once out of the inn yard, urged him into a gallop toward the Goole road.

All had gone well, as he'd expected. The weary bailiff had surrendered his master's money with grim resolve, then been surprised, even grateful, when Jeremy had dumped nearly half upon the road again before leaving.

"Next time don't tarry when you've obligations to meet," Jeremy'd advised him sagely. "I never do," and he'd tipped his hat and galloped back into the trees, circling around before heading north toward Howden again.

But when he'd reached the crossroads, he'd had to change his destination. A cloud of dust was rising along the distant ridge. It could only be a troop of soldiers marching from somewhere to somewhere, and although they'd no cause to suspect a lone traveler outright, Jeremy made it his policy not to tempt fate. He'd ridden southward instead and spent the day near Garthorpe. The weather had not much improved. Although he'd longed to get some sleep under an obliging tree, the drizzle forced him to keep to the cover of a smelly barn. Either the farmer was remiss or the cow was ill-tempered, but she had spent the afternoon lowing incessantly, keeping him from a sound sleep. He had awakened feeling heavy-headed and surly. The skies had cleared—one small blessing—but it was still chilly and he had ridden back toward Howden with little thought for anything but Bess' company and a soft bed in which to sleep.

It had happened so suddenly, it was still unclear in his memory. He'd come over the hill above the inn. It had been just a little past midnight, he'd reckoned, and he'd been surprised that the inn was dark already. Most nights at least a few of the local people and, of course, the inn's patrons, were up for a bit of drink and cards. Perhaps the chill had sent them to bed early, he'd supposed as he'd kept riding, but the hair on the back of his neck had risen.

If only I had listened to that premonition, he now reproached himself. *If only I had turned around.* He had sensed danger. Why hadn't he acted upon that perception? If he had done so, Bess wouldn't have had to warn him as she'd done. The bloody redcoats would have had to abandon their ambush plans and pursue him through the frosty night, and he knew he could have eluded them. He wouldn't have returned to the inn, maybe for several months. Too risky. Bess was a smart girl. She'd have understood.

But he'd kept riding, casually dismissing his foreboding. He had been tired. He had been cold. He had been lustful.

He'd seen the muzzle flash before he'd heard the report. Someone was shooting at him! He hadn't hesitated an instant. He'd pulled Satin around so sharply, he had nearly unseated himself, then dug his heels into the horse's sides harder than was necessary to coax him into a full gallop, heading westward across country. He hadn't wanted to return the way he'd come and risk being trapped at the river near Howden Dyke. It was only after he'd gone nearly a mile that a thought occurred to him. Why had his assailant fired from such a distance? He'd been well beyond the range of even the finest rifle.

He'd kept riding west and made it nearly as far as Barmby-on-the-Marsh before the rush of energy that had driven his escape suddenly abandoned him and he had to sleep or fall from his saddle. Despite the cold, he slept outside, next to a huge roll of hay that offered some concealment and warmth. He awoke near dawn, brushed himself off as best he could, then rode on into town. The breakfast smells from a shabby little tavern on the outskirts beckoned to his hungry stomach, and he ordered more than his usual fare. It was in the middle of this Epicurean pleasure that his world had once again turned on end.

His memory was strangely murky from that point on. He remembered someone coming into the inn, excited by some news, telling it with eager relish. He had only half-listened. He knew no one here, so it could be of little concern to him. It was only when questions were asked to get more of the man's tale that Jeremy's spoon had frozen halfway to his mouth and his heart had begun pounding like a damn drum.

"What, Hobbs' daughter? Why'd she shoot herself?"

"I told ya. Ta warn ol' Jeremy off. They was waitin' for 'im, see. 'Ad 'er showin' in the window so's he'd ride up unsuspectin' like and they could nab 'im."

"But you still haven't said why she kilt herself," someone else asked. By this time, Jeremy had lowered his spoon and sat staring' at the table before him. Bess was dead? Bess was dead? That shot he'd seen! That explosion in the night air! That had been the moment of her death? And he had ridden away!

As he was meant to, he realized immediately. As she'd intended him to. But why? Why had she killed herself?

"...tied to 'er, they did, so's she wouldn't try shoutin' to 'im, I guess. But she went and pulled the trigger 'erself afore he could get close enough ta be taken."

"A bad business," someone said sadly.

A bad business?! A bad business?! It's a fuckin' disgraceful business! he had wanted to scream. How had the authorities known he was coming? How had they known?

His mind had seized upon the answer in an instant. He'd been betrayed. Not by Hobbs, surely, for he had as much to lose as Jeremy. Never by Bess! No. Except for the off-chance that one of the guests had overheard his plans and alerted the redcoats, there was only one person at the inn with enough rancor towards him to want him dead. Tim Mott! Tim Mott! *Tim Mott is a dead man!*

How exactly he had gotten from that moment of clarity in the tavern to the time he'd awakened upon the Thorne prison floor was a mysterious puzzle of bits and pieces. He absolutely did not remember leaving the tavern or riding Satin toward Howden. He *did* remember deciding upon his sword to dispatch Mott. He wanted to be close enough to see the man's pain, wanted to twist his hand at the last to make sure the bastard suffered more. He was already relishing the moment when he'd heard the explosion of powder and felt something reach into his gut with a tearing fire, ripping his breath away. He remembered two more blasts, had felt the balls entering his thigh, and remembered thinking in surprise, *My leg's been blown off.*

That was all until the prison floor. And the pain...

Jeremy opened his eyes and looked around his comfortable London parlor. He thought now as he'd thought then that he didn't deserve to be alive. He'd been stupid and careless. He had followed one mistake with another. He shouldn't have gone to see Bess the night before the robbery. He shouldn't have kept on when he'd seen the inn darkened so early. And then, when she'd sacrificed her life to warn him, he had thrown that precious gift away. Only the efforts of a puny boy in a stinking prison had kept it from being a total waste.

What a goddamn idiot he'd been! He didn't deserve to be alive. His whole life had been a useless, selfish waste of breath.

He glanced at the pistols he'd laid on the table and sighed. Useless or not, Bess Hobbs had wanted him to live. Whether he had wanted her to or not, she had purchased his life with her own. He felt tears slipping down his face and he didn't try to stop them this time. There was no one to see, no one to reproach him for his weakness of spirit just now. He thought of her bright smile when last he'd seen her. He thought he could almost smell the rose water in her hair as he held it and kissed it, could almost hear her answering laughter. All that loveliness had vanished in a flash of gunpowder. He realized suddenly that he had been angry with her all these months for being lovesick and foolish. He had wanted to shout at her for wasting her life over him, as if being able to berate her could somehow alter what had happened.

He wanted to speak to her now more than ever. Perhaps he would still scold her just a little for loving him too much. But mostly he wanted to thank her for being brave and strong and selfless. He had not deserved it. He realized he did not feel angry with her anymore, just saddened by the waste. The world needed more good hearts like Bess', that was certain.

A pair of pale blue eyes flashed through his mind's eye and he let out a weary sigh. There was *another* good heart that he'd neglected. He wondered what Lillie Tolver was thinking about him now, if she thought of him at all. Surely she must believe that she was right. She had told him he wouldn't come back and he hadn't. When he'd come to the split in the road at Borwick, he had hesitated, though only for an instant. Swing east the way he'd come, back toward Leeds and the people he'd left there, or keep going south? There wouldn't be much difference travelwise. Both would bring him to London and his search for Philip Bramhearst.

But the way south was less complicated. No Benjamin Twigg. No Lillie Tolver and her family. He'd taken the road south, dismissing any regrets. It was kinder not to intrude in their lives again. Another chapter closed.

And what to do now? *Sleep*, came the simple answer. His tears had dried, but instead of feeling better, he felt drained of energy. His greatest desire was to fall asleep where he sat, but he knew he'd pay for such folly with a stiff neck in the morning. He took a deep breath and pushed himself to his feet. *What will you do now?* the question persisted. *What will you do?*

The knock on his door was so light, Jeremy wasn't sure whether it was indeed a knock or just the wind rattling a bit of loose wood somewhere. It was a cold afternoon and he was not planning to go out for several hours, nor was he dressed to receive any guests. His shirt was barely tucked into his breeches and his hair wasn't tied. *Damn*, he thought with a frown. *Probably Orser. What's he doing up and about so early?* He wasn't really in the mood to see anybody after last night's reflections, though he'd avoided revisiting those troubling thoughts since he'd risen at noon.

He pushed in his shirt, quickly put on his coat, then threw open the door with an irritated sigh.

Two startled brown eyes met his and his mouth dropped open dumbly. It was as if his musings of the night before had conjured up an unlikely apparition to vex him by the light of day.

"Miss Pettygrew," he greeted, finally remembering himself and bowing slightly. "I... This is an unexpected pleasure."

Although the portico around the door offered some concealment, she glanced behind her nervously then pressed forward. "May I come in, Mister Harwood? Please. Before I'm seen."

Jeremy stepped back with only a puzzled nod and she hurried inside.

"May I take your things?" he asked, wishing again that he'd hired a man, for even this simple task took on intimate implications if he were the one performing it. She nodded and he took her cloak and bonnet and hung them beside the door. "Please," he said, stretching a hand toward the parlor behind her. "Shall I offer you some refreshment?"

"No, no," she stammered, turning toward the parlor, then turning back so suddenly that they nearly collided. "Oh, oh, I'm sorry," she said, sounding close to tears. "I shouldn't have come here, of course. I don't know why I did. That is, I've some notion of why I did, but I have reconsidered."

"Are you in need of assistance?" he asked. He had not expected his concerned question to be met with laughter bordering on hysteria.

"Indeed, Mister Harwood," she admitted through her strange amusement. "I sought to escape, just for a little while, from the prison of my life, but now that I am here," she shrugged, her laughter finally dying, "I find that I am too much a coward to proceed." A tear slipped down one cheek and she quickly wiped it away.

Jeremy was no fool, at least about some things. What would bring an unescorted lady to a gentleman's door in the middle of the day? Only two things he could think of—overwhelming necessity or an illicit assignation. As Rosalind Pettygrew seemed not to have been pursued by ruffians to his door, he must assume it was the latter. The trouble was, he had not been a party to arranging a tryst. She must have realized by now the awkwardness to which she'd subjected both of them with her headstrong actions.

"I'm most flattered—" he started.

"You've met him!" she blurted out. "He was telling me this very morning, as he does every morning whether I will it or no, about last evening's doings. He mentioned your name, among others, and proceeded to regale me as usual with his poor opinions of everyone. I think he does it to make himself seem less wanting in good qualities. He called you a foppish hanger-on and Orser's toady. I couldn't bear it. I actually excused myself with a headache. You've *met* him, Mister Harwood. How am I to endure such a man for a husband? I had thought to overlook his physical flaws, but how am I to overlook his mean-spiritedness? How am I to bear the children of such a vile...such a contemptible—"

She bowed her head and wept.

Jeremy took her arm and led her into the parlor, guiding her into a chair and pulling up another to face her. She continued to cry, her head bent so low it looked as if she wanted to disappear.

"Rosalind?" he said quietly, then laid a hand atop her clenched hands to get her attention. "Have you told your father of your dissatisfaction with this match?"

She shook her head and raised a bereft visage to him. "He wouldn't care."

"Why? Most fathers care for their children's happiness."

"My father has run through our available monies," she admitted. "Some bad dealings or something. We've properties, of course, and standing, but with Stephen's settlement after we're married, my family will be able to live as they did before. They're all depending on me."

"Then it seems to me your father should have to be the one to marry that lump of meat, not you," he commented dryly, and she laughed despite her tears. "It also would seem that any man with two eyes could see how unsuitable a creature Mister Lacey is. But if you haven't told your father of your unhappiness, then you cannot expect other than what has been arranged. Perhaps there is less necessity for the match than you believe. Perhaps your father would find another remedy to his problems if he knew how you abhorred this man."

Even as he said it, Jeremy doubted the matter could resolve itself so easily, but he was glad to see that his words had lessened her tears and that her eyes held hope where there had been none before. She nodded and placed a hand on the side of his face.

"I know I shouldn't have come," she admitted, smiling a little through her watery eyes, "but I'm glad that I did. When I heard him speak of *you* so disparagingly, knowing all the while what a worthy gentleman you are, I could not help but hate him even more than I already do. And when I compared him to you, and compared the feelings that you stir in me to those he inspires, I... It was selfish, I know, but I wanted just a little happiness for myself. It never occurred to me that you might refuse me."

"I didn't," he reminded her. "You thought better of the matter, that is all."

She took her hand from his cheek and averted her eyes. "An opportunity I may one day regret not taking," she said quietly, then looked at him with renewed boldness, though Jeremy suspected much of it was feigned. "If I reconsider, would you refuse me?"

Jeremy smiled and stood up, helping her to her feet as well. "Not because you lack appeal, Miss Pettygrew. But as you have not yet reconsidered, and since your charming presence here serves neither of our resolves, it's best if you leave now. May I escort you home?"

She thought a moment. "I want to say yes. I even want to you to go with me when I face Father, though I know that would never do. But I have imposed upon you more than I ever should have—"

"I would like to see you home, Miss Pettygrew. In truth, my sense of honor would not allow me to let you venture away unattended. We are friends, after all, or at the very least, civilized people."

Her smile was filled with so much gratitude, Jeremy could not help but smile in return, though as he did so he had a premonition of trouble. There was bound to be trouble when one involved oneself with other peoples' problems, and Rosalind Pettygrew had a *huge* problem, literally.

"Who the hell are you?" Sir Thomas Pettygrew demanded. "I don't recall having made your acquaintance, so you've no business being acquainted with my daughter."

Jeremy inclined his head deferentially. "Jeremy Harwood, sir. I have, in fact, just recently made the acquaintance of *all* your daughters. I—"

"Harwood? Of the Cumbria Harwoods?"

"A cousin, sir."

"Hmm. Well, you've still no business here. Good day, Mister Harwood."

"Excuse me, sir," Jeremy said, with just enough brash to make Rosalind's father raise an eyebrow as he turned back toward his unwanted guest. Jeremy pressed on. "I don't mean to intrude, but may I inquire after Miss Pettygrew's well-being."

"You may not." He started to go again.

"Excuse me, sir, but I must insist. You see, she has confided something of her situation to me—"

"Is that why you're camped out in my parlor? Hoping to secure her affections from Mister Lacey—"

"Not at all, sir," he interrupted. "I only wish her happiness and I do not see that as a likely outcome if she marries Stephen Lacey."

"Rosalind's happiness is none of your concern."

"Perhaps not, but it certainly must be yours." He waited for the man to respond, but when he didn't, Jeremy took a breath and continued. "I don't know whether you've had the opportunity to spend time with your future son-in-law, sir, but as a fellow bachelor, we move in the same circles." What harm in letting him think he'd spent more than just one regrettable evening with the lout? "I hesitate to defame any man behind his back, but perhaps matters as important as marital alliances might excuse such slander." Again he paused, expecting a rebuff, and again Sir Pettygrew remained silent, his eyes narrowed but curious. "Stephen Lacey is as crude a man as I have ever met, sir. He is tolerated only because of his connections and for no other reason. He is contemptuous of everyone around him yet seeks to secure the good opinion of others by resorting to a flood of the coarsest jests imaginable. He drinks and eats to such excess, it is revolting to spend all but he briefest periods of time in his company. He spits when he talks, sir. Is this the man you would have for a son-in-law? Is this the man you would ask your daughter to..." He wanted to say, "take to her bed," but thought better of it. "...to endure for the rest of her life? Although I am only briefly acquainted with her, Sir Thomas, I know a kind heart when I see one, and I would not want to see that kindness squandered on the likes of Stephen Lacey."

Still the baronet said nothing and Jeremy finally lifted his chin. "Am I to have the courtesy of a response, sir?"

Rosalind's father pursed his lips in seeming annoyance. "My daughter is currently crying in her room, Mister Harwood. She told me of her misgivings in such a rambling string of hysterical mutterings, I dismissed her entreaties as some sort of maidenly apprehension. She's been engaged these nine months, Mister Harwood, and this is the first I've heard of her doubts." He paused a moment, then shook his head. "Your presumption is extraordinary, young man, but I cannot dismiss all of what you say. I will consider matters further. Now leave my home, Mister Harwood. You are not welcome here."

"Why is that, sir?"

"Another presumption? Very well. You are a threat. It's obvious my daughter has taken a fancy to you, and it's just as obvious why she'd prefer you to Lacey. But you've nothing to offer her, Mister Harwood."

"I never supposed I did," he said honestly.

Sir Thomas Pettygrew seemed taken back by the admission. "Very well. We understand each other then. Good day, sir."

Though Jeremy felt less than satisfied with the outcome, he could see by the baronet's resolute stride that he would not be imposed upon further.

Chapter Nine

Jeremy avoided social invitations the following week, pleading illness. He became his former reclusive self, spending the mornings walking or riding and the afternoons reading, and found he preferred such idle pursuits to the whirl of society. London's booksellers were treasure troves of variety, and the prices were so much better than in York or Sheffield, he could buy two volumes for what one had once cost him. His first purchase had been Henry Fielding's *Joseph Andrews* and he begrudgingly found the late magistrate's writing most admirable. He determined to read *Tom Jones* next, despite its lengthiness.

He knew he should be dealing with Tim Mott, but what difference would it make *when* the vermin eventually died. Besides, the weather was not the best for traveling north. In a month or two would be better. And he had prospered at cards in the last weeks. Despite the poor showing he had made the night of Varnley's murder, which he thought could be blamed on being more than distracted by his disgust for the man, he had managed quite well since then and had set aside a considerable sum. He wouldn't have to go back to Scotland for awhile yet. He had never tarried as long in town and though he knew he would not be forever contented with such an aimless existence, it suited him now. He could not think about the future. There was too much of it ahead of him.

It was nearly supper time and he was just finishing dressing to go eat at the public house down the street when there came a pounding at his door—a fist being applied with all possible force, it seemed, for the sturdy door shook with the blows. This was not a friendly caller, that was certain, and Jeremy scooped one of his pistols from the dressing table and cocked it at his side.

"Open the door, Harwood," came a commanding voice.

Rosalind's father?

"Who are you?" Jeremy returned, unable to quite suppress the temptation to vex the blustering man at his door. "I'll know before I willingly admit a ruffian, which by your pounding I might well suppose."

An exasperated sigh was audible from the other side. "Let me in, Harwood. 'Tis only Sir Pettygrew, not some damned brigand."

Jeremy unbolted the door but kept the pistol at his side. He barely had time to step aside before the baronet barged past him and strode haughtily into the parlor.

"Why, come in, sir," Jeremy bowed, slamming the door shut and striding after his unwelcome guest. "And now who is being presumptuous, Sir Thomas?"

"I have just cause and you know it, you debaucher."

"I must ask you to leave, sir."

"And if I don't, will you to shoot me?" the man challenged, nodding to the pistol.

"Not unless you give *me* just cause."

The baronet drew himself up and examined his host. "God, you've a cool head for a scoundrel. But I will not be so easily handled, Mister Harwood. I have come for my daughter. Where is she?"

Jeremy tried not to show his surprise. Rosalind was missing and her father sought her here? "Why would she be here, sir? As I told you before, we were only briefly acquainted—"

"She's not here? But her sisters thought—"

"You may search my humble lodgings," Jeremy volunteered with a wave of his hand.

Sir Pettygrew squinted suspiciously. "If she is not here then you know where she is."

"I have not seen your daughter since I left her in *your* care last week, sir. Are you sure she isn't shopping for a new bonnet or—"

"Damn your eyes, she isn't shopping! She's been gone since after supper last night, or so we think. That is the last anyone has seen of her."

Jeremy motioned for the man to sit down, then did so himself. "This is alarming news to be sure," he said, uncocking his pistol and laying it aside. "But she has not come here, nor have I had word from her."

"But she knows where you live," the baronet said, his tone accusing. "Pamela told me she'd come here before, and unescorted! Do you deny it?"

"I cannot, though I agree with you that it was an ill-advised visit, one which, I assure you, I did not solicit. Did Miss Pamela also tell you that?"

"We have sent word to every person to whom she might have gone and have had no luck," Sir Thomas admitted, and Jeremy finally heard the voice of a concerned father, though whether that concern came from love or a desire to maintain appearances, he couldn't quite tell. "Do you know of anyone else to whom she might have turned for help?"

"I don't. The only other acquaintance I have in common with your daughter besides yourself and her sisters is Mister Lacey."

"She would not go to him," Sir Thomas said flatly. "Not if he were the last man living."

"Her words?"

Sir Thomas nodded.

"Then you did not release her from her obligation to marry him?"

"I hadn't decided yet. I suppose she took my reluctance for refusal. May God never bless you with female children, Mister Harwood! They're a damn lot of trouble!"

Jeremy had to smile at the baronet's outburst, then sobered again, remembering its cause. "May I assist your search for her, sir? I'm presently at loose ends and would gladly—"

"No thank you, Mister Harwood," Sir Thomas said as he stood. "*You* are the last person I would send looking for her. A case of the hound to the hare. But do me, or at least her mother and sisters, the kindness of sending word if you *do* hear from her. And tell her our only concern at this point is for her safety."

Jeremy nodded and was about to show Sir Thomas out when the man quitted on his own with a slamming of the door.

Jeremy had no idea where an unattached, highborn lady might seek aid in general or where Rosalind Pettygrew would go in particular. He knew about the lower classes, of course. They went into service somewhere, either as cooks or maids or, if they were unlucky, as bar girls or whores. Jeremy didn't think Rosalind was desperate enough to escape her impending marriage by falling that low. What else then? Her family had checked relatives and known friends to no avail. It had been too spontaneous a departure for her to have solicited for a governess' position, though certainly some young ladies of her station were forced by circumstances, or lack of comeliness, to support themselves that way. Jeremy mulled over the problem throughout supper. His help had been refused, but he had never let other men's stubbornness determine his course before. He felt somehow responsible for having brought Rosalind home, though becoming her lover would not have been a wiser choice. He sighed as he climbed the steps to his apartments after supper. *This is what comes from getting involved*, he scolded himself.

He poured himself a drink once inside and sat down to think further on the problem of Miss Pettygrew. It was hard to put himself in a woman's shoes, but he made the attempt. *Where would I go if I didn't want to marry that pig of a man?* he asked himself. *Where would I go if I didn't want to be discovered by my family?* Surely not to another family member, no matter how distant they might be. They would be obligated to reveal her whereabouts to her father in time. Friends would be under less accountability, but if they were known, Rosalind must know she might be found there. What about unknown friends? *And how am I to know of them if they're unknown?* He chuckled to himself and took another sip of gin. In mid-sip, he had a thought. Actually, two thoughts. What had been the name of that governess Rosalind and her sisters had been so happy to see the day before Elliot Kingsley swung? Miss Wickam? Hatwick? Knatwick! God, a needle in a pin shop to find a spinsterly ex-governess or her sister Clara or Carla or whatever. Anyway, wouldn't the family have had the same notion? They might have already sent inquiries to dear Miss Knatwick.

But not to Missus Whitcomb he'd warrant. Her sisters had snubbed the woman contemptuously. Would it even occur to them to suggest that their sister might have sought refuge with an actress? Had they even deigned to remember her name? Jeremy smiled and slugged down the rest of his drink. Madge Whitcomb was his best lead. It was still early. Plenty of time to take a stroll over to Drury

Lane and see if he could find out where Missus Whitcomb was currently performing.

He did not find Missus Whitcomb right away, but he found someone else that momentarily distracted him from his search for Rosalind and left him feeling cynical, even hostile, towards females in general.

When coming away from the Royal, having been told by a disinterested fellow taking money at the door that no such actress was performing there at present, try the Fortune, Jeremy saw the older gentleman he'd previously seen with his mother entering a card house across the street. The man was alone this time. Without thinking, Jeremy altered his course, crossing the street and entering the club.

The older man had not yet found a table and Jeremy tarried at the entrance, pretending to be searching for someone. At last he saw the man start toward a corner table with some open chairs and headed that way himself.

What he was doing, he did not know. Curiosity again? But whereas he had trusted his father with the information that the highwayman, Jeremy Knox, was still alive, he would not dare trust his mother with that knowledge. She was too careless to guard such a secret. He might find himself a wanted man again if he wasn't careful.

Jeremy observed the man, who introduced himself genially as Quinton Selby, while they played cards. And though he might have pretended inattention, Jeremy listened to Mister Selby's every word, waiting to glean whatever information he might about his mother, waiting, too, for an opening in which he might inquire about her. It was an hour and several drams of whiskey later before Mister Selby gave him that opening.

"Come on, gentleman," he feigned a plea after losing yet another hand. "Be kind to an old man. I've a demand upon my purse for a fancy smock before the season opens."

Jeremy hesitated only a moment. "Does that 'demand' favor purple satin cloaks as well?" he asked casually.

Selby looked amazed but unembarrassed. "She does, sir. But how would you know such a thing."

"I thought I had seen you before," Jeremy informed him. "Near Christmastide. I hope you do not take offense, sir, but it was the lady that first caught my eye, not yourself. And she wore that purple cloak."

Selby smiled. "She *is* an eye-catcher, my Lydia."

"Ah," Jeremy said with a knowing nod of his head. "Lydia Knox."

"You know her?" Selby asked, suddenly wary.

"Who does not?" was Jeremy's simple reply, and a couple of the other players chuckled. "Really, I mean her no disrespect, sir. I only meant that I know *of* her," he clarified, hesitating once more before adding, "though more of her son."

"Ah, that daring scamp!" said a mustachioed man beside him with an approving smile. "Glad I never crossed paths with him, of course, or I'd be lighter a few shillings. But I liked his style. That I did. And he made a good end of it, I hear. Shot down trying to avenge his missy."

"I heard they hanged him at Thorne," said another.

"Shot him. Hanged him. Makes no difference in the end."

"To his mother it might," Jeremy said soberly, watching Quinton Selby's face as he spoke. "I hope Mistress Knox is enduring her grief well."

"It grieved her kind heart mightily at the time," Mister Selby said sadly, then added with a wink, "but nothing a pretty muff and a new cloak wouldn't cure. That very cloak you saw her in, young man, was the one that turned her tears to smiles again."

"I am glad," Jeremy said over the laughter of the other players, "that she was not inconvenienced by tender feelings for too long."

"Another excellent example of the inconstancy of a woman's heart," the man with the mustache laughed. "Even a mother's heart. Listen, gentlemen, and remember it well. And do not expect to be long remembered by your doting wives, grateful lovers, or loving daughters. Your widows will be glad they may spend your money at leisure, your lovers will soon find another means of support, and your daughters will be glad you can no longer meddle in their lives."

The other men nodded, grinning with grim acceptance of a bitter truth.

Jeremy nodded, too, but more from conformity than feeling. He was having an unexpectedly difficult time accepting the fact that a satin cloak had vanquished his mother's bereavement. It should not have surprised him. He remembered well her self-pitying reaction to Eleanor's murder. Her selfishness had driven him away in disgust. Had she exhibited any of the usual anguish at her daughter's death, he might have felt duty-bound to stay and comfort her. But her tears had been for herself, not Eleanor. And her tears for him had dried at the sight of a bit of purple satin. It left him believing that the man beside him spoke the truth. Women were incapable of feeling deeply for the men in their lives. He wondered that he had not fully understood that until now. He wasn't certain whether such disaffection was an innate flaw in that sex or whether it was a response to the all-too-frequent callousness of men toward their women, but the truth of it left him feeling oddly dispirited.

If a man's own mother could not even be counted on to grieve for him, what other woman could he ever count on to truly love him? *Listen and remember*, his companion had advised. *And do not fool yourself into expecting it.*

The Madge Whitcomb who greeted him backstage was much altered in appearance. She cackled in character as he approached.

"By the pricking of my thumbs, something wicked this way comes," she hissed.

"You mistake me, ma'am," Jeremy replied in hushed tones, for the closing scenes of *Macbeth* continued beyond the heavily curtained backdrop. "I seek only a comforting word concerning the welfare of a mutual friend of ours."

The witch inclined her scraggly, bewigged head, her heavily lined eyes squinting in wariness. For a moment Jeremy almost thought her capable of conjuring a hex upon him. Then she smiled.

"As I've only met you in the presence of dear Rosalind, I assume you seek word of her. But why here? Do you not know her family? The Pettygrews, lad. Seek your comforting word there."

"She has left their protection," he informed the crone. "Her father told me that he has exhausted all leads and been unable to find her."

"And he sought *your* help?"

"You do well to be surprised," Jeremy grinned companionably. "No, madam, he refused my help. *A hound to the hare* I think were his words."

The actress chuckled, her bosom bouncing beneath her tattered costume. She took a step forward and reached out a hand, adorned with long, false nails, to touch his arm in seeming comfort. "But you look for her anyway. *Are* you a hound after the hare, Mister Harwood?"

Even through the ghastly makeup, Jeremy could not mistake the salacious gleam in Madge Whitcomb's eyes. If it would help him to find Rosalind, perhaps he should feed the woman's obvious love for titillating scandal. If she *were* harboring Rosalind, perhaps pretending to be enamored of Miss Pettygrew would help his cause.

"I find I cannot stop thinking about her," he said. That was true enough, though friendly obligation rather than love made it so. "She came to me once and I did not have sense enough to protect her then. She obviously does not want to risk being so unkindly rebuffed again. But I am worried for her safety. You know the world, Missus Whitcomb. It is a cruel place for the defenseless. A dangerous place. I don't think our dear Miss Pettygrew appreciates her situation."

The sound of shouting and swordplay was building to a crescendo beyond the backdrop. The witch only looked at him with an assessing eye.

"You are a man of feeling, Mister Harwood." she finally said. Her breathing seemed to have quickened, her bosom rising and falling as if she had just exerted herself in some way. She took a deep, quieting breath and let it out slowly through parted lips. "I don't know where she is, but you're right, my dear boy. I *do* know the way the world works. We must put our heads together and find her."

"Lay on, Macduff!" Macbeth shouted fiercely, his voice penetrating the farthest reaches of the theater, even back stage. "And damned be him that cries, 'Hold! Enough!'"

"It's almost time for my curtain call," the witch whispered as other cast members back stage suddenly became active, scurrying by to find their places. "Then I must put myself to rights, of course. Come to my rooms in about an hour, Mister Harwood. We'll discuss what might be done for dear Rosalind then." She gave him the address, then hurried away, leaving Jeremy with an uneasiness he could not shake.

It was too much in one night. The day had begun well enough, had even progressed all the way through the afternoon with no premonition of disagreeable prospects. Since then he had been called to task by an angry, insulting, overbearing father, discovered the true shallowness of his mother's feelings for him, and now stood facing further blatant evidence of feminine duplicity.

But her breasts *were* beautiful. And large. Once freed from the confines of their clothing, they had seemed to swell to magnificent proportions. He felt himself harden in primitive response at the sight. His mind might be repulsed by her willingness to usurp her friend's desired paramour, but his body was not, especially as she stepped closer, her eyes full of obvious yearning. His eyes strayed once more from her face to her breasts.

"Go ahead, lovey," she said breathlessly. "I love a man's hands on my tits, and you've got such nice hands. Masterful hands." She pushed forward a little more, her long fingers sliding around his waist.

"Is this what you call putting our heads together?" he asked, but his voice was not condemning as he'd intended. She might be ten or more years his senior, he thought, but they seemed no obstacle to his lust. He wondered with a smile what had become of the ugly hag that had pronounced Macbeth's doom just a few hours before? Vanished into the night air to be replaced by yet another apparition, this time a queen of infinite variety. Damn, what's the harm? he thought, his hands finally molding themselves around her offered breasts. She sucked in an appreciative breath.

"We'll talk later, lovey," she sighed.

And what of Rosalind? he wondered momentarily. *Am I betraying her in this?*

Madge let a hand drop to his crotch and trace the outline of his erect member through the fabric of his breeches as she nuzzled closer. *Huzzah for betrayal*, he thought cynically, and even harbored a momentary contempt for the absent Rosalind and her naiveté. Madge's wandering hands soon freed him from his pants. Her touch was warm and smooth and skillful. He bowed his head and sought her lips, his hands still reveling in the silken roundness of her huge breasts, toying with the dark nipples where they rose hard against his thumbs.

They had not even ventured far from the door before she had begun her seduction, speaking to him of her need as she slowly undid the little buttons down the front of her gown. Telling him, as she'd slipped her bodice off her shoulders and let it fall to the floor behind her, how she had recognized him as a young man of "promise" since the first moment she'd laid eyes on him. Complimenting his figure as she'd approached him invitingly. Even invoking Rosalind's name—that same "dear Rosalind" she supposedly wanted to help—in her praises. "Dear Rosalind certainly chose a handsome devil this time," she'd cooed. "A young fellow who's able, I'm sure, to give a lady what she needs."

"Come on, lovey," she panted now, tugging on the lapels of his coat to encourage him to the floor. "Give it to me good, sweeting, and I'll do for you, too."

It would be a pleasant exchange if nothing else. How could it be otherwise. All thoughts of the lost Rosalind and his contemptible mother disappeared completely as he willingly obliged her appetite…and his.

Chapter Ten

There had been no talking afterward, or at least not much. She had again insisted that she did not know where Miss Pettygrew was and, upon reflection, could not think of anywhere else Jeremy might look for her. But he was welcome to come back looking again if he wished. He'd left her with a careless kiss and one last caress of her ample bosoms. He wondered with a sigh if he'd be lucky enough to encounter another such pair in his lifetime. A return visit was a tempting idea.

In the morning, however, he shook his head in mild contrition. *Bad plan, Jeremy*, he told himself. In fact, lingering in London did not hold much appeal. He missed the wider spaces of the countryside more and more. He realized that part of the attraction of his former "profession" had been that it had meant traveling the open roads and just "being" in the world. No schedules. Few worries beyond his own needs. Few people to whom he must answer.

He did not plan a return to robbing, of course. He knew he could never go back to what he had been. Fear prevented him, but lack of desire for the work was an even more compelling deterrent. Still, he must find something to do with his life, something that would satisfy him as he had once been satisfied. He missed being happy.

Happiness was a tricky thing, he realized. He'd been happy as a child because he had known no better and because his mother, for all her conceit, *had* managed to provide the basic comforts of food, clothing and shelter. Children are happy as long as they feel safe. He'd been less happy as he'd grown older and realized fully just who and what his mother was...and who and what *he* was. Still, he had managed a degree of contentment in mastering his surroundings wherever they'd lived. He had enjoyed growing to be a man strong enough to work with the smithy in Penrith. Sweating had even made him happy.

Then there had been the year or more following Eleanor's death. He had been unhappy then and attributed his unhappiness to grief, but now he realized it had also been lack of purpose that had laid him so low. No longer a brother or son, he was only a young man adrift. It was not until he had taken to highway robbery that he had regained a degree of happiness. His purpose? To steal without getting caught and to enjoy all the luxury that his stolen prizes could buy—fine clothing, a fine horse, good food when available, and the security of lacking for nothing. Even the possibility of capture and death had added to his satisfaction each time he avoided those consequences. Yes, he'd been happy. Happy with his notoriety. Happy with the women he'd bedded. Happy to be riding the roads with no obligations.

Happy until that chilly night when he'd seen a muzzle flash from the Running Lion and heard the explosion of gun powder echoing up the hill. It still echoed in his dreams sometimes. It marked the complete changing of his life and his purpose. Survival, not pleasure, had become paramount. Now that he *had* survived, it was time to remake himself into another creature again.

No longer a brother and son. No longer a highwayman. But who, then? He didn't know yet but he somehow knew the answer did not lie in London. He wasn't cut out for the indolent lifestyle of society. It was too much effort for too little gain and too great a chance of ruination by drink or bankruptcy. He did not want to pursue a deeper acquaintance with anyone he had met so far and, in fact, would prefer to avoid most of them. He could not forget that although he had enjoyed some of the culture London offered, he had also murdered a man here. In short, London was a nice place to visit, but no one in their right mind would choose to stay, at least not for very long.

It was more than time to leave. He should have left already.

He would go tomorrow.

No, too sudden. He could not ignore the fact that he had made certain connections here that he might want to profit by someday. An unexplained departure would invite not only suspicion but enmity. And he was using the name of Harwood now. Despite his true status in that family, he found he did not want to discredit it unnecessarily.

He looked around the sunlit dining room where he sat alone over a sloppy breakfast of eggs and smiled. He had been lucky to find such a place. Would the landlord want to continue renting to an absentee tenant? It would be nice to have a place in Town, but his future was so uncertain, he didn't know whether it would be worth the expense. The old Jeremy had never stayed anywhere for long and never called any place home. Permanent lodgings were just another encumbrance. Most men, however, saw belonging somewhere as essential to their welfare. Perhaps he would have to force some permanence upon himself if he were to make his life more normal. Besides, this place made him happy most days, and wasn't happiness what he sought? He would talk to the landlord today.

He would say his good-byes within the week. Farewell to Viscount Orser who, for all his drinking and gambling had kept their shared secret well. Farewell to the viscount's friends who had welcomed a commoner into their gaggle on Orser's say-so. A casual dropping of the information to the public room keepers, tavern keepers, and shop keepers with whom he'd become a regular patron, with a thanks for their services.

He thought about his brief search for Rosalind, unsolicited though it was, and wondered if he should continue it while he stayed. It wasn't his concern, really. The problem from which she fled—an unwanted connection with the repugnant Mister Lacey—had been a problem since long before *he* had met her. It had, in fact, been the reason for their meeting in the first place, for her sisters had said they were putting by good memories to see her through the impending dreariness of her marriage. He was not responsible for her infatuation with him. He could not help it that, when compared to Mister Lacey, he looked like the man of her dreams. Even his mother's elderly lover, Mister Quinton Selby compared well with Mister Lacey. Almost *any* man did. He had just been in the wrong place at the wrong time and drawn her interest.

As I recall, you *approached* her, his memory chided him. True, he had spoken first, complimenting her loveliness, telling her she would be the last beautiful thing Elliot Kingsley would see. He had been in a mood to socialize that day and it had seemed a safe flirtation. Did he owe Rosalind Pettygrew anything just because he had flattered her at a vulnerable time in her life? He sighed. Perhaps a little. Perhaps a bit of concern at least. He would follow his other lead, find her old governess and see if she harbored the fugitive girl. After that, he was out of ideas, time, and inclination.

It had not been so difficult to locate Miss Knatwick and her sister Clara after all. He had done it in the course of a day, with the unlikely help of Viscount Orser's cook. He had gone to Orser's home that afternoon to tell him he would be leaving soon and to thank him for his assistance "in all things." The viscount had been glad to see him after so long an absence, was glad to see he was well, and was glad when Jeremy accepted an invitation to dine with him and some of the others that evening. They fell into conversation and Jeremy mentioned the missing Miss Pettygrew.

"Can't say as I blame the girl," Orser had commiserated. "Can't stand Lacey myself. But I don't fault Pettygrew for rejecting your proffered help, either. If I had a daughter trying her fool best to ruin her reputation forever, I'd not send a gent like you to find her."

Jeremy told him of his idea to locate Miss Knatwick and before he knew it, Orser's cook, Missus Jenny had been summoned up to the sitting room.

"If my wife were here, she would know how to find such a person, for she has always been the one to engage the help. But Missus Jenny is the only knowledgeable female on the premise. If she doesn't know, she might know who would."

She did. Not precisely Miss Knatwick's address, of course, but who she had last worked for. When Jeremy left Orser's home with a promise to return for supper, he made his way to Miss Knatwick's last employers, fabricated a lie about being a nephew returned from the Continent in search of his aunt, and soon had the address of Rosalind's old governess in his pocket.

Miss Knatwick looked surprised to see him. She was even more surprised when he told her why he had come. No, she had not been contacted by the family and wondered why, for she and her charges had always been close, or so she had thought.

"Rosalind knows, however, that although I would gladly let her stay with me as long as she wished, I would be duty bound to tell her family that she was here."

"Even if she were trying to escape an impending evil?" Jeremy asked.

"Marriage to Mister Lacey might not be ideal, Mister Harwood, but it would have its compensations. Ardor is of less consequence than security for a woman."

Jeremy returned her assertion with a quizzical stare, then remembered the position from which Miss Knatwick spoke. A woman who had never known true security, who had been at the beck and call of spoiled children and their parents her entire adult life, might indeed find the idea of marriage to even a Stephen Lacey a blessing. She had no children of her own and now, at her age, never would. When she became too old to be a fashionable addition to even a country gentleman's household, she would have to get by on whatever she had put aside and hope it lasted until she drew her last, lonely breath. No, Rosalind would not come to this woman, he realized, not if she sought a sympathetic heart.

He rode back to his apartments to change for supper with a mixture of regret at having failed and relief because he had done what he could. Rosalind had hidden herself well, it seemed, and it would take someone who knew her far better than he did to find her. He could leave London with a clear conscience.

A knock at the door? It was late, after midnight by now, though he'd dozed off over a book, so maybe it was later yet. He rubbed his eyes and tried to force himself more quickly to alertness. Perhaps he had dreamed it.

The rat-tat-tat of an impatient knock sounded again and the receding clopping of hooves and cab wheels on cobbles. It was no dream. He had a visitor. Wearily he dragged himself to the door and laid a hand upon it.

"Yes," he said. "Who is it?"

"Rosalind," came a woman's whisper.

He shot the bolt back and opened the door. A swirl of bustling skirts and perfume—vanilla, he thought—scurried past him, but before he had even shut the door behind her, she turned and struck his face with a stinging slap of her little hand, then flounced into the parlor without a backward glance.

I don't like her, he fumed, following her into the parlor with the intent of throwing her back out the door. Perhaps she deserved Stephen Lacey as a husband after all.

"How *could* you choose that lowborn strumpet over me?!" she demanded, having seated herself imperiously on the sofa where he'd been reading. She picked up the open book, glanced disinterestedly at the cover, then closed it and tossed it aside. "Well?"

"Miss Pettygrew—"

"Rosalind."

"Miss Pettygrew," he repeated, undeterred. "I'm not sure to whom you are referring..." though he thought he knew. Two gorgeous breasts came to mind. "...but it scarcely must matter to you. We have no understanding, you and I. And might I point out that it is more *likely* for a gentleman to choose a low-born strumpet, as you call her, for the very reason that she *is* low-born. Most gentlemen do not make it a practice to ruin society's unwed daughters, not if they value their lives."

Rosalind's red lips were pouty and her brown-eyes stared at him in hurt confusion. "I see," she said, and sounded like she *did* finally understand. "Still, it hurt to hear that you and she... That you... She told me *exactly* what the two of you did, Mister Harwood, to let me know what kind of man you truly were and to warn me off."

"Yet here you are," he said pointedly, "against your friend's advice."

"She's no longer my friend," Rosalind said sullenly. "She never was, that false creature. Well, I suppose I should have known that an actress can *act* like a friend, but I really believed she cared. She was so good about taking me in when I told her about Mister Lacey. She seemed genuinely sympathetic, even cried with me..."

Her voice trailed off and she looked away. Her eyes had a dolefulness that finally inspired him with some compassion for her.

"I'll get my coat," he said quietly. "You need to go home."

"*Again* you will deliver me back to face my wretched future?" she asked without looking at him. She shook her head and slowly stood up, fixing him with a disappointed look. "No, I'll just go, thank you."

"Where to, may I ask?"

"I don't really know. But I will not marry that horror of a man. I'd rather be dead."

"Your father said he had not made up his mind—"

"I'm just a woman, Mister Harwood. My options are limited. I was raised to be a lady who could carry on polite conversation, keep the servants in line, and give birth to some man's children. That is all. If I cannot do that, then I am worthless to my family. I was willing to fulfill that obligation, despite Mister Lacey's repugnant form, until I got to know him better...until I compared him with you. I cannot overlook his personality any longer. I will not endure his attentions. And now that I have run away, I realize that I have lost *all* chance for another match. Even Mister Lacey may reject me at this point, for who knows how many men I might have been with during my absence."

"Your family has been discreet in their inquires, Rosalind. I don't even think your fiancé realizes *why* you are gone. For all the world knows, you are visiting an aunt or something."

"Perhaps." She looked at him then, and besides a new hopefulness in her eyes, he saw also open adoration and something like determination. "I cannot help how I feel about you, Jeremy. Every time I see you, my heart aches with it."

He smiled sadly. "Then let me put your mind and heart at rest, Miss Pettygrew, by assuring you that you will not have to see me much longer. I have decided to quit London within the week."

"No!" she exclaimed, her voice breaking as she spoke. She rushed forward and threw her arms around his shoulders like a clinging child. "Don't go! You mustn't! I cannot bear that I will never even see you somewhere by chance."

"I thought seeing me made your heart ache," he reminded her, returning her embrace as platonically as he could, though he couldn't totally dismiss the allurement of her chest pressed against his, the scent of vanilla rising from her hair, or the way her little hands kneaded at his back in desperation.

"If I weren't a baronet's daughter, would you love me?" she asked, her voice muffled against his chest. His hesitation in answering made her release him just enough to turn her head up in question.

"Are you grown enough to hear the truth?" he asked, doubting that she was but seeing no way out of this awkwardness without speaking it. "If you are asking if you are a desirable woman, then the answer is yes. If you want to hear that I would like to bed you, Miss Pettygrew, again the answer would be yes." She smiled at his admission—her full lips showing a row of pearly little teeth—and a satisfied gleam came to her eyes. "But if you are asking whether I am the sort of man who would pledge his undying devotion to you...if *that* is what you mean by love...then the answer is no. No, Miss Pettygrew. I'm not sure I am capable of anything more than desire. Do you understand?"

Her smile had lessened slightly at this last confession, but she made no move to release him. "I am not so silly as you think me," she said softly, her arms tightening again. "I never thought of you as a replacement fiancé for Mister Lacey. Your position in the world makes that quite impossible, of course."

Now *she* was speaking the hard truth and he found, for all its accuracy, that he did not enjoy hearing it.

"You have nothing to offer me, Jeremy, except the pleasure of your company. If we were discreet, we might be mutually satisfied. Do *you* understand?"

Where was the naive girl who had cried and pouted and slapped him for being intimate with her supposed friend? What was she about now? "I understand well enough. But have you forgotten, Miss Pettygrew? You're *still* a lady." The pressure of her hands on his shoulders and the enticing press of her belly to his belied his words. "And if you have any hopes for another alliance, it would be unwise of you to encourage me further. I am not a scoundrel to spoil innocent maidens."

Ah, but she was making it difficult to remember virtue. He had never slept with a virgin he realized perversely. Even Bess, as young as she had been, had been deflowered long before he'd taken up with her. Virginity was not such a prized commodity among the lesser folk, but he knew it was sacred to the nobility, at least while marriage deals were being negotiated. If he forgot that, her father would have redress in court if not at the end of a dueling pistol.

"What if I were to tell you that I'm *not* an innocent maid, Jeremy, so you needn't feel hesitant on that count?" She smiled enticingly at his look of disbelief and slowly kissed the side of his jaw several times, finally flicking the end of his chin with her tongue.

"You surprise me," he said, and meant it. Someone should have fired the girl's chaperones, he mused, for they had done a poor job of it. Not only had she been despoiled before her wedding night, she now coaxed his ardor like a practiced seductress. He reluctantly took her arms and held her away from him. "Still," he insisted with forced conviction, "I *am* leaving within the week. I want no obligations here."

"And I ask none. If you are really leaving, then leave me with a wonderful memory. Please, Jeremy. Please."

"What if I leave you with child instead?" he countered, but his resolve was weakening.

"Then I'll marry Mister Lacey as scheduled and pass it off as his. It would actually be a comfort to know that it was not."

She had an answer for everything. Convenient but unnerving. Something told him to refuse her, and quickly, but she was becoming more appealing by the moment. And he had realized during her entreaties that he had never bedded a lady. Too dangerous. Too well guarded by their fathers and husbands. Were they finer than other women? Softer? Whiter? Smoother? Did their more educated minds bring some extra quality to the act? He might never know if...

"You will do me no favor by refusing me," she insisted, reaching out to tug his shirt out a little, then slipping her hands beneath it. He felt her shudder with delight, then hesitate momentarily when her fingers found the scar beneath his ribs.

"I was shot once," he said matter-of-factly. "If that changes your opinion of me—"

"Oh, no," she said, stepping back and unbuttoning the bottom of his shirt. Her long fingers tentatively touched the pink circle left by the bullet, her eyes bright with obvious fascination. He looked at her as she examined him and could not fault her beauty. Her chin was small and pointed, her neck long and curved. What he could see of her breasts through the thin fabric of her gown looked promising, and when he touched her there, he found a nipple already hard with anticipation. She inhaled sharply, then smiled in delight.

"No floor for me," she whispered teasingly.

Had Madge told her even that?!

"Take me to your bed, Jeremy."

He paused only a moment, then swept her into his arms and up the stairs. Even with her miles of skirts and petticoats, she was light and he momentarily wondered whether she would disappear altogether once her clothes were shed.

She did not. She looked more fragile in her nakedness than other women he'd bedded, but not unpleasantly so. *Like a porcelain knickknack*, he thought as he ran his fingers along her body. But warmer than porcelain. And much softer and smoother, too. He liked the way her little hands explored him as well, kneading the muscles on his arms, running her palm down his belly, and finally, curiously, touching his rigid member, her eyes wide with an almost childlike fascination. He could only suppose that her other encounters had been less leisurely, though perhaps she was merely enjoying the allure of the forbidden as he was.

He wanted to treasure this exchange, not rush to fulfillment. Rosalind Pettygrew was a rare jewel, to take delight in and to cherish. And to remember. Perhaps she had been right to insist upon this tryst. Christ, it *felt* right. He groaned as her fingers shyly encircled his organ, then ran his own hand up the inside of a silken thigh, his fingers pushing gently into the dark, slick hair between her legs. "You're so lovely," he whispered, slipping two fingers into her…and getting an unwelcome surprise.

He might have never been with a virgin before, but he'd been with enough other women to know there was something different about Rosalind Pettygrew. His fingers had encountered a barrier just inside her nether lips and she had flinched with the pressure.

"Don't stop," she pleaded when he looked at her with accusing eyes.

"You lied to me," he said, his hand still teasing her swollen nub, in part to torment her.

"It doesn't matter," she panted. "I want you, Jeremy. Please don't stop."

The selfish bitch, he thought. *The beautiful, selfish little bitch.* He wanted her, too, but he would not take her. He had no wish to end up on the wrong end of a pistol again, especially one held by a justifiably outraged father. But neither could he bring himself to pull away completely. She was so smooth to touch. The smell of her filled his nostrils and he moved to lie between her legs, his hands separating her thighs as he lowered his head. He would have this at least, he thought ruefully, and give her something to goddamn remember. He cupped his hands around her buttocks and teased her with his tongue until she lurched forward and shuddered again and again, gasping like a pale white fish.

He raised himself quickly then and grasped his own member with angry need. He had meant to torment her, but he had increased his own desire in doing so and needed his own release.

"What can I do?" she asked timidly.

He was surprised she would even care to ask, but took full advantage of her unwitting generosity.

"Put your mouth around me," he said, his breath quickening even at the thought. She looked at him in surprise for a moment, then smiled a little embarrassed smile and knelt before him. "Move a little," he gasped when her red lips closed around him. It took only a few strokes of her mouth and an accidental sweep of her tongue to bring him to his own climax. He nearly laughed when he saw the dismay in her eyes as his seed filled her mouth. *Another memory for you*, he thought dryly.

"Get dressed," he said coolly, getting off the bed and retrieving his own clothing from the floor where he'd strewn it. "I'm taking you home now."

"No! I won't go!"

He paused in buttoning his breeches and fixed her with an angry glare. "I've no further use for you, Miss Pettygrew. In fact, you're of little use to anyone until you're either properly married or properly ruined. Who is your physician?"

"My physician? Doctor Edwards usually sees us in town. Why?"

Jeremy shoved on his boots and tucked in his shirt. "Be dressed when I get back," he said coldly. "And if you're gone, I'll hunt you down with my last breath and strangle that pretty little neck of yours."

She smiled, thinking he jested. Then, noticing his expression, she had the sense to look frightened. He didn't doubt that there was murderous rage in his eyes. He felt murderous. She was just another conniving, self-centered female who hadn't cared if she caused his ruin along with her own so long as her selfish desires were fulfilled. She had come here not once but twice, both times with wanton notions that, if acted upon, could have gotten him killed. Could *still* get him killed, he reminded himself. He should have known that first day he'd met her that she was trouble, hiding her engagement ring and yet teasing him with encouraging glances. Were all women deceivers? Even Bess? He stalked out of the room, pushing his cynicism to the back of his mind. He had arrangements to make if he were to escape discredit and maybe even a damn duel.

The rented carriage pulled up in front of the Pettygrew home near dawn. Inside was a quiet Rosalind, an equally silent Jeremy, and a sleepy Doctor Edwards. The three made their way inside to the exclamations of the help and an immediate appearance by Sir Thomas and his wife still in their nightclothes.

"I return your daughter to you, sir," Jeremy announced with a mocking bow. "She foolishly appeared at my door again, and since I had no desire for you to castrate me on the spot, I have brought along your own physician so that he can assure you of her purity."

"Father, I'm so sorry," Rosalind pleaded, her eyes filling with tears. "I just couldn't marry Mister Lacey—"

"Has this man touched you?" her father interrupted, his eyes never leaving Jeremy's.

"I have touched her, sir, but not violated her. She is still marketable goods." He saw Sir Thomas' fist clench and thought the baronet would strike him for his impudence, but the man kept his fist at his side.

"I won't marry that dreadful man," Rosalind was sobbing into her mother's arms. "I'll die first. I'll run away again."

"He has withdrawn his suit," her father said, still looking at Jeremy with murder in his eyes. "But if this young man speaks the truth, then perhaps, in a year's time, we will seek elsewhere for a husband. Can you see my daughter now, Doctor?"

Missus Pettygrew escorted her weeping daughter up the stairs, followed by the weary doctor. Jeremy turned to leave.

"Where are you going?" demanded Sir Thomas.

"Home. It has been a trying night, rejecting silly females and searching out doctors. I need some sleep. You know where to find me if you want to shoot me."

He thought he saw a hint of amusement in the baronet's eyes as he turned away again. If he were lucky, he would never see the man or his troublesome daughter again.

Chapter Eleven

Jeremy exalted in the sense of freedom that swept through him each morning as he rode north. It was early March, still more winter than spring, but even just three days out of London, Jeremy felt so far from its influence that the last three months spent there seemed more of a dream than a reality. Perhaps they were. Perhaps he still lay on a prison floor in a feverish delirium.

He took a deep breath and blew it out forcefully just to feel the cool air in his lungs and see the vaporous cloud escape his mouth.

No, this was real. He was alive and it was March of 1761. England had had a new king for the last year, though the exchange of one bloody George for another made little difference to most folks.

He had lingered at his first stop, St. Albans, walking the morning away, and had only gone as far as Barton by nightfall. To Bedford only the next day, but ah, what a glorious supper he'd had at the Groggy Dick. Missus Dick knew well how to crust a shepherd's pie. He'd never tasted better.

Now Pat cantered easily down the road toward Kettering. Perhaps they would get there today, perhaps only to Rushden or Higham Ferrers. It didn't matter. He was enjoying the journey too much to hurry it. He could have taken the more easterly roads, but he did not like the countryside so well there.

He tried not to dwell on his final destination. Though he had determined upon it before he'd quit London, he was not wholly content with his decision. Still, it was better than drifting aimlessly as he'd been doing the last few months. Already Tim Mott had lived six months longer than he should have. Would that the blast that had killed Bess blown off Mott's cursed head instead, but such rudimentary justice was sorely lacking this side of heaven. He'd lost much of his resolve during his idle days in Town. He would be killing out of dispassionate duty now instead of blind rage. Perhaps that was better, but it did not *feel* better.

He'd had time to think things through after he'd attended to the distraction of Rosalind Pettygrew and her capricious designing. He had retraced in his mind the steps that had gotten him to where he was. Utter necessity had driven him to Scotland, but after that, he had determined his own course, indulging many a whim along the way. He had met his father. That had been a better encounter than he had anticipated, but looking back on it, he realized that it had taken something from him—his edge of anger. No longer could he harbor the same bitter resentment toward an unknown enemy. He had looked Daniel Harwood in the eye and found much to admire. He had recognized his father's strength, but he had also recognized his weakness and heard a man's regret. Yes, some of his anger was gone and with it, a bit of his own strength, for Jeremy had learned to use anger to keep himself safe in a hard world.

Still, he had followed his hate to London, there to kill a perverted animal if he could. He had not found that an easy task after all and had almost lost the nerve to proceed. Only circumstance had moved his hand in the defense of another, so he could not credit his own courage or resolve with accomplishing the deed. It had just been dumb luck, if having the justification to kill a man could be called lucky. He was glad afterward that Philip Bramhearst lived no more, but more for the sake of the man's potential victims than from any feeling of vengeance fulfilled. Eleanor had still died terribly and was still dead. That could not be altered no matter what he did.

Though in London he had seen the death of one hate, another hate had been reborn. He should have left sooner, he thought in retrospect, before his vague notion of feminine deceit had had a chance to evolve into a new-found conviction. He had always mistrusted mankind in general, but he had wanted to believe that women, who seemed so essential to a man's happiness, were better, somehow, than the men with whom they consorted. He had believed that women were truer, more loving, and more caring than men. That was why God had ordained them to be helpmeets and mothers. Despite his own mother's wantonness, he had believed her to be essentially good. She had kept him and his sister well enough over the years, had been there with a comforting hand on their foreheads when they were ill. She had finessed schooling for him, hadn't she? He had believed that his mother wouldn't be a whore if men had not betrayed her loving nature. Men were to blame; women were only their victims.

That basic belief had altered the night of Eleanor's murder, of course. He had discovered the great, tragic truth as his mother sobbed before him in self-pity. Lydia Knox was a selfish, self-centered harlot who would willingly use her own flesh and her children's blood to further her desires and greed.

He had told himself in the years that followed that his mother was the exception. Most women were not so self-indulgent. They cared about their families, husbands and children. He had experienced the love of many women, or so he thought. Lately, when he had reconsidered his past, he wondered if he had been mistaken. Women had desired him, certainly. Some had been anxious for the coins he would leave them, but they had convinced him of their affection, too. The truth was that they had enjoyed his body as he had enjoyed theirs, used him as much as he had used them. Love did not motivate their actions, he now saw, only self-gratification.

Love did not motivate many marriages either, he'd observed. Security was the stronger glue. Two together had a better chance than two alone, and with the added complication of children, it was in a woman's best interest to marry, and marry as well as she could. Among the high-born, marriages were brokered for financial and political gain, but it was not so different for the common folk. Women set their caps on whoever could support them the best. A farmer was better than a tailor, a smithy better than a cobbler. For all he might be the kindest, most honorable man in town, the rag and bone man did not inspire many matrimonial aspirations. Commerce then, not love, ruled women's hearts.

Madge Whitcomb and Rosalind Pettygrew had been an inspiring pair. The actress had been willing to overthrow friendship for sexual gratification with less thought than one gives to choosing a pair of shoes. And Rosalind, that child in a woman's body, hadn't cared who she hurt in her mad rush to make herself happy. Not that he cared a fig for any of her set, but she had not treated her own people well either. She had ignored the scandal she might bring upon her parents and sisters. She had convinced that obese bore, Lacey, that she cared for him for nearly a year. And Jeremy had not liked being made a fool nor having his precarious position jeopardized just because she had decided that he would make her happy in bed.

And what of Bess Hobbs? She had given her life for him. What could be more selfless than that? Surely he could not group little Bess in with the rest of these women.

She didn't have a chance to betray you, the voice of his new cynicism whispered. *If things had gone differently, she, too, might have shown her true colors soon enough. Why was she with you at all? It wasn't just happenstance that Tim Mott developed such a loathing for you, you know. He and Bessie had an understanding before you came along, or so she'd implied.* 'Oh, he were sweet on me for a time,' she'd said to explain the man's hate-filled stares when Jeremy was about, 'but that's over now.' For her, maybe, but obviously not for Mott. *A rich, well-dressed highwayman was better than a poor, ill-kempt stableman.*

He didn't want to believe that what the new voice whispered was true. It made the beautiful things that he remembered about his time with Bess seem ugly. He didn't want her memory to be tainted by his pessimism, but he couldn't quite banish the voice in his head either.

A vision of Quinton Selby's winking face flashed before his eyes, not for the first time. And his voice saying, "Nothing a pretty muff and a new cloak couldn't fix." He had only heard that confirmation of his mother's heartlessness ten days ago, yet the words were burned into his brain, still throbbing like a newly-lain brand. It had hurt, more than he wanted to admit to himself, to know just what value his mother placed on him. It shouldn't have surprised him. It shouldn't have wounded him as if he were a short-pantsed schoolboy. But it had.

Was he really ready to believe that no woman was trustworthy? That no woman could truly love a man? Or could he believe that deeper, more soul-chilling thought—that *he* wasn't worthy of true love even if a woman *were* capable of it. After all, not even his own mother—

Enough! It matters not! You're not some flaming philosopher trying to solve the riddles of life, he scolded himself as he rode, his face now as dark as the day. *Not some milquetoast poet ready to quit living if I can't secure that illusory sentiment called love. Not worth the having, perhaps, even if it exists.*

What *did* exist was that need for purpose he had acknowledged needing before. He would go to the Running Lion, there to kill Tim Mott as he should have done already. Then he would go to Leeds and check on Benjamin, give the boy some more money as he'd promised. Show Lillie Tolver that she was wrong about him. Then to Carlisle again if his father didn't find his close proximity an embarrassment. He would check with him first, though why he should let his absent father's feelings determine his course, he wasn't sure. Wherever he ended up, he could try smithing again for a time. He was certain he could still do it well, after his hands toughened up a bit. He enjoyed being around horses. They were easier to deal with than people.

Two days later, Jeremy rode through the streets of Nottingham. It was still early enough to visit a few of the shops. He could almost feel the money in his purse yearning to be spent. He had often purchased his embroidered shirts and lace collars in Nottingham, for except for the French products available for three times the cost in London, Nottingham lace and embroidery was beyond compare. He passed by the little establishment he had once frequented. He knew to go elsewhere. He did not want the able little shopkeeper to recognize him.

He bought only one shirt and collar, tucking them into his already full travel sack instead of wearing them. Perhaps he never would. They were too much like something Jeremy Knox would wear. Dangerous. But maybe, at some distant party, perhaps back in London someday, he would feel anonymous enough to do so.

The Trip to Jerusalem was busy that night, crowded with a soon-to-be bridegroom and his fellow celebrants. Jeremy chose a back table at which to eat, with his back to the wall and a fairly clear view of the tavern door. *Never turn your back to the door. Keep an eye on the blokes around you. Never drink to excess. Don't call attention to yourself.* He had fallen into his old patterns without much thought as he traveled further into the area he had once frequented as a highwayman. He kept his hat on, his head slightly lowered, wary but still able to find amusement in the antics of the bridegroom and his rowdy friends. He hoped for the groom's sake that the wedding wasn't the next day for to judge by the volume of ale that was going down his throat, he'd be in no condition to say his vows. Then again, he thought darkly, maybe that was the perfect condition to be in for such an occasion.

The woman who served him seemed to have singled him out as a possible tumble, but he was in no mood for dalliances of that sort. His sullen response to her flirting finally seemed to convince her of his disinterest and she left him alone. It occurred to him that if he fell into *that* old pattern again he risked being forever jaded as far as women went. On one level he had accepted their mercenary nature and had decided he was better off not being deluded by romantic claptrap. On another level, so far to the back of his mind that he barely had a glimpse of it, was the hope that he was somehow wrong. From that same place came an instinctual warning. Indulging in casual trysts would bring about the death of that small hope. For now, he would remain celibate.

A thatch of dirty blond hair through the murky glass caught his eye when he glanced up from his food and he straightened in alarm and squinted his eyes to catch some further view of it. It was gone, lost in a jumble of other passersby. It couldn't have been! Surely old Tim would not be this far south of his rat hole. Another, similarly grimy pedestrian passed by and Jeremy relaxed a bit. The bloody hostler was haunting his waking thoughts now. The sooner he was dead, the better. Tomorrow he would ride through Sherwood to Cuckney, maybe even push for Worksop. To Doncaster the next day, if the weather held. And then for Howden. *Three days, Mister Mott,* he mused, taking a deep draught of ale. *Three days and you will join the rest of the damned in hell.*

The hair on his neck had been prickling since his phantom glimpse of Tim Mott through the thick windows of the Trip to Jerusalem. He had the feeling that he was being followed, but for all his close perusal of the roadsides, forests, and village alleyways, he could see nothing to confirm his suspicions. The weather moved in near Tickhill and kept him from making it to Doncaster that day. Irritated by the delay, for now he could think of little else but dispatching Tim Mott and then getting on with his life, he ate an early supper and went to bed. He wanted to get an early start.

It was still raining the next morning but the downpour had lightened to a drizzle so he decided to press on. He wouldn't make the Running Lion by nightfall, he knew, but he'd be within striking distance the next morning. *You've been granted a bit longer to live, Mister Mott,* he thought, and wondered at the justice of Providence. *If vengeance is the Lord's, why hasn't He taken it by now?* Jeremy fumed.

It was little more than gray with the approaching dawn when he made his way to the stables behind the Grey Stone Inn. The stableman wasn't even up yet. Cacophonous snores came from the little room just inside the door. *It's a wonder he doesn't set the horses skittering*, he thought with a smile, but all seemed quiet, the soothing sound of munching coming from several of the stalls he passed.

"Hello, fellow," he greeted Pat quietly, laying his traveling bag aside and taking the horse's nose in his hands as the beast stuck its head over the stall door. "You game for the day?" he asked, as if he expected an answer. He took Pat's bridle off a hook beside the door and slipped it on with a few easy movements, then hoisted the saddle off the wall, stepped into the darkened stall, and flung the saddle up. He needed no light to secure the straps. He had done the task many times and in full darkness. He gave Pat's side a firm slap to get the horse to exhale any excess air, then pulled the buckle tight.

His eye caught the flash of metal behind his right shoulder. He attempted to straighten and turn but wasn't fast enough. The knife caught him in the soft flesh between his shoulder and his shoulder blade. He heard as well as felt the metal strike bone. The blow jarred his teeth to the root, and then vanished.

Before the blade could descend again, Jeremy reached around with his left hand, made a snatch for a retreating wrist, and caught it. His assailant tried to twist the knife into his arm, but Jeremy wrenched it upward and heard the man grunt in pain. Still, his attacker did not relent and had the advantage of being upright whereas Jeremy had not regained his posture yet. The man's strength, fueled by a rage—Jeremy could feel trembling in the man's taut arm—kept him from straightening up. He was off balance and knew if he went down, he would die. Pat had skittered away from the fracas but was banging his hooves against the floor as if he might make a rush for the stable door and safety. He would knock both men down if he did.

Though his right arm felt strangely numb, Jeremy forced it over to the pistol in his waistband. He fumbled to pull back the hammer, but his thumb didn't seem to have any strength so he used two fingers instead. He fleetingly wondered if he'd end up shooting himself as he grasped the readied pistol and attempted to tug it from his pants. His assailant suddenly pressed in and he stumbled but didn't go down.

He was loosing the struggle. He was running out of time.

With all the strength he could summon, he pushed himself around, the pistol now insecurely in his hand, and fired into the solid darkness behind him. The flash of the powder, deflected by the nearness of his attacker's body, burned his hand, but the bullet had found its mark. The dark shape slumped to the ground, falling over his feet.

Jeremy kicked free of the weight and stood panting for a few moments, trying to focus on his assailant, but the man remained a quiet, dark lump on the ground.

"Here, what's going on!?" came the hostler's frantic voice. He was hurrying through the stables with a newly-lit lantern. The wick had not been turned up properly and the dim light threatened to go out with every careless swing.

"I've been attacked," Jeremy said simply, managing to return the pistol to his side, then search out his wound with his good left hand. His fingers were immediately overrun with blood.

"Gaw, you're stuck good," the stableman gasped. "Is 'e dead? Who is 'e?"

The pale light of the lantern swung over the prone figure, but he was laying face down. All that could be seen was a matted thatch of blond hair.

"I don't know," Jeremy said, still panting from his exertions, but his mind was reeling at the possibility. Could it be...

The stableman cautiously approached the body and toed it over with his bare foot. "Do you know 'im?"

"No," Jeremy lied. "I've never seen him before."

The hostler shook his head. "Well, 'e's deader'n Jesus," he said, crossing himself absentmindedly. "Ya'd best get that tended to inside," he added, nodding to Jeremy's shoulder.

Jeremy shook his head. "No. I've got to be on my way."

125

"Ya can't just leave," the man said with a frown. "You've shot a man. Got to see the magistrate seems to me. And 'ave Missus Stone look at that 'ole in yer back for ya bleed out."

"It's not that bad," Jeremy argued. It *did* feel as if the wound were running less profusely. He pushed past the man, stepped over Tim Mott's wide-eyed corpse, and grabbed Pat's bridle with his good left hand. "Get out of the way. If the magistrate needs to speak to me, tell him I've gone to Leeds. The Tolver's furniture shop. But tell him, too, that I was attacked by this man and shot him in self-defense."

"Says you," said the hostler warily. "'Ow am I to know it fer the truth. I din't wake til your pistol let loose."

Jeremy stared at him in disbelief. "You can see he stabbed me in the back," he said as patiently as he could manage. "How else could it have happened?"

"I ain't no judge," the man admitted. "I say ya talks to Squire Fellows." He held up his lantern and shook his head. "Yer almost as white as this here corpse, lad. Ya ain't gonna make it to Leeds anyway."

"Move aside," Jeremy ordered and heard the panic in his own voice. The stable man moved reluctantly out of the stall and Jeremy guided Pat past Mott's body. He had to get out! If he could just get on his horse and ride away, he wouldn't have to worry about the shaking in his legs or the odd lights that danced about in front of him. What if they accused him of murdering Mott?! He'd hang at last, but this time he would be blameless. It angered him to considered it.

"Hand up my bag," he said, taking hold of the saddle and managing to hoist himself atop his horse. He dropped heavily against Pat's neck, unable to straighten himself, and just lay there for a time, comforted by Pat's warmth.

It was no use.

"I'm dying," he said simply, his voice muffled in the horse's mane. His own voice sounded far off. *The bastard killed me*, he thought, and wanted to laugh at the irony but couldn't. Perhaps Providence had taken a hand in things after all. What other power could explain the impossible circumstance of the man he had sought to kill finding him first and managing such a stealthy attack? Jeremy had underestimated Tim Mott. He had not thought him capable of executing such a plan. Had Mott been the one following him since Nottingham? Had he spotted Jeremy along the streets somewhere and set about trailing him for this purpose? Why had he been so far from home?

Ah, he would never know that now. He was dying, or dead already. He could feel God's arms around him, carrying him like a child. It was a wonderful relief, a wonderful peace to let go of everything.

Chapter Twelve

Heaven smelled good. Or maybe it was Hell, but it smelled heavenly. Perhaps Missus Dick had passed away suddenly and been swept up to heaven, there to cook her shepherd's pies for the angels.

Heaven had clean bedding, too, though not as fine as he had expected. More like rough cotton than soft linen. Maybe God had decided he didn't deserve the finest stuff. That was reserved for the saints and other good folk. Still, the pillow against his cheek was soft enough. He lay on his stomach, his arms at his sides, and he smiled. It was so good not to have to worry about anything anymore. He'd left all that behind him and as soon as he could convince his eyes to open and his body to move, he would find God's dining table and help himself to that glorious-smelling food.

"Jeremy?" came a voice at his ear. "Is ya awake agin?"

No! It can't be! He frowned with the effort of opening his dry eyes. The room would not focus until he had squinted several times. *Where the hell am I?* he wondered. And why was Benjamin's gnomish face peering at him from his bedside?

"Why are you always here when I wake up?" he croaked gruffly, but he could not be disappointed at awakening on earth for long. The smile on Benjamin's face was too exuberant.

"We come ta look after ya," was the boy's explanation. "A gent named Squire Fellows sent word fer us ta come, said ya might be dead when we got here, but ta come anyways."

"We?"

"Me, Mister Sam, and Miss Lillie," he said happily. "We was mighty happy ya weren't dead when we got here, though Miss Lillie, she'd already cried some just in case."

Jeremy smiled at the boy's vision of the world. "You got here quickly," he commented. "It would have taken me at least a couple of days."

"More like three with the wagon. Mister Tolver sent it just in case we had ta cart back yer corpse."

Jeremy frowned and tried to bring his arms up to his side so he could push himself over and get a better look at the boy. Three days? Another two at least for the squire's man to get to Leeds with the message and find the Tolvers. And how long since then?

"Christ, I can't move," he complained.

"Ya oughtn't ta try," Benjamin explained. "Missus Stone said she thought ya'd died a couple of times that first day, and the bleeding just wouldn't stop fer all her stitchin', like a flood inside somewhere, she said. Yer arms is tied ta yer sides so's ya won't open things up agin."

Jeremy tried to make himself relax, but he couldn't do it, his breath coming in short pants. The pillow, once comforting, now felt as if it would smother him. "Get someone!" he ordered. "Get someone to help me turn over!"

Benjamin was gone without a word, his feet pounding over the wooden floor like a scuttering rat, then pounding down some unseen stairs. Soon another, lighter footfall ascended, though in just as great a hurry.

"Oh, dear God, you're awake," came Lillie's voice, though her face was not yet within sight despite his attempts to see behind him. When at last she came around the bed and knelt down beside him, he could not help feeling suddenly safer. Perhaps this was heaven after all. With her pale blue eyes and wisps of golden hair escaping from her cap, she looked exactly as he imagined an angel might look.

"I want to turn over," he said quietly. "I can't breathe like this."

She nodded and her face vanished. He felt the weight of the blankets leave his back and the chill air on his bare legs and feet. Then she was untying the strips of cloth that he now realized bound his forearms to his body. It was a relief just to be able to move his arms a little, though he could feel immediately the tenderness behind his shoulder when he move his right arm.

"There now," she said, her face suddenly back before him. "Let me do the turning, mind. You mustn't put any strain on your arm at all, Jeremy. Benjamin, hold his arm still while I move him."

Jeremy felt the boy's hands on his forearm, a human replacement for the cloth restraints, but he didn't fight him. He closed his eyes and forced himself to submit to Lillie's ministrations as she slipped a hand beneath his chest, careful not to jostle his arm, then levered him onto his left side. He felt her weight upon the bed and realized she was half-kneeling, her arm around his back to keep him from falling back too roughly. The only trouble was, once it was done, he was so far over on the little bed, he was close to falling off the other side.

"Oh, dear," she lamented. "Help me, Benjamin. Pull him back this way, but try not to hurt him. No, Jeremy, don't help," she scolded when she saw him attempting to lift himself back. "This will just take some time."

It did, but at last he was lying on his back in the center of the narrow bed with his pillow properly fluffed and the covers pulled to his chin. Although he hadn't consciously exerted himself, his heart was hammering uncomfortably in his chest and his head was spinning. He just lay there for a time, his eyes closed, willing himself to recover his equilibrium. Somebody's hand, he thought it was Lillie's, rested on his covered left arm, like a mooring for his drifting thoughts.

"Too hot," he said.

"That's the fever."

"No, it's the damn blankets," he said, trying to smile so she'd know he wasn't truly complaining. He felt the covers folded down to his chest and sighed, surrendering himself to sleep again.

"How long has it been?" he asked the dozing girl at his side. It was night outside the window, but a stubby candle in the corner of the room gave off just enough light for him to make out his surroundings. It was a tiny room but probably one of the best at the Grey Stone Inn, for that is where he supposed himself to be. He watched in fascination as Lillie came slowly awake, her eyes appearing confused for a moment as she tried to adjust to her dimly lit surroundings. Then she looked at him, remembered where she was and why, and laid an anxious hand on his arm.

"How are you?" she asked. "Are you in pain?"

Surprisingly, he didn't feel much more than tenderness where his shoulder rested against the bed, and overwhelming fatigue, of course.

"No, I'm better," he assured her. "How long has it been?" he asked again.

"Nearly four months," she replied, her tone suddenly a bit frosty.

"Four months? Impossible. Oh," he said, realizing. "No. Not since I left Leeds. How long have I been laying here like a side of beef?"

She smiled a little and looked down with embarrassment. "Of course. Well, I think Squire Fellows said you were attacked last Thursday morning. At sun up it'll be Wednesday. Six days then, nearly a week."

"Are they going to hang me once I'm able to stand up for it?" he asked.

"Goodness, no. Squire Fellows assured us you'd been absolved of any blame. That dreadful robber obviously deserved what he got."

Jeremy closed his eyes again. "That he did," he agreed wearily. "But he wasn't trying to rob me. He was bent on murder, pure and simple."

"Why on earth would he want *you* dead?" she asked. "The stableman said you didn't even know him."

Jeremy opened his eyes again and looked at her, wondering whether to trust her with the truth. When she reached up and smoothed a bit of hair off his forehead, he made his decision. She was one of the few people who knew who he was and that he was still alive.

"I *did* know him," he said flatly. "He was the hostler at the inn...the inn where Bess died. He's the one who betrayed me to the king's men, the one responsible for what happened. I was coming north to kill him," he admitted bluntly.

Lillie's hand paused, then fell away from his face. "Oh."

"Oh, what?"

She smiled sadly and shook her head. "Nothing. Just Benjamin thought you were on your way to see us." She paused. "So did I. Don't tell him the truth. It would hurt him to know."

"But I *was* planning to come there," he argued, starting to rise, then stopping abruptly when he felt the sharp pull in his back. He settled back onto the bed and waited for the pain to pass.

"It's all right, Jeremy," he heard Lillie say. "It doesn't matter."

"I *was* going to come," he said, not looking at her. "After I killed Mott, I was going to stop in Leeds, to give the boy the money I'd promised him." He paused and looked at her solemnly. "To prove you were wrong about never seeing me again."

"Well," she said with a faint smile, "I was nearly right, wasn't I, though I'm just as glad you didn't die just to make it so."

"Now I can die contented," he said dryly. "I've won an argument with Miss Lillie Tolver."

"Don't you even think of dying yet," she whispered in a scolding voice but he saw the glisten of unshed tears in her eyes. "Please, Jeremy. You will try to get better, won't you?"

He nodded and shut his eyes from sudden weariness. "Of course. I've no choice, it seems, if my body cooperates." He took in a breath and let it out slowly. "I thought I was dead already. I remember God holding me in his arms, but I suppose that was probably just the stableman carting me up here. It felt good, Lillie, not to have to worry anymore."

"Worry about what? You're safe again. I won't let anyone hurt you; neither will Benjamin. You'll get well and we'll go home."

He nodded again. He did not have the strength to tell her that becoming entangled with people again, even the people of a loving family, was exactly what worried him.

"I've been smelling that divine fare below stairs for a fortnight now, yet end up eating this damned broth everyday," he fussed, letting Lillie ladle in the watery sustenance since he'd discovered he could only manage to spill it on himself if he used his left hand.

"Hush now," she said soothingly. "Missus Stone said you can start eating something more substantial tomorrow. Broth is best for now."

He took another spoon full, then shook his head. "No more," he said grimly. "Send in Benjamin."

"I'll help you. What do you need?"

"To relieve myself, woman," he said irritably. "The boy holds the piss pot for me. How do you think I've been managing?"

"I hadn't thought," she admitted, blushing and looking away. "Benjamin's not here. He's gone to fetch eggs for Missus Stone."

"Then someone else," he snapped. "And hurry. All that damned broth's gone right through me."

Lillie hurried around the bed and grabbed the chamber pot from beside the window. "I've helped my father when he's sick," she explained in forced merriment.

"I'm not your father."

"But you *are* sick. And there's no one else right now."

Jeremy let out an exasperated sigh, his frown deepening. "I don't know if I'll be able with you watching," he said tersely.

"Then I won't watch."

"You'll end up spilling piss everywhere," he predicted. "Christ, hurry up then."

She helped him scoot to the edge of bed, then positioned the chamber pot between his legs, averting her eyes when she'd done so.

"There, Mister Harwood. You may piss away."

He couldn't keep from smiling as he pulled up the nightshirt Mister Stone had loaned him and took aim. It took a while, but finally the fullness of his bladder won out over his self-consciousness.

"Stay there a moment," she ordered when he was done, carefully carrying the pot over to the window and dumping it into the alley below. She helped him settle back into a sitting position on the bed, then straightened the covers around him.

"Do you want some more?" she asked, picking up the bowl of broth again.

"Not damned likely."

"I'm glad to hear you are so ill-tempered. It can only mean you are feeling better."

He frowned at her for a moment, then a chagrined smile crept over his features. "About time, I'd say, wouldn't you? I feel like I've been in this bed for a thousand years."

"Only two weeks," she smiled, settling into her customary chair and picking up the mending she'd agreed to do for Missus Stone.

"It seems longer," he complained. "Perhaps I could get a book to read."

"I'll ask about one when I go downstairs next time. I thought you liked our chats."

Did he hear hurt in her voice? "I only meant I must be a great bother to you, worse than a baby, surely."

133

She smiled but did not look up from her work. "Oh, indeed. And with none of the benefits besides. Babies, at least, are cute and loveable. You're fine to look upon, Jeremy, but more prickly than I had remembered."

"Much has happened since I left," he said sullenly.

"So I've supposed, though you'll not speak much about it. What you *have* shared has not seemed so bad. You made important friends in London and spent the winter in…comfortable recreation."

He had spoken only of theater and social engagements, but her tone implied more. "You make it sound…sordid." Had she guessed at things he'd omitted? His face felt suddenly hot and he wondered if he were blushing. *Damn*! He'd often cursed her seeming perceptiveness, but surely discerning the true nature of his "recreation" would take more than mere intuition. Was she a witch then, this angelic-looking creature sewing diligently beside him.

"I merely envy you your season of leisure," she amended. "'Twould be a rare treat for anyone."

He thought she was going to stop there, but no. That was not Lillie's way. "You've gone from a cranky baby to looking like a toddler caught nibbling on a pie," she commented with a knowing glance in his direction. It made him blush anew. "But if your pursuits *were* sordid, Jeremy, you're right not to tell me. 'Tis none of my business."

How disappointed she'd be in me if she truly knew me, he thought, and felt more remorse at the notion than he'd supposed he would. Well, there was no undoing the past—

"And it was a good thing to meet your father," she continued, oblivious to his self-recriminations. "I envy you that as well."

She'd told him about her real parents in one of their recent "chats." For all she called Mister Tolver "Papa" —for she had never known another—he was, instead, her great-grandfather! Had tragedy and the King's service ever struck another family so soundly he wondered? Both father and grandfather killed in separate wars with France. And the good wives of the Tolver family? Mister Tolver's had died of natural age just a few years ago, but Lillie's mother had died bearing Martha, and the elder Missus Tolver had been killed by a careless carriage on the narrow street behind the furniture shop not many years later.

"Still, I've no cause to complain," she hurried on, perhaps embarrassed that she'd implied something lacking in her upbringing. "I couldn't have had better care than with Papa and Nana."

He watched her long fingers now as they worked the needle expertly through the cloth. "I've meant to ask," he said. "How can your father be managing without you and Sam for so long? I've put him at terrible inconvenience, I'm afraid."

"I've two other sisters, Jeremy. They can look after things well enough without me. And Sam went home a week ago, as soon as we knew you'd recover. I hope you don't mind, he took your horse."

"My horse?"

"Well, we'll need the wagon to get you home. You'll be ready to travel soon, but not on horseback, I think."

Jeremy frowned. "You keep talking about bringing me 'home,' Miss Tolver. I don't have one."

"*My* home then, you beastly man," she scolded lightly, not taking her eyes from her sewing. "You should try being civil to folks who care about you, Jeremy. You'd be a better man for it."

He relaxed back into the pillows and looked out the window. A better man. He'd thought, at twenty-six, that he was as formed in essentials as he'd ever be. Perhaps he was right to a degree, but Lillie seemed to take it for granted that a man could change. Who was right?

His father said *he* had changed since his youth, but Jeremy had to take his word for that, his personal knowledge of the man encompassing less than an hour.

A *better* man. Yes, he'd always known he was flawed but took it as a given that human beings in general were flawed. Sometimes downright rotten. He hadn't thought his own flaws particularly grievous by comparison.

"I'm sorry," Lillie said quietly. When he looked over at her he saw she had laid her sewing in her lap. "I didn't mean to hurt you, Jeremy. 'Twas unkindly said."

"But truly said," he admitted. "But I don't know how to be a better man, Miss Tolver. Or perhaps I know but I can't quite manage the transformation."

"You could start by trusting people," she offered. "You're always so detached, so indifferent…or pretend to be."

He nodded and looked away again. "I know. I would like to trust people, but I have experienced too much of treachery. My intellect will not let me forsake my distrust so easily."

"Do you even try?"

"No," he admitted. "I haven't the luxury. Despite my poor opinion of this world, I still want to keep living in it. Trusting people can get you killed."

"And distrusting people keeps you safe?" She shook her head and took up her sewing again. "You have almost been killed twice this year, Jeremy. It seems that your distrust did not protect you either time."

Her self-righteousness made him feel suddenly defensive. "It *would* have if I had heeded it more fervently!" he snapped. "If I had been *more* prudent, those soldiers wouldn't have even known I was coming back. There wouldn't have been any damned ambush. Bess wouldn't be dead now. If I had *listened* to that voice of distrust, Miss Tolver, I wouldn't have ridden down that hill when I sensed danger. My mistake was *trusting* that I would be safe at the Hobbs' inn. I didn't turn away when I should have. Then, like an arrogant idiot, I trusted that I was more than man enough to dispatch that weasel Mott. Instead I discovered that a troop of soldiers with loaded muskets beats a hothead with a sword any day of the year." His self-reproach spilled over into another anger he'd never before vocalized. "I trusted my mother to protect my sister from harm and instead she sold her to a perverted murderer who strangled the life out of her before she'd even reached the age of twelve. I trusted her to love me, too, just for being her son, and discovered she grieved for my supposed demise not a minute longer than it took her to convince her besotted lover to comfort her with pretty gifts. I—"

He stopped when he saw the look of horrified dismay on Lillie's young face. Much of what he'd revealed was new to her, and for a moment he regretted his rash words. Those things were private. And he had upset her, he could see that clearly enough from her ashen face and the hand she'd pressed to her chest. Then he remembered her provincial faultfinding.

"You haven't the first idea what you're talking about, Miss Tolver," he said cuttingly. "It's all a pack of nonsense, this trusting business, put about by those too stupid to know any better or by those with evil intentions so that they may dupe their trusting victims more easily. Wives, trust your husbands so that we may indulge our passions where we may without the nuisance of a scolding. Husbands, trust your wives with your hearts for then you will be blinded to the true reason she has thrown in her lot with you— security and self-preservation. Subjects, trust your monarch and your government, for while you foolishly believe they have your best interests at heart it will be easier to pass laws to steal your property and wealth, even your freedom and life—"

"Stop," Lillie said, her eyes now streaming with tears.

Yes, he thought, *it hurts to hear the truth but it's better for her to know it now. Better than being deluded, maybe even hurt, when she discovers it the hard way as I have.* He thought she was leaving in anger when she threw her sewing aside and stood up. But she did not run out the door as he expected but ran, instead to him, sitting down close at his side and taking his face in her hands.

"Oh, you poor man," she said, her tears still falling. "Oh, Jeremy you're so wrong. It doesn't have to be like that. Bad things will always happen, but in the meantime God has given us times of joy and beauty—"

He turned his head to one side, then another, trying to free himself from her touch, and her words. He took hold of her wrists then and pushed her hands away, but she only leaned closer. "Times of love, Jeremy. Not every mother betrays her children. Not every husband and wife are unfaithful to each other. *We* make the world better, *ourselves* better, if we choose trust and love despite the risks. You'll miss so much if you go on as you have—"

"Why do you care?" he challenged her. He wanted to push her away more forcefully, knew he could if he tried, but something held him back. As mistakenly naive as she was, he did not want to hurt her feelings, this girl who had cared for him so tenderly over the last few days. "I told you before, Miss Tolver, I'm not worthy of your concern. And I don't *want* to be rescued from my solitude."

"Yes you do. I can see it in your face."

"The only thing you should be seeing on my face is pity. Pity for a witless girl who doesn't have sense enough to believe her own eyes when she sees the evil around her." He let go of her wrists. "Leave me be, Miss Tolver."

"I love you," she said softly, her pale eyes sad, her lashes still wet from her tears.

"No you don't," he said with quiet scorn. "And I certainly don't love you, so there's an end to it." He leaned back in the pillows and closed his eyes. He felt her weight leave the bed and he almost opened his eyes again, almost caught her hand and pull her back down beside him, almost decided to play the game and say the words he knew women loved to hear. *I love you. There will never be another. We'll be together forever. I can't live without you.*

All lies.

He kept his eyes closed, his hands at his side. "If you have stayed to take care of me because of this infatuation, I'm sorry for it. You can go home if you wish. I can hire someone until I'm better. And I'll make sure you're compensated for the time you've already spent here. Would that be fair, Miss Tolver?"

When she didn't answer, he opened his eyes and found the room empty.

Chapter Thirteen

Benjamin came up with his food that evening—a real plate of food this time. By his cheerful demeanor, Jeremy was sure that Lillie had not told him of their falling out. It was plain that Benjamin thought the sun rose and set on Lillie Tolver, though whether from puppy love or brotherly devotion, he couldn't quite determine. Jeremy could manage better with solid food than he had with the broth, though Benjamin still cut his meat for him. He even forced himself to use his right hand for most of the meal, slow-going though it was. His shoulder and back were throbbing by the time he'd finished, but he didn't complain. His leg had done the same at first, but walking on it had eventually paid off. He knew if he weren't to lose all strength in his arm, he had to use it if he could.

"You're sweatin' like a pig," Benjamin commented as he took away the tray. "You all right?"

"Wonderful after that fine meal," Jeremy assured him. "Just a bit tired."

"Right. I'll come back later afore I goes ta bed."

But Jeremy couldn't sleep even though he was bone weary. Not only was his shoulder throbbing, his thoughts would not quiet. *Damn Lillie Tolver*, he thought when more than an hour had passed and still he could not sleep. He kept seeing her rushing toward him, her arms outstretched, like a mother running to scoop up an injured child. She had cried for him, grieved for his coldness of heart. She had said she cared for him, even loved him. Christ, was he to be plagued his entire life by silly women who threw their hearts down before him and then were surprised when they got trampled underfoot?

Well, he wouldn't be going back to Leeds with her, of that he was certain! It wouldn't be right, nor would it be kind, knowing now how she felt about him.

139

The door squeaked open and Benjamin popped his head in. "Ya ready fer yer bedtime whiz?" he asked with a smile.

Jeremy nodded and pushed himself to the edge of the bed. It was getting easier and easier. When the deed had been accomplished, he tried standing up, quickly sitting again when a wave of dizziness overtook him.

"'Ere now, don't do that ifn someone's not with ya," Benjamin scolded when he turned and saw. "Jesus, yer white as a sheet agin. Lay down. Lay down. I'll get Lillie."

"No!" he ordered, then softened his tone when he saw Benjamin's determined look. "No, don't bother her. She's done too much already. I just need to sleep, that's all."

"Ya sure?" the boy asked, still worried.

Jeremy nodded and settled back again. He was beginning to hate this bed. Benjamin helped him pull up the covers, then started out.

"I wonder if you could ask the stableman...what's his name?"

"Mister Oaks," Benjamin informed him. "He's a great fella. Ben showin' me all sorts o' tricks ta carin' fer horses."

"Would you ask Mister Oaks to come and see me tomorrow when he has a free moment? I've been wanting to thank him."

"Fer what? He just carried ya in."

"Please, Benjamin. I would like to speak with him."

Benjamin shrugged. "Sure, I'll tell 'im tanight."

"Thank you. And by the way, I owe you my thanks as well, you and Lillie, for coming to help me like you did."

"'Course we'd help ya," he said. "You're our friend." Then he waved a dismissive hand and left the room.

Again Jeremy could not fall sleep, but it gave him time to sort out his quickly forming resolution to quit Tickhill as soon as possible. He would ask Mister Oaks to get him as far as Doncaster. There he could catch a coach, to where it didn't matter, though north would do. To Carlisle. Would his father help him if he needed it? Possibly. If not, he would manage on his own. He would leave Benjamin some money, though less than he had planned. Mott's attack would mean a drain on his purse since he felt duty-bound to pay for the room and meals. And he had to leave something for Lillie, too. He had determined on that the moment she had told him she loved him. That would square things between them, compensate her at least a little bit for her nursing of him. What a damned nuisance he'd been, but she had borne it well. And the family had Pat. They could sell him if they had no use for him. He'd buy another horse when he could ride again.

This time she'll be right, he thought as he started to doze off. *This time she won't see me again.*

Mister Oaks hesitated to agree but relented when Jeremy made it sound as if Missus Stone and Miss Tolver, who he seemed to think were Jeremy's guardians, knew about his plans to leave and had approved. He was right glad to see him recuperating so well, he said, and no thanks necessary for doing what was needed for another soul in trouble.

Now Jeremy's only worry was that if he delayed his departure by too many days, Mister Oaks would inadvertently let a word drop and set the guardians after him to stay. True he hadn't seen Lillie since yesterday, so perhaps she wouldn't try to detain him, but Missus Stone was a no-nonsense sort and he didn't want to face her disapproval. He was leaving whether she willed it or no, but it would be more pleasant to avoid a confrontation.

Now that Lillie no longer sat with him, he spent the day exploring his capabilities. He could use his right hand well enough, but there was little strength in it. He had regained some movement in his arm, though he could not raise it higher than his shoulder without pain, nor would it move very far from his side. Against Benjamin's advice, he started standing every hour or so and discovered that the more often he stood, the less dizzy he became. By the end of the first day, he was even walking around his bed, though very slowly. He figured that if he fell he'd at least have half a chance of hitting something softer than the floor.

The next morning he made even more progress, venturing across the room to the window, looking out at the dreary alley separating the inn from a cobbler shop, then tottering back to his bed. At midday he took a different route, toward the wash stand, caught his reflection in the tiny mirror, and immediately called for Benjamin.

"I need a shave and a bath," he told him.

"What? Now?" Benjamin asked in surprise. "Ya ain't goin' no where. Why bother?"

"If a bath is too much trouble to arrange, just a shave'll do."

In the end he had both. Mister Stone brought up the wash tub, Benjamin carted up the hot water kettles to fill it, and Mister Oaks was recruited to help them get Jeremy into the tub and out again. As he crawled back into bed that afternoon, he not only felt presentable, he felt ready for travel. Mister Oaks had given him a dubious look when he'd suggested leaving the next morning, but had finally nodded in what Jeremy took for agreement. "I'd be willin'," he'd said, "but it can wait if you're not up fer it come then." Jeremy planned on being "up fer it" before dawn.

"You've been right quiet," Benjamin commented as they shared their supper together. "You feelin' poorly?"

Jeremy looked up. "Did you say 'you'?"

Benjamin reddened with embarrassment. "Lillie's been learnin' me a bit, 'cuz I asked her. Don't want ta talk like a idiot all my life."

"And how is she?" he asked, ignoring Benjamin's original inquiry.

"Lillie? Fine, far as I can see. She's been helpin' Missus Stone wash and mend the linens most o' the day. You want me ta send 'er up?"

"No, no. I suppose she's helping Missus Stone to help pay her way here. I hadn't even thought..." He *hadn't* considered the position he'd placed her and Benjamin in and it made him angry at himself. "Fetch my wallet, boy. Time to tend to business."

"There'll be plenty of time 'fore we leave."

"It's on my mind now," he said.

The boy did as he was told and whistled when he saw the notes Jeremy pulled from the pouch.

"Here's for Missus Stone to cover yours and Lillie's expenses these last weeks," he said, handing the boy the money.

"This here's way too much," Benjamin protested.

"Whatever's left over, Lillie can have it for nursing me, all right. You see she gets it in the morning."

Benjamin nodded, looking honored by Jeremy's trust.

"And remember I promised you some of our 'aunt's' money?" he reminded him with a smile. "Here's your inheritance, then. Not as much as I'd hoped to give you, but probably enough to buy an apprenticeship. Perhaps Mister Tolver would take you on."

"He already tried," Benjamin admitted. "I ain't got the hands fer wood, he said. But I'll find somethin'. You can help me decide later."

Jeremy couldn't tell him there wouldn't be a later. He planned to stay well clear of the Tolver household for the rest of the foreseeable future. He nodded, though, not wanting to diminish the happiness on the boy's face.

"And this is for my debts so far," he said. "If anything is left over, Missus Stone can have it for putting up with my irritable self."

"Ya— *You* ain't been too surly," Benjamin laughed.

"Of course I have. It's my nature, I'm afraid." He closed the wallet and gave it back to Benjamin to lock in the drawer. "And to prove it, I'll ask you to get the hell out now and let me sleep."

Benjamin smiled. "Right. See you in the mornin'," he called back.

Not if I'm lucky, Jeremy thought, his chest feeling strangely heavy as the boy disappeared through the door and he realized he'd probably never see him again.

It was still dark when he rose and lit a candle, just one to guide his way, then set about dressing. His shirt, vest, and coat had been mended and washed, with little of the stain remaining from the blood that had drenched them. He dressed slowly. It was only three or four in the morning. He had time to conserve his strength and move carefully. Although he only meant to spare everyone the trouble of his care—and Lillie the pain of caring more than she should—it felt for all the world as if he were a criminal slipping away from his jailers while their backs were turned.

He tried to shake the feeling. His debts were paid, and more. He had kept enough to see him through for a few weeks, for he could tell as he pulled on his boots that he was still in need of convalescence. His shoulder felt like a smithy's hammer was ringing out a shoe on it, and strangely, his lower gut and right thigh—those old, long-healed wounds—ached, as if in sympathy with his shoulder. After he'd tied back his hair, one of the more difficult tasks for it involved raising his

143

bad arm and reaching behind his head, he settled back on the bed again, allowing his heart to stop pounding and the pain across his back to subside. Mister Oaks would still be snoring away at this hour, and although Jeremy planned to rouse him for an early departure, there was still plenty of time. He lay back against the head board and closed his eyes.

He awoke with a start, realized he'd slept, and glanced in alarm toward the window. He relaxed when he saw it was still dark, but dawn was not far off. The women would soon be up to begin the day. Did Lillie start the bread for Missus Stone? Would she be up already, meet him as he left again with reproach and condemnation? Look at him with pitying, hurt-filled eyes? The thought drove him out of bed. He gathered his travel satchel, stuck his hat on his head, and carefully made his way down the stairs and through the back regions of the inn. Only a sleepy dog raised its head, wagged its tail uncertainly and then, evidently deciding that anyone moving like a dead man walking was no threat, settled back to sleep again before Jeremy had even shuffled as far as the door.

The morning air had a nip to it, but it was not uncomfortably chilly, a good promise for the day and the journey ahead. He shut the back door quietly, then looked out across the yard. It was not too long of a distance from there to the stables under normal circumstances but to Jeremy, already winded by his trek through the inn, it looked a mile. He stood a few moments, then took a fortifying breath, straightening his back as he step out. Slow but straight, he told himself, hoping to appear to be a whole-bodied man to any casual onlooker. He still wasn't certain that Mister Oaks would take him to Doncaster even if he appeared well, but Jeremy was *certain* he wouldn't consent to doing so if he were looking at all ill. Jeremy hoped the lack of light would hide any lingering paleness.

When he reached the stable, he paused again, resting his left hand heavily against the frame and willing himself to breathe more slowly. He could hear the vibrating snores of Mister Oaks on the other side of the rough wall and he tried to slow his breathing to match their cadence. His legs were shaking a little. *I have to sit down*, he thought, wishing it could be on the seat of a wagon already heading for Doncaster. He pulled open the door and sank onto the first bale of hay with a sigh. The stall walls might be hard but they felt as comforting as his lately-abandoned bed at that moment. He considered closing his eyes, just for a little rest, then decided against it. He wanted to be gone, the sooner the better. He allowed himself only a few minutes to regain an appearance of health, then rose and knocked at Mister Oaks' door.

"Good morning, sir," he greeted cheerily. "Might you oblige me now with that lift to Doncaster?"

Mister Oaks rubbed his eyes then squinted. "You sure are an early one, Mister Harwood. 'Twere this time o' the mornin' you was struck down as I recall."

"I'll hope for better luck today," Jeremy said with a smile. "Shall I come back later then?" He prayed the answer would be 'no.' He wasn't sure he'd make it back to his room. He saw Mister Oaks trying to think through a sleepy haze then, praise God, shaking his head.

"But if ya want to get this early o' a start, 'twill 'ave ta be my lad Reggie who drives ya."

Jeremy's face spread into a relieved grin. *Better yet*, he thought, for he would be more likely to prevail against any misgivings young Reggie might have should he start to feel poorly along the way. "No problem at all," he assured the sleepy hostler. "I'm just grateful for the ride."

"You heading to York from there?" The man's question was a casual one and Jeremy answered him in like manner, speaking the lies with practiced ease.

"Most likely, or perhaps to London. I can't decide which uncle upon which to impose myself."

Mister Oaks chuckled. "I'll tell Reggie to hitch up the little cart. It ain't elegant but it'll get ya there. Ya can wait in the hall. I'll send him ta fetch ya."

"No, I'll wait here. I like horses better than people most days and I haven't been around them for quite a time." He waited until the big man had nodded in ready understanding of such a sentiment and turned back into his rooms before he attempted to walk to the nearest stall. When he reached it, he leaned against it for support, murmuring to the little gray mare within. He was rewarded with a nuzzling of his extended hand. "You'll be a good girl and not let on that I'm near to fainting, eh? That's a good lassie. Sorry I haven't anything for you," he apologized in quiet sincerity, for the mare pushed at his hand with obvious expectation of finding some treat. "Forgot to filch an apple from the kitchen as I passed through. Too busy trying not to fall flat on my face."

When fourteen-year old Reggie came into the stables a few minutes later, he was full of enthusiasm. "Won't be long 'fore I have us hitched and off," he announced. *Probably excused from some of the more menial chores he usually does*, Jeremy mused, guessing at what would make a boy so eager to drive to Doncaster and back.

"The sooner the better," he said with pretended vitality. "Perhaps I'll be lucky enough to catch a coach today if I'm there early enough."

With obvious intentions of pleasing the man responsible for his unexpected adventure, Reggie returned with the little cart in a manner of minutes. Jeremy tossed his travel satchel into the back and made his best try at hopping effortlessly onto the seat beside the boy. His bravado nearly caused him to succumb to the lightheadedness that had threatened him all morning. He shook it off and held on with white-knuckled determination as the boy snapped the reins and they started out of the inn yard.

He wanted to look back but he dared not. The attempt might be his undoing, toppling him from his precariously held perch. And if either Benjamin or Lillie happened to be watching him leave, he did not want to remember the look of reproach he would most certainly see in their eyes.

The seven miles to Doncaster were accomplished with enthusiastic speed by young Reggie, who dropped Jeremy at the nearest coach house with wide-eyed gratitude for the extra sovereign that was pressed into his hand. He wasn't likely to notice Jeremy's frail appearance while staring at the unanticipated treasure.

Jeremy smiled and waved as the boy drove away, then groaned and sank slowly onto a narrow bench outside the inn. *Well, what now, you great fool?* he asked himself. *You'll not make it far, even by coach, in your condition. They'll be burying you beside the road somewhere.* He sat on that narrow bench for nearly a half an hour before his head had stopped spinning enough to trust it with supporting his body.

"Good morning, my good man," he greeted the landlord hoarsely, trying to make it sound as if his throat were painfully swollen. "I'd like a room please, one I can stay in for a few days as I've taken a bit of the quinsy, I think."

"Yes, sir, I've just the one."

"And when do you expect a coach through for Carlisle or Gretna?"

"Had one through three days back," the man informed him. "Probably another within the week."

"I'd like to go with it if there's room. Can you see to that for me if it comes by? And can I have my meals brought up so I can rest." He took several notes from his wallet. "I'll just pay for three days now and settle the rest when I leave."

"Very good, sir," the innkeeper said with a grin at the proffered money. "I'll show you up right off."

It was a dark hovel of a room, with one small, grimy window and no amenities but a sad-looking bed and a crooked table. *A proper hole for a wounded animal*, he mused darkly as he lay down on the bed and let fatigue overwhelm his senses. *But at least if I die here, I'll die without a lot of silly clamor.*

Chapter Fourteen

Something was wrong. Even though he felt stronger daily and his equilibrium was less easily lost, he was continually hot. An infection had set in, that was obvious. It left him feeling constantly feverish and glassy-eyed. Still, when the coach came through six days later, he was on it. He had no clear plan other than reaching his father's locale and appealing to him for help if need be.

It was a four-day coach trip to the Scottish border, though he'd be getting off several miles shy of that in Carlisle. The first stopover was the worst. Leeds. Logic told him that Lillie and Benjamin would be back there by now, but he knew it, too, because he could feel their nearness somewhere in his gut. He took to his bed early that night, not just out of bone-deep weariness but because he feared even the chance that they would wander into his life again. He could not suppress a sigh of relief when the coach pulled away the next morning.

That day passed in a blur of fitful dozing and ended in a sweat-filled night. Through sheer strength of will he managed to shave the next morning without cutting his throat.

When the carriage headed more directly north, he thought he felt better. He was able to focus more on the scenery that bounced by the window. He actually joined in a conversation with the other four passengers near mid-day. The subject was horses—it seemed two of the men were breeders for a Scottish lord—and he was always anxious for any tidbits of knowledge on equestrian matters. The elderly lady on the far side of the coach was just offering an opinion on which color looked best with an equipage when there was a shout outside and their own carriage jostled to a stop.

Even in his feverish state, Jeremy knew what was about to happen. He had not let himself be unprepared as so many of his former victims had been, for his two pistols were readied, one at his side, the other tucked into the waistband of his breeches. He had only to determine whether the odds favored him before proceeding. He lay his head against the side of the coach and shut his eyes.

"Outside, ladies and gents," came a harsh voice. "Come on, come on."

"Oh, heavens defend us," the lady declared tearfully.

Jeremy could feel the coach rocking about as its other occupants began to file out. He heard muttered curses from one of his fellow travelers and the lady still crying outside.

"It's your lucky day, mate," came the harsh voice again. "Here's a gal ta tickle your fancy."

"She's a bit old but she'll do," came the laughing response.

More than robbers maybe, Jeremy thought. *They mean to have their fun with us, then either leave us disgraced or, more likely, dead.* He'd run into this kind before. It wasn't just the money that drove them, but the satisfaction of overpowering their marks.

"Here now, you in there," came the harsh voice, closer than before. "Wake up and get out or I'll blow your head off."

"He's been ill," came the voice of one of the horsemen. "He's probably passed out."

"Well, he'll never know what hit 'im then, will 'e. Hey, Rab, maybe he'd be more ta yer likin', eh? He's a comely fella. Looks too weak to fight much."

The clopping of hooves approached the other side of the coach and Jeremy sensed the arrival of the other bandit. He hadn't heard any others, though that didn't mean that there weren't any.

"Just rob us and be done with it," ordered one of the passengers outside. "You needn't murder the man."

"Shut yer hole!"

It was all the distraction Jeremy needed. He knew that both highwaymen either had their heads in the coach windows or were very near. He prayed his right arm would cooperate as he reached beneath his jacket for his pistol. His left hand already held his other pistol. It took only a moment after opening his eyes to target the harsh-voiced robber at such close range. And he wasn't inclined to be merciful. He aimed at the man's head and fired. He heard the lady screaming but had no time to stare at the horror of the brainy mess he'd produced with the first shot. He turned his gaze and his second

149

pistol at the astonished Rab and pulled the trigger. He meant to hit him between the eyes but at the last minute his arm faltered and when the smoke cleared, there was a neat hole in the man's neck instead. It didn't matter. He was just as dead when he slipped off his skittering horse and fell with a thud against the door of the coach.

Now I'm screwed if there's another, Jeremy realized, and waited helplessly for whoever might next appeared. It seemed the elderly woman was in a fit of hysterics, or was another robber holding her hostage? *Ah, well, I've done my bit.* He took in a deep breath and tried to get control of a belated fit of trembling.

"You all right?"

It was one of the horsemen, scrambling back into the coach. He produced a handkerchief and wiped Jeremy's cheek. Only then did he realize that some of the last man's blood had spattered him.

"I'm fine," he said, pushing away the man's helping hand more from embarrassment than ill-temper. "We'd best be gone quickly, though. These men often work in teams and the gunfire might draw the others down."

It was a strange feeling to be obeyed and treated as if he were some sort of authority which, given his past occupation, he supposed he was. And they called him a hero, too, an appellation against which he would have protested more vehemently if he'd had the energy to do so. But the encounter had left him drained of reserves. He contented himself with leaning back into the corner of the coach as the others hurriedly reboarded and the driver urged the horses forward. The elderly woman had regained some of her composure and turned all her grateful attention on him, fussing over his well-being and extolling his heroism with ever more effusive praise. *Christ, I'll be a bloody saint by day's end*, he mused, but smiled at her as graciously as he could, reminding her that it had been in his interest as much as anyone else's to have acted as he did. At a break in her adulation, he asked one of the other men to reload his pistols for him.

"In fact, take charge of them 'til we reach Penrith. I'm afraid I'd not do myself credit if we were to meet another challenge today."

"You certainly did yourself credit enough for one day, Mister Harwood. We're indebted to you. If there's anything…"

But he did not hear more, allowing the rocking of the coach to lull him into a soothing sleep.

* * *

"You take care now, lad," one of the horsemen bid him as he left the coach.

"We'll see he's settled before we go on," the lady, a Mistress Hardy, assured him, for she and her escort—a fellow named Mister Herbert and whom Jeremy took to be her servant turned man-friend—were also getting off in Carlisle. She motioned for Mister Herbert to take Jeremy's travel satchel, then guided him with a protective but firm hand into the inn where they had stopped. He had the odd feeling that she had adopted him as a son and though he thought to protest, he knew a juggernaut when he met one. Mistress Hardy was not to be deterred from her admiration of him for rescuing her from, as she put it, 'certain debasement and death.' He wondered, though, whether she wouldn't have been a great deal more trouble to her would-be rapist than he might have supposed.

"Now I have put two halves together, dear boy, and realize you must be related to the Lord Harwood of these parts. Is it not so? I've never met the gentleman, for we certainly do not move in the same circles as he, but of course he's known to all."

"I'm his cousin," Jeremy said easily.

"Oh, then you'll be going to his care. That's a comfort."

"Not immediately. I didn't have time to inform him of my arrival. I'll be staying here until I send word."

She nodded understandingly. "Then we'll make sure you're looked after before we move on to our own little nest in Hickby. No, no! No trouble, I'm sure, for we can never repay the services you rendered so nobly on our behalf. Come along now, here we go. You're looking quite fatigued again. Immediate rest is in order."

During the next several days—Jeremy was uncertain as to their number—he slept. Then he slept some more. Time moved from moment to moment with no particular direction. He did not think of what to do next. He did not make plans for the future. He did not think about the past, about who he had been or what he had done or what had been done to him. Occasionally the face of someone would worry at the corners of his mind—Bess' black eyes and red lips,

151

Benjamin's gnomish smile, the thin-lipped smirk of Philip Bramhearst, the dull, lumpish features of Tim Mott glaring at him from the shadows of the Hobbs' stables, his mother's pretty, pointed nose and scheming eyes, and a pair of sky-blue eyes that saw him too keenly and shone with too much affection. He dismissed each with an inward shrug of ennui. He ate when the landlord sent up his meals. He looked out the window at nothing in particular. And he slept whenever the feeling overtook him, which was often. He did not know if he had been at the Carlisle inn for three days, a week or longer when there came a knock at his door different from the hurried little knock of the kitchen boy with his meals. It didn't matter. He had dressed earlier but was lying down again and he didn't feel like getting up.

"Come in," he bid, neither annoyed nor cheerful. He was too disinterested to be either.

The door did not open immediately and he thought his visitor might not have heard him. Then the knob finally turned, the door opened with smooth confidence, and a familiar but little seen face appeared before him.

"Good morning, Jeremy," Lord Harwood greeted soberly. "I hope I'm not intruding."

Jeremy pushed himself up to a sitting position and started to rise, but his father motioned him to stay, closing the door behind him and pulling the one chair in the room over next to the bed.

"I can see why I've not heard from you. You look dreadful."

"Do I?" Jeremy asked, sincerely curious. "I haven't thought to look lately." He leaned his back against the pillows and frowned. "How did you know I was here?"

"A Missus Hardy sent an oddly-worded inquiry after your well-being. She wished her best regards to my heroic cousin and seemed to assume you were recuperating from your malady in my care. When you didn't show up, I made some inquiries of my own."

Jeremy nodded.

"So, what is the matter with you?"

"I don't know. I think the wound may be harboring an infection. I should have regained my strength by now, but all I'm good for is sleeping the day away."

"The wound? What sort of wound?"

152

"A not-so-proverbial knife in the back," he said grimly, then explained what had happened as best he could remember through the haze of unconscious periods, fever, and fatigue.

"And you say this was the man who betrayed you to the authorities? The man you were intending to kill?" The baron shook his head and smiled wryly. "I continue to be amazed by the many coincidences that comprise most men's lives." He fixed his son with a steady look then, one that Jeremy supposed was reserved for errant servants or his own half-siblings. "You will let my physician look at you, this afternoon if I can arrange it."

Jeremy nodded his acquiescence. He realized he had not been clear-headed enough to have taken that obvious action himself. Of course he needed a doctor. He wasn't getting better.

"And you will accept my hospitality, convalesce at my home where we can look after you properly." He looked around the little room with ill-hidden disdain, then back to Jeremy.

"I don't know."

"What don't you know? Surely that was your purpose in coming here, wasn't it? To seek my help?"

"I don't know. I wasn't well. I couldn't stay were I was, so I just came here. I suppose I *did* hope you'd at least care enough to bury me if I didn't survive."

Lord Harwood was silent for a few moments, his face as expressionless as Jeremy often knew his own face to be. "I don't know you, for all you are my son," he finally said, "but, yes, I suppose I would care enough to bury you. And I care enough not to let you die from neglect either. Will you come?"

"Won't it be...inconvenient, not to mention discomforting, to have me about. What will your family think?"

"My wife knows the truth of the matter, but your sisters and brother have been told that you are their cousin. I think, when they see you, they may suppose otherwise, but they will not speak of it unless I do."

"Obedient children." He did not mean it to sound unkind but heard the bitterness in the remark. He had never been given the opportunity to be this man's obedient—or even disobedient—son. "I'm sorry. I don't mean to be churlish. I'm just not very practiced at accepting help graciously. It has rarely been offered and I learned early that asking for it could be risky, could even be perceived as a sign of weakness."

"If I may be blunt, you *are* weak, Jeremy. You're at least twenty pounds lighter than when I saw you five months ago, and you were thin then." The words were spoken sternly, but there was a tenderness to them as well. "It's time to let someone help you."

Jeremy looked at his father's face, so like his own, and saw, if not exactly love, at least understanding. He let out a pent up breath, suddenly overcome by weariness and resignation, and nodded. "Yes," he said. "Yes, I'll go with you."

Once installed at Harwood Manor, Jeremy saw little of his father and even less of the other family members. He wasn't exactly surprised. He'd had only a momentary expectation of being welcomed into the bosom of a new-found family—a fleeting vision of himself one day riding beside his father and his half-brother across Harwood lands sharing manly pride in the place, then later teasing his little sisters, and maybe even his father's wife, about some foolishness or other.

The cold stare of that woman and the uncomfortable glances of his half-siblings when being introduced to him had dispelled any illusions he might have momentarily cherished. He would be tolerated only, for his father's sake, nursed back to health and then politely sent on his way.

The doctor arrived less than an hour after his own arrival. He was businesslike and spoke only to Lord Harwood, not Jeremy. He would need to do some minor surgery, he said, to drain a large pocket of infection. Did his lordship want that performed on the premises or at his surgery in town? Daniel Harwood thought it best to be done at the manor so that Jeremy wouldn't have to be moved afterward and the two men decided that, since the doctor's leisure served him then, that it should be done immediately.

Jeremy listened with dull resentment. Had he no say in the matter? Was he such an insignificance in the lives of these great men that he was not even to be consulted regarding his own treatment. Still, he kept quiet. He realized through the headache that plagued him that he wasn't quite up to making decisions. What did it matter after all? If the quack killed him, perhaps it would be just as well.

The quack didn't kill him. In fact, Jeremy felt so much better upon awakening the next morning that he remembered his previous musings with bafflement. His view of life had never been a cheerful one, but he had always given self-preservation a high priority. He could only think it had been the infection that had stolen that instinct from him. He was glad it had returned. As he gazed around at the big, bright, elegant room in which he lay, the morning sun streaming through the windows and nary a dust mote in sight, he was glad he was alive. His essential pragmatism, however, had not been affected by the splendor of his surroundings. He would let himself be cared for because it was the wise thing to do. The sooner he got better, the sooner he could leave. He was not wanted here, that much of his fever-muddled memory he trusted, and he had never been one to stay where he wasn't wanted.

His father and the doctor looked in on him after he had eaten his breakfast with the help of a lad from the kitchen. All was well. His father stayed to make some polite conversation about nothing in particular, then left. The next two days proceeded in like fashion. The third day, only his father came.

"Doctor Bremerton tells me you should be ready to rejoin society today. I'll send in my man to help you dress, then take you down."

Jeremy frowned only momentarily, then planted a grim smile on his face and nodded his consent. "Very well. I want you to know that I appreciate all you've done for me. I will always be grateful. My regards to Doctor Bremerton as well."

Lord Harwood nodded then gave an almost embarrassed shrug. "Not only are you my son, you are a fellow human being. Both obligated me to help you if I could. I'm just glad I was able to do so."

Fairchild, Lord Harwood's valet, was sent in to help Jeremy dress, but the man seemed a complete dunce about dressing for travel. He looked at the clothes Jeremy had laid out and shook his head, offering a flimsy shirt and expensive dinner suit which he had brought with him and which he said his master had sent for the occasion.

"Please thank Lord Harwood," Jeremy said tolerantly, "but I'm afraid those won't be warm enough."

155

"Are you chilled, sir? I could ask the maid to build up the fire, then see to it that the parlor is well heated."

"What good will that do me?" Jeremy asked, starting to think the man was a simpleton. "No, if you'll just help me with what I've laid out here, then pack my other things into my valise, I'd appreciate it."

"But sir, where are you going?"

Jeremy frowned at what seemed like presumptuousness in a servant even to him. "I'm not sure yet but it is *my* concern, not yours."

Fairchild seemed completely taken back by the answer. "Of course, sir. I only meant... Will you excuse me a moment, sir?" He laid the garments he had brought with him over a chair and scurried out of the room.

So much for help dressing, Jeremy fumed. He could manage. He did feel nearly himself, if a little wobbly on his feet. He shed the robe that had been loaned him and with his good left hand managed to work his shirt over his head, carefully lifting his still-tender right arm into the sleeve. He was just shrugging his other arm into a sleeve when Fairchild returned, accompanied by his father.

"What's going on here?" his father demanded, seeming more bewildered than angry.

"I'm dressing," Jeremy answered matter-of-factly.

"Fairchild seems to have the impression that you are preparing to leave."

Now it was Jeremy's turn to look bewildered. "I am. You asked me to."

"I did not such thing."

"But... You said it was time to rejoin society."

"I meant to come down from your room. To walk and regain your mobility. To sit with us, enjoy the library perhaps...or the conservatory."

"If I can't read, you mean."

"Again you mistake me. I meant that the tranquility of the conservatory might suit your recovery better than the mental exertions of reading."

Jeremy felt like a scolded child, and rightly so, he realized. "I'm sorry. I thought you would welcome my departure."

"I will, when you are well enough to do so, for then you will have recovered yourself fully and be able to live your own life again. Until then, let it be clear that you are welcome here. I'll have no more of these martyred pretensions."

Jeremy returned his father's hard gaze with one as stern. "'Twas no pretension, sir, nor did I aspire to martyrdom. I merely accepted the awkwardness of my being here and concluded that you would want me gone."

"All in good time," his father answered, his tone gentler than before. "Now please, let Fairchild help you dress so you don't cause yourself further injury. I'll be back when you're finished."

The cold eyes of Lady Harwood that Jeremy remembered upon his arrival seemed less so now. Actually, they were almost friendly. Almost. There was still that reserve about them that communicated some distrust, though she had obviously set aside some of that feeling upon seeing how heavily he had leaned upon his father's arm to walk. Here was no dangerous highwayman to threaten her family's security. Here was only the unfortunate by-product of one of her husband's premarital liaisons.

"Sit here, Mister Harwood," she greeted, indicating a comfortable chair generously filled with plumped pillows. "Would you care for some biscuits and tea?"

"Thank you, no. I'm still quite satisfied from breakfast."

"Perhaps later then. You are looking better than when you arrived. I hope you are *feeling* better as well."

"Much." He leaned back into the chair, suppressing a sigh. No use appearing too contented. He didn't want his hostess to think he was unaccustomed to such luxury nor that he was settling in too permanently. "I'm glad for this opportunity to thank you, as I've thanked my...your husband, for opening your home to me and seeing to my comfort so solicitously, especially considering the circumstances."

Lady Harwood glanced at her husband, then back to Jeremy. "I'm a plain speaker, Mister Harwood, so let me speak plainly now, then we shall have no occasion to do so again, I hope. I harbor no contempt for either you *or* your mother, for she had nothing to do with me. You are my husband's son and that relationship can only make you dearer to me, especially when I see his likeness so profoundly in your person.

"I cannot excuse your former profession so easily, though I understand that hard necessity often motivates such desperate enterprises. And according to Missus Hardy, who has continued to communicate her best wishes and extol your heroism in daily missives, you have so far turned your life around that she credits you with the destruction of two such robbers as you once were."

Jeremy took a deep breath, then shook his head. "I'm afraid Missus Hardy gives me more credit than she should, or rather attributes my actions to nobler causes than are accurate. I, too, am a plain speaker, and I would not have you indulging similar false notions. I shot those men because they seemed intent on murder, not robbery. *Self*-preservation motivated me more than heroism, I assure you. And also..."

He paused, considering whether it would be prudent to continue. She had granted him shelter in her home, but she had also given him a dispensation of sorts for his criminal behavior and he did not deserve it. "Lady Harwood, I cannot let you excuse me of my past misdeeds. They were not motivated by hard necessity but by greed, that most despicable of inspirations. I enjoyed the lifestyle other peoples' money provided me. I liked good food, fine clothes, and everything else abundance of funds makes possible. I told myself I was only taking from those who were too foolish to protect their extra coin. I prided myself on never harming my victims, but of course every time I held a man at gun point, I risked that very thing. I was arrogant and prideful, and my thoughtless self-indulgence eventually led to the death of a young girl whose only crime was in valuing me more than she should have. It nearly cost me my own life as well. If this were a just world, it would have. That is why I no longer ride the roads—self-preservation and a feeling of obligation to that girl. No moral awakening. No lessening of pride. Not even much of a change of heart, for I still desire those fine things I once stole."

To his surprise, Lady Harwood smiled at him. "But you *have* changed, whatever your reasons, and that is to your credit, Mister Harwood, whether you'll accept it or not. You have discovered the error of believing that your actions affect only you. You have been given a second chance to live more rightly."

Jeremy did not return her smile but he nodded politely, still reluctant to admit she might be correct.

"Now we have an understanding, I hope, and you will no longer feel so uncomfortable here."

"And what have you told your children about me?"

"We've told them," Lord Harwood put in, "that you are the son of my cousin, that you were born in Jamaica but that my cousin died while you were just a baby and you and your mother came to England to live with her mother's family near York." Lord Harwood seemed to take satisfaction in the fabrication.

"Do these parents have names?" He did not mean to sound peevish but something about his father's easy dismissal of their relationship felt...what? Bad? Wrong? Did it actually pain him to hear his existence explained away so glibly?

"Michael was my cousin's name but as he was never really married, I haven't mentioned the name of your mother to the children. You may choose one of your liking."

"Elizabeth." It came out so readily, it surprised him. Bess' full name, he realized. Well, in a sense, she had been responsible for his new life. The mother of his future, whatever he chose to make of it.

Lord Harwood nodded his acknowledgment, as did his wife. "That should do. Now, some tea?"

The 'children,' as their parents referred to them, were older than Jeremy had first supposed upon meeting them the day of his arrival. Their features bore the elegant stamp of their mother which, like her, gave them the appearance of greater youth than they possessed. The eldest daughter, Portia, he had taken for sixteen. She was twenty. The second daughter, Viola, was sixteen. He had thought her to be closer to thirteen or perhaps fourteen. And his half-brother, Edwin, whom he had thought was surely no older than twelve turned out to have fifteen summers to his credit.

Their mental endowments—which Jeremy noted once he had had a chance to converse with them a while—did, indeed, reflect their true ages, especially Edwin's, whose serious nature and general astuteness made him seem even older than his fifteen years. Jeremy found he liked his half-brother very much but also found his questions the hardest to answer. The boy was no fool. Any inconsistency in Jeremy's replies could undo the flimsy net of lies the adults had constructed.

"So you grew up in Jamaica?" Edwin asked upon the occasion of their third conversation. He and his sisters had contrived to take their afternoon tea in the library where Jeremy had taken refuge.

"No, I was born there but left before my memories begin, I'm afraid."

Edwin looked disappointed. "How unfortunate. I have always had a fascination for the Caribbean. I'd like to go there someday, wouldn't you, just out of curiosity?"

"I haven't your fascination, I guess. My mother did not speak admiringly of the place, especially since it was responsible for my father's early death."

"It must have been hard growing up without a father," Portia put in sympathetically.

"Yes," he said, able at last to speak with total honesty, "though I'm not certain I appreciated that lack as a child. One tends to accept the circumstances that one is born into until one is exposed to a wider experience of the world."

"That's so true!" agreed Viola. "When I was little, I never would have imagined that people actually lived their lives quite comfortably with never a servant to their name, yet it's a much more common situation in the world than our own. Maybe even preferable."

Edwin laughed. "Vi, you'd succumb to a fit of nerves within the week if Bonnie wasn't at your side to see to things."

"I wouldn't!"

"You would," put in Portia, "and so would I, for we have become accustomed to such leisure. But I dare to say, Edwin, that all of us would eventually adjust to a change of circumstances if necessity dictated. It is the nature of mankind to adapt. Don't you agree, Mister Harwood?"

"I do."

"'Mister Harwood' sounds so horribly formal," Viola said poutily. "Mayn't we call you Jeremy? You are a cousin after all."

For some reason, Jeremy found himself looking to Portia for advice. She returned his look of askance with a smile.

"If you would not be offended by the familiarity, it would not be considered improper, especially within the family."

Within the family. Yes, he supposed he was now. Although they thought of him not as a brother but as only a distant cousin, he was at least that to them. He belonged to a family again, if only remotely.

"Jeremy it is," he said to Viola, who seemed quite pleased with having been responsible for the change.

"Do you enjoy riding?" Edwin asked.

"He's not well enough for that yet," Portia reminded her brother, her tone protective.

"I didn't ask him to go riding, I just asked if he enjoyed it?"

"I'll go further than that and admit that I love it," Jeremy answered.

"Then when you are well again, I will lend you the use of Robbie if you like. He's the finest horse in our stables. I'll wager you've never ridden one better."

"He's a monster!" Viola warned. "Not a nice horse at all, for all Edwin worships him."

"He isn't! Not if you know how to handle him."

"I'd like to see him," Jeremy conceded. "Though I may need a less-spirited mount for a time."

"Tomorrow? If you're up to it, we could take a turn to the stables together."

"It's too far," Viola said.

"Yes, stop pestering him, Edwin," Portia scolded.

Jeremy looked at the three faces around him and found himself smiling with honest amusement. "I shall decide when I awake in the morning," he told Edwin in what sounded suspiciously like a big brother's authoritative tone. "But if not tomorrow, then as soon as I'm able. I promise."

The next two weeks passed by quickly if lazily. Spring was on the land and with it enough good weather to afford many walks in the gardens around the house and to the near-lying parks. He was often in the company of his half-siblings and even, occasionally, his father, though that gentleman always kept a polite distance to their exchanges. But to Portia, Viola, and Edwin, there was no need for reserve now that they were all acquainted, and they treated him with affection and openness, sharing stories of their growing up and hopes for their futures with him as if he were a dear friend. At first he was uncomfortable with such intimacies. It almost felt as if he were betraying their trust by not telling them who he really was. But as the end of the second week approached, he realized he looked forward to getting up each morning because it meant being with one or all his siblings at least some part of the day.

The library was another enticement to linger. If he could read everything upon the shelves, he knew he would be a happy man forever. There was no time for that, of course, so he contented himself with reading bits and pieces of as many volumes as he was able.

"You're always in that stuffy old room," Viola chided him one evening at dinner.

"You only think it's stuffy because you don't appreciate the acquisition of knowledge," Portia defended him. "It's the best room in the house to some of us." She looked at Jeremy and gave him a single nod of accord.

"And you're always dragging him out into the gardens, Vi," Edwin put in, "so he's getting his share of fresh air as well. A few hours of stuffiness won't harm him."

Lord Harwood laughed. "Neither would they harm you. You'll be back to school soon. Best see to reviewing some things."

Edwin nodded, looking suddenly sorry that he had attracted attention to his lack of study lately. He seemed to be always off riding or at least hanging about the stables. Jeremy could understand that passion, of course, since he shared it. He hoped he could soon indulge it, for his shoulder barely pained him anymore and he had regained some of his vigor.

"Who's for liars whist this evening?" Viola asked.

"I'm afraid not my dear," Lord Harwood excused himself.

"That would be nice," Lady Harwood nodded to her daughter.

"Who else? Jeremy?"

"Perhaps a hand or two."

"We've been pressing you too hard," Portia told him, looking at her sister and brother accusingly before turning a sympathetic face his way again. "You look tired. We will not take any offense if you choose to retire early rather than play cards."

Jeremy smiled at her concern. "I *am* a bit tired, but I think a few hands of cards will be a pleasant prelude to sleep, at least I usually find it so."

"Much better for the digestion, too," Lady Harwood said sagely.

"Oh, good," Viola said happily. "Liars whist is always more challenging when Jeremy plays. I never know what he's about."

"That must mean he's a good liar," Edwin commented with admiration.

"I hope that's not true," Portia said, giving him a shy smile, "for I have come to depend upon his word."

Something in her gentle tone troubled him. He glanced discretely at his father but Lord Harwood seemed not to have noted the exchange. Nor, it seemed, had his wife. In fact no one had given Portia's earnest declaration any import, but something had stirred in his subconscious. Was it a feeling of guilt...or apprehension?

Chapter Fifteen

It was time to leave. Everything instinct told him he should go.

He wasn't sure exactly why a sense of foreboding had settled over him, he only knew that the old prickle of apprehension he had often heeded on the road had been plaguing him for the last two days and it made him nervous to ignore it. He had been ensconced at his father's home for almost a month. Surely it was time to go, ill premonition or no. That morning he spoke to his father.

"I feel I should be moving on now."

"Nonsense. You're still far from well."

"I assure you, I am so far recovered that I fear you'll discover me for a fraud if I let you treat me as an invalid any longer. And I cannot in good conscience continue to impose myself upon you and your family—"

"Impose!? You are the current mode, sir, and keep my other children quite entertained and out of *my* hair. I haven't heard so many admiring accolades for a visiting relative since my wife's brother from India came two years ago with all his stories of tigers and rajahs and the like."

"And I quite enjoy their company as well," Jeremy admitted, "but I cannot continue here as a stricken charity case when I'm quite able to fend for myself again."

"It's only been three weeks or so. Give yourself more time. Here." Lord Harwood reached behind him and plucked two fencing swords from their places on the wall. He tossed one to Jeremy.

An easy catch usually, and Jeremy instinctively reached out. The sword fell to the carpeted floor of his father's study.

"En garde," Lord Harwood said, waiting for his son to retrieve the fallen rapier and take his stance.

Jeremy willed his body to perform the familiar task. He knew how to handle a sword well—another skill he had once prided himself in. At first it seemed he might be an able adversary, but after only a few parries, his father easily disarmed him and brought the point of his weapon meaningfully up to Jeremy's vest button.

"You're dead," he said grimly. "Are you usually so easily bested? Do you always sweat like a horse after only two minutes of exercise? Tell me you don't feel like collapsing into that chair and staying there the rest of the morning." He lowered his sword. "Tell me all that and I'll be ready to agree with you that you're ready to fend for yourself again. Do you even know where you would go?"

Jeremy thought quickly, for up to that moment, he had not. "To Scotland first, for some of my money. Then to London. I've rooms there."

"A long trip. I go to town myself in a month. Perhaps you would consider accompanying me when I do."

Jeremy looked at his father in speechless wonder, amazed on two counts. First, that his father should be desirous of his remaining as long as another month and secondly that he wanted his company on the road. It surprised him even more when he felt tears stinging at the back of his eyes. He quickly blinked them back and covered them with a frown.

"Did our contest hurt you?" Lord Harwood asked, moving forward with a steadying hand on Jeremy's arm.

"No sir, not at all." He took a steeling breath. "I'll stay as long as you'll have me and be glad of your company south."

"And as for me," Lord Harwood admitted with a chuckle, "I know I'll be with someone who's acquainted with the roads better than most men *and* can acquit himself well in a pinch according your Missus Hardy."

Jeremy smiled. "We'll hope for an uneventful journey. I, for one, have had enough of such adventures for a while."

"Father's agreed to give a ball!" Viola greeted Jeremy and her other siblings as they returned from a walk to the stables a week later. "I only just heard him telling Mother that it was all right."

"Oh, God, do I have to go?" Edwin complained. "I hate those silly gatherings."

165

"No, you don't," Viola said merrily, "for it is in two weeks and you'll be going back to school in one."

Edwin let out a relieved sigh. "But poor Jeremy shall not escape so easily. How I wish I could do something to save you from such an ordeal."

Jeremy smiled at his brother. "I don't anticipate such an occasion with dread, Edwin. I quite enjoy a good soiree."

"You're kidding," Edwin exclaimed in wonderment.

"Well, 'tis not so fine as a good gallop on a spring morning, but dancing with pretty women is a close second."

Edwin grinned. "Speaking of riding, we're still on for tomorrow, aren't we?"

"You're not going to ride that monstrous Robbie, are you?" cried Viola.

"No, we all agreed he is too much yet for Jeremy to manage with his injury," Portia put in. She did not see the look Jeremy exchanged with Edwin nor, thankfully, did Viola.

"Father will be going with us, I dare say, but even if he cannot, I know these lands front to back."

"Just a short ride," Jeremy reminded his eager brother. "I cannot let my fair cousins worry longer than that over my welfare."

"Do you have something to wear for the ball? If not, I'm sure one of father's suits would do well if taken in a bit. You are of nearly the same coloring."

"Nearly the same?" Edwin said in disbelief. "That's rather an understatement, Vi. He is father's very image."

"Not so similar," Portia protested, tilting her head to one side and looking at Jeremy more critically. "Jeremy's hair is a bit darker, his face a little longer, and his eyes have not the tilt of father's."

"*Do* you have something to wear?" Viola asked again, unable to hide her irritation at the constant diversions away from the topic closest to *her* heart.

"Stop fretting about it," Portia chided. "It's not likely to be a very grand affair at this time of the year, especially if it's to be put together in just a fortnight. I'm sure Jeremy's own attire will suffice."

Jeremy couldn't help but be amused by the murderous glare the younger sister fixed upon her superior-sounding sibling. "You'll be happy to know, Miss Viola, that I possess an extremely becoming lace cravat and a new linen shirt. And I shall place myself in your capable hands and show you the jackets and waistcoats I have with me. You can decide if they will do for your ball."

Viola beamed with pleasure, then gave her sister a dismissive toss of her head.

"See what a lot of trouble it all is," Edwin commented sagely. "I can't see that I shall ever find pleasure in it."

Jeremy approached Robbie with a soft word, gently taking hold of the bridle and caressing the stallion's black neck with easy confidence.

"Ah, he remembers you," Edwin said. "He knows you admire him, too, so he'll give you a good ride."

"You're sure you don't mind giving him up to me this morning?"

"No sir. Father gave him to me last year and I've longed to show him off to someone who'll really appreciate him. Portia and Viola don't like him at all so consequently he doesn't like them much either. Shows his bad side whenever they come around."

Jeremy ran an admiring hand down the stallion's neck one more time, then took hold of the reins and swung himself easily into the saddle. Robbie skittered a little to one side as Edwin mounted up on a big gray beside them, but a firm hand soon quieted him. Damn, if it didn't feel good to be back atop a good horse again, Jeremy thought with a joyful smile at his little brother as he followed him out of the stable yard and toward the rolling expanse behind the manor house.

"Let me know if your shoulder starts to hurt you or if you tire," Edwin called over his shoulder. "We'll take it slow."

"To hell with slow," Jeremy shouted with a laugh and knocked his heels into Robbie's sides. As he expected, the horse sprang forward with an effortless leap and galloped past a wide-mouthed Edwin toward the open field. Jeremy could feel the stallion trying to take his head, but he held him back just enough to show the animal who was in control. As they approached the forested boundary, Jeremy reined in the black horse and spun him around to see where his brother might be. Robbie reared a little in protest, not wanting the fun to be over.

Edwin and the gray were not far behind and overshot Jeremy's position by several yards before the boy managed to stop him and bring him back. He smiled at Jeremy with unconcealed delight.

"Magnificent," Jeremy greeted his brother enthusiastically. "He could have run to the moon if I'd let him."

"He's nearly done that several times," Edwin admitted with a grin. "He gets his head every now and then and just takes me with him. I've had to wait until he tires before he'll mind the bit again."

Jeremy frowned. "Does your father know this?"

"Of course not. He'd say I mustn't run him or forbid me to ride him altogether. I don't want that."

"But it's dangerous, Edwin. Surely you know that."

For just a moment the look on Edwin's young face turned petulant and Jeremy expected he'd have to deal with a fit of teenage pique. He was prepared to stand firm. If Edwin couldn't control this fine but headstrong beast, then he shouldn't be riding him at all.

"Will you teach me to manage him?"

Jeremy grinned in relief and admiration for his brother's unusual maturity. "If I can. You're correct when you presume that this horse knows who will hold him and who will not." He nudged Robbie forward and started back toward the house, Edwin falling in beside him. "He knows you love him so he doesn't try to trample you into the dust as he does your sisters. But he also knows that you don't know how to keep him from indulging his fancy to run. And he loves to run. I can feel his impatience even now, quivering with every step. And where are my hands?"

Edwin's eyes left Jeremy's face and looked. "Nearly upon his neck."

"Relaxed?"

"No. Tightly clenched. It looks like you're holding back a coach of four."

"Nearly," Jeremy said with a smile. "And my legs?"

"Also tense, knees in on his withers."

Jeremy nodded. "And still he could go if he really wished to do so. With a horse like this, it is a matter of wills and whose will shall prevail at any given moment."

"I've a strong will," Edwin said matter-of-factly.

"Yes, but that is only half of it."

Edwin frowned for the first time that morning. "Even recovering from a grievous injury, you are stronger than me. I won't be able to manage him for years."

"You're strong enough now, but here's the trick. You can *never* let down your guard with him. He must always feel you are holding him back. If you abandon yourself to the exhilaration of the ride, he will abandon his allegiance to your command, at least while the fever to run is upon him. Do you see?"

Edwin nodded but he looked unsure.

"He's a young horse. I'm sure your Father had him well trained before he gave him to you, but Robbie's forgotten some of that, I fear. He's trembling like a new-broke. You've been letting him have his way for nearly a year and he's grown used to it."

Edwin's face brightened. "*You* ride him while you're here. That should remind him."

They were nearing the stables and Jeremy stopped. "That will only be part of it. We must teach him—and you—that he should obey any rider upon his back." He turned Robbie around. "Is there a place we could go where we will be less conspicuous than in these open fields?"

Edwin nodded and pointed to a ridge of trees. "Beyond that is a fine field."

"Then let's begin today."

"You're not tired?"

Jeremy was touched by the genuine concern in the boy's voice. In truth, his shoulder felt a bit tight. He knew it would probably throb later, but he'd manage it. "*You're* going to be doing most of the work," he said. "I'm just along for the ride."

"Where do you go each morning?"

Portia Harwood seated herself across from where Jeremy was reading and fixed him with a steady gaze. It was clear that she would not go away without an answer to her question.

"Edwin and I? We go riding, of course, though I'm afraid I can't tell you exactly *where* we go. Edwin leads and I follow."

She seemed to consider his reply for a moment, then shook her head. "I only half believe you, Cousin. Edwin's demeanor has been most curiously variant this last week after your rides together. At first he was sullen, visibly tired, and short-tempered with everyone. Then, the last two days, equally exhausted but jubilant. And today, *you* rode out on Robbie but Edwin rode him back."

"What? Have you been spying on us from some upper window, Miss Harwood?" He was surprised to see her blush to the roots of her hair at his question. He had meant it only to tease her and deflect her curiosity, but her distress was apparent as she bowed her head and stared at her clasped hands. *Had* she been "spying" then? On him? That vague feeling of apprehension that he had felt during the last two weeks again prickled the hair on his neck. Damn!

"He's Edwin's horse. Why shouldn't he ride him?" he hurried on, placing a mask of ignorance upon his face to discourage any confessions of love she might feel obligated to make to explain her discomfort.

Portia looked up at him again, some of her composure regained. "I love my brother, Jeremy, and worry for his safety. I can't quite put my finger on what it is, but I know you two have a secret. I see it in both of your faces each day."

Now that his brother was well on his way to being not only Robbie's owner but his master as well, Jeremy saw little harm in revealing their secret. "Yes, but 'tis not much of a secret, though Edwin considers it so. I've been working with him to control that great beast your father gave him. He's a good horseman, your brother, but he hadn't the will to handle that horse if it got a notion to run. Now he does."

"*You've* been giving Edwin riding lessons?" He did not miss the incredulity in her voice.

"To him *and* to Robbie. The horse had gotten used to having the upper hand. We've been confusing him, swapping riders every few minutes until he didn't know who might have control of his bit. He's found it much easier merely to obey than to try to outsmart whoever's riding him. What? Why are you laughing?"

"My brother has had some of the finest riding teachers in England, Jeremy, and the life long tutelage of our father. And *you* have managed to improve his riding in less than a week?"

His eyes narrowed. He had been mistaken a moment ago. She was not harboring a secret passion for him, only a secret contempt.

He felt his back stiffen at the insult. "As I said, Edwin was already a good horseman," he replied tightly. "I only sharpened his skill a bit. He confided to me that he had often lost control of Robbie. I, too, care for his safety, Miss Harwood. Rather than risk that or your father's withdrawal of riding privileges, we decided to tackle the problem together. If I was of any assistance to him, that is all the gratification I require."

Her laughing face had so far transformed that she now looked to be on the verge of tears. "You're angry. Oh, Jeremy, I'm sorry. I would not offend you for the world. I..." She fell suddenly silent, staring down again at the clenched hands in her lap.

He wasn't sure of what he should say, if anything. Her reaction to his curt reply renewed his earlier suspicion that she might have a secret infatuation for him. Why hadn't he foreseen this possibility? Why hadn't her father or mother? *They* might have predicted their own daughter's inclination for romance. She did not know they were so closely related. Even first cousins married, after all, and she supposed him to be more distantly related than that. He should have left a fortnight ago when the foreboding had first come upon him. Perhaps it wasn't too late. If he was right—and as the silence between them lengthened, he was almost certain that he was—then, for his sister's sake, he would rather have her enmity than her improper love.

"Are you satisfied that I have not harmed your brother?" he asked churlishly.

"I never said—"

"Your inquiries implied it, and more. You distrusted my intentions."

"No."

"You must have. I might even have supposed you suspected me of buggery, Miss Harwood."

Again Portia blushed, but her face had hardened into disdain, too. "I *never* meant to imply such a revolting explanation for yours and Edwin's behavior and it is brutish of you think me capable of that. It is even ungentlemanly to speak it."

He stood, for now that she was angry as well as distressed he could justify leaving.

"Please excuse me, Miss Harwood, but I have never claimed to be a gentleman."

"Until now you have always seemed one," she said, her voice catching in a sob.

"Perhaps your brother was correct, then, when he supposed me to be a good liar," he replied coldly, then tossed the book he'd been reading down on the sofa and strode from the room. When he heard a few muffled sobs, he resisted his inclination to turn around and comfort her. His sister was crying yet he must pretend it didn't affect him.

It was the biggest lie he'd ever had to tell.

Chapter Sixteen

When he stopped to consider the sudden and unexpected turn his life had taken in less than an hour, he mourned for all he might be about to lose.

His own sister was, if not in love with him, at least infatuated with him. The line had been crossed and she would probably never feel that easy, familial love for him again. For her sake he might have to sever all ties with his new-found family, at least until she was married to some other fellow and looked upon him as no more than a girlish crush. Until then, she might dislike him for rejecting her affection. Maybe she always would. It hurt him to think so, for he liked Portia and had looked forward to years of companionship with her and the others. When supper came, he almost did not go down. What if there was a scene that ruined his hopes of any future affiliation with the family at all? The thought of a permanent separation brought him nearly to the point of weeping. Was he destined to always lose what he loved?

In the end he convinced himself that he must go down or risk more prying inquiries after his health and disposition. He braced himself before entering the dining hall. He did not want to appear jovial and further hurt Portia, but neither did he want to look as bereft as he felt. He took a deep breath, fixed a look of general cordiality upon his face, and went in.

"There you are, Jeremy," Lady Harwood greeted. "I trust you've had a satisfying day?"

"In most respects, ma'am." He glanced at Portia but she was talking with her sister.

As the evening progressed, Jeremy began to realize that he had not gained Portia's enmity as he'd half hoped. He was surprised by the pluck she showed, for although he had quarreled with her, insulted her, and left her in tears, she talked to him as politely as ever. No one

173

else in the family would have suspected that anything was amiss between them. He glanced at her curiously, trying to read whatever might be revealed in her eyes, but she avoided any direct eye contact with practiced poise.

She could hate him or love him or think nothing of him at all for all she revealed that evening and throughout the next day. The suspense was unnerving. He wondered if he could endure the uncertainty of her feelings much longer. Then an idea that might salvage the situation, at least temporarily, came to him as he awoke the next morning.

Edwin was leaving the following day. What if he were to offer to accompany his brother to school? It would get him away from Harwood Manor in an honorable endeavor, raise little objection, and might even be welcomed by his father and Lady Harwood. The only one that might object was Viola, for she spoke of nothing but the approaching ball and how proud she would be to present her handsome cousin to all the eligible ladies in attendance. He had decided not to ruin her fantasy by pointing out that the penniless, distant cousin of a baron was far from being a tempting marriage consideration. He would ruin her plans irreparably by leaving, but it could not be helped. He had to get away.

"I'm sure Edwin would be delighted," Lord Harwood said, but he did not seem as enthusiastic as Jeremy had hoped. "It's not necessary, of course. 'Tis only a two-day journey. He has come and gone a dozen times over these many years in the good company of our head groom."

"I had thought of it more as a companionable enterprise rather than one of necessity," Jeremy replied. "Edwin and I have become quite good friends."

Lord Harwood nodded. "I've noticed. I'm glad of it." He paused. "And might we expect you to return after seeing Edwin to school?"

Jeremy shook his head. "I think it's time I leave. I know it is. And I'm able again. Shall we fence once more to prove the truth of that?"

"No. I can see you are well enough." His face, usually so unreadable, appeared troubled.

"I apologize for leaving before your own journey to town," Jeremy added. "I had looked forward to that."

"So had I. It is still not impossible. You could even be back in time for Viola's ball. She will not forgive you for missing it. She had high hopes of you meeting your future wife from among our guests and settling close by," he said, smiling grimly at the thought of his youngest daughter's certain tantrum.

"I will try to resign her to the rightness of my leaving. Perhaps if I tell her I go to meet my true lady love, her sense of romance will prevail over her disappointment."

"Do you?"

The image of Lillie's sweet face, kept so long at the back of his mind, suddenly swept through his senses and he closed his eyes at the unexpected and painful longing. "She has dismissed me from her heart by now if she knows what's good for her. I did not leave her well." He wasn't leaving Portia well either. It seemed to be a habit of his new life to run away, though with Portia there was at least good reason. Lillie, he had realized when his mind had cleared of its fever, had deserved far better from him.

"Will you take some fatherly advice this late in your life?"

Jeremy opened his eyes and nodded.

"Women are different creatures than we men. Whereas we are inclined to be practical, logical, and unforgiving, women often place a higher priority on the heart of things. They will love when we would condemn. They will forgive when a man feels honor bound to stand firm. They do not always follow the wisest course, choosing instead the most loving course." He hesitated before continuing. "It's clear that you care for this woman. Don't assume she will not forgive you just because you would not forgive yourself. It's a fair wager when dealing with women that their love will stand more tests than ours."

Jeremy frowned. "I have not found that to be true, sir. In fact, it's been my experience that most women are self-serving and deceitful," he said simply.

Lord Harwood looked at him with such profound sadness that Jeremy was afraid his father was about to cry. It panicked him to think he might.

"Oh, God, Jeremy, I'm so sorry I abandoned you to Lydia's care. I shall never be able to forgive myself for that. I robbed you not only of a father's care, but now, it seems, the simple pleasure of being able to love someone."

Jeremy did not want his father's remorse, but he could not quite bring himself to deny the justice of it. It *was* partly Daniel Harwood's fault, but certainly there were others, including himself, who must answer for any faults in his character.

"Each man must take responsibility for his own failings," Jeremy said. "Perhaps I choose to distrust women out of some unconscious willfulness."

"If that is so, I will pray for you to realize it soon and banish it from your life," his father said passionately. "I would not like to think of you living a life empty of true companionship. It is not always easy, but it is the best part of being alive I have found."

The two men fell silent for a few moments. So much had been said…and left unsaid. Lord Harwood finally broke the hush.

"Let me know where you are? Where I can reach you? For one thing, it would be awkward explaining to the children why you just vanished from out lives and for another," he added with a steady look, "I'd like to know."

The news of Jeremy's leaving hit the household like a sudden spring storm when Lord Harwood announced it at luncheon. Edwin was, as predicted, overjoyed. Also as predicted, Viola refused to believe Jeremy could be so cruel as to abandon them so soon before the ball.

"You cannot go!" she pleaded. "What will my friends all say? They will think I've been writing them lies, that's what!"

"Mother and Portia can tell them Jeremy exists," Edwin said practically. "Really, Vi, don't be so theatrical."

"I shall never forgive you, Jeremy," she said, ignoring Edwin's admonishments. "You cannot abandon me for so slight a reason as seeing Edwin to school. It won't do."

Jeremy glanced at his father, then, briefly, at Portia. "Would you forgive me, Viola, if I told you I leave also on a mission of the heart?"

He saw Portia straighten involuntarily and it grieved him to wound her more than he already had but…

"What?" cried Viola. "You are already in love? Why haven't you said something before now, letting me go on and on about seeing you settled?"

"You were so happy making plans, I did not want to ruin your fun. But it reminded me that I have neglected her for too long. I need to see her, to apologize for being away so long."

"What is her name? Oh, she cannot blame you for being absent when you tell her how grievously that dreadful robber hurt you. Shall I write her a letter attesting to your infirmity so she shall forgive you more readily?"

Jeremy smiled. "It might do more to make her jealous, being penned by a pretty young lady," he teased. "I'll have Edwin write my excuses."

"He'll look like a fellow conspirator," Viola reasoned. "Better it should come from Father. What is her name?"

Jeremy paused and looked again at Portia, whose steady gaze at her plate broke his heart. No one else seemed to notice her distress. "Her name is Lillie," he said. "She may not have me after the wretched way I've treated her, but I've nothing to lose but my pride."

"Oh, this is so exciting!" Viola exclaimed. "I forgive you everything if you will only write and tell me whether you are successful in your suit or not. It's better than a novel. Dear Portia, why are you crying?"

All eyes turned to where Portia sat with tears slowly running down her cheeks. Jeremy wanted to reach across the table and wipe them away, but although he alone suspected the cause of her sadness, he only stared in empathetic support like the rest of her family.

"I shall miss him, that is all," she explained.

The house was quiet. Everyone had gone to bed long ago, but Jeremy could not sleep. He was packed and ready to leave with Edwin and the groom in the morning. His father had given him the gray gelding 'for as long as you need him,' a generous gift and one which Jeremy would have refused if not for the fact that he needed a horse. He planned to return it as soon as he bought another of his own.

In his restlessness, he wandered down to the darkened lower floors of the house, unsure of his destination. He considered going out for a bit of fresh air, then remembered the trouble he'd caused on an earlier occasion when he'd been mistaken for a prowler by one of the grooms. He didn't want to cause a similar commotion tonight. He just wanted to be alone.

He walked quietly from room to room, standing for a minute in each elegant archway or door before moving on to the next. Each room held more memories than he would have thought possible to accumulate in so short a time. *I'll miss this place*, he realized. *I'll miss these people—my family. When will I see them again?*

When he came to the hallway lined with the portraits of his predecessors, he sucked in a breath of wonder. The moonlight was shining directly through the tall windows opposite the paintings illuminating them in eerie splendor.

The moon cast his own shadow along the wall beneath each ancestor as he ventured down its length. He remembered the first time he had come here—was it only six months ago?—and how he had longed to stop and stare as he was doing now. He had done so several times since his return, but never with such a feeling of solitude. There had always been the worry that someone would come upon him and wonder at his lingering. When he stood before his grandfather's portrait, he noted how like him he and his father were, yet different, too, of course. The former Lord Harwood had a ruddier complexion and light-brown eyes. His wife's portrait, forever beside him, testified to the origin of Jeremy's own darker eyes and fairer complexion and to the shape of his brow, too, which was different from his father's.

"Must you go away?"

If Jeremy had been armed, he might have run her through, so excessive was his surprise at Portia's trespass into his private reverie. He had seldom in his life let down his guard so entirely as he had just done, for he had never felt safe enough to do so. He had thought himself free at last to be incautious. She had proved him wrong and it made him unaccountably angry at her intrusion.

"What are you doing here?" he asked testily.

"Like you, I could not sleep. There is so much left unsaid—"

"And better left that way," he interrupted.

Portia pursed her lips defiantly and gave him the scolding look he had come to treasure, for it invariably was motivated by her deep concern for those around her. "It isn't better, Jeremy. Things left unsaid are often regretted. You're leaving tomorrow, and I fear you'll be gone for a long while, perhaps forever. I would always regret not telling you how I feel—"

"I cannot let you declare yourself, Portia." His heart was pounding in panic. "You cannot know... It would change everything."

Portia frowned, the hurt in her eyes threatening to spill over in tears. "Would it be that terrible to hear?"

"Not terrible, no." *Yes, more than terrible. Oh, Christ! I was so wrapped up in my own good fortune at knowing my family, I didn't think...* "'Tis enough I know," he said, trying to placate her. "And I'm sorry for any hurt I've caused you. I did not think to warn you off. You were like a sister to me—"

"But I'm not," she argued tearfully, taking hold of his upper arms in sudden desperation. "We are only cousins, Jeremy. I know you love another now, but if she should reject you—"

"Please stop," he commanded, pushing her gently away and holding her at arm's length. "Believe me when I tell you, Portia, I will only ever regard you as a sister. I will only ever love you as a sister."

"But I'm not!"

"You are." The words were out before he could stop them. He watched as her face grasped their import, then felt her tense up beneath his hands and pull away. And he realized at that moment, when he saw the look of despair and the beginnings of self-loathing on her young face, what he should do.

"Don't worry," he said soothingly, almost as would talk to a skittish horse. "I won't be back to plague your life. I promise. You can be secure in that."

"Never come back? I don't want that."

"You say that now, but I think you'll be glad of it someday."

"Oh, what have I done?" she asked, looking away in confusion.

"Nothing wrong, that's certain. It was *my* fault, and your father's, too, for not being wise enough to anticipate where our lies could lead. You must exonerate yourself of any blame, Portia. It is not your fault."

"And yet I love you," she said, looking at him like a curious child, as if she were seeing him for the first time. "I love you and it is not right that I should."

"I'm sorry," he said again, that phrase sounding hollow and inadequate. "Will you be all right? Shall I wake your mother?" He wasn't sure what desperate act such circumstances might precipitate in a young woman. Portia surprised him by laughing.

"Don't be silly, Jeremy. I'm not about to do myself harm just because I've fallen in love with the wrong man. If that had been my philosophy, I'd have been dead several times over by now, for you are not the first to win my heart, nor even the second."

He knew much of it was false bravado, but he admired once again his sister's fortitude. "I'm relieved to hear that."

She looked down at the floor for a moment, then back at him with sad eyes. "I shall always be embarrassed by this, but it would cause me even greater pain to think you were staying away from your own family just because I... You've come to know me fairly well these last weeks, Jeremy. I am not a weak woman."

"No. You're one of the strongest women I've ever known."

She smiled again, her eyes misty. "Then good night, Jeremy. And do not be gone too long. Now that I know who you are... That is, I would like to know you better. You are, after all, a dearer member of this family than I had realized."

He watched her turn and leave the gallery like a queen departing her council chambers. He hoped someday her knowledge of their true relationship would, indeed, inspire a more acceptable affection for him, the love of a little sister for a big brother.

He had missed that sort of love for too long already.

Chapter Seventeen

He told himself he wasn't stalling but he knew he was. It was easier to *think* about going to see Lillie than actually doing it. He sat in his new parlor, a glass of gin in one hand, awaiting the first dinner his new cook would put before him.

Upon leaving Edwin at his school in Lancaster, he had ridden north again with Mister Upton. He did not accompany him 'home' however, leaving the groom's company on the outskirts of Carlisle and continuing north into Scotland. He had lingered there almost a week, making the excuse that he had to arrange for the bulk of his money to be secured to a bank in Leeds, the rest upon his person. It was a risk he was taking, for if his true identity were discovered, any money in an English bank would be reclaimed by the crown. Of course he'd probably be at the end of a rope by then, but his heirs, if any existed, would be left penniless. *Ah, well, worry about that when it happens*, he thought.

Now he had been in Leeds for five days, avoiding the area of town where he might happen upon Lillie or Benjamin or *any* of the Tolvers. He had excused his delay by telling himself he needed to find rooms first and see to his banking, not to mention arranging for a servant or two—a cook and a house boy at least—before he would be able to take the time to see the Tolvers.

In truth, he wasn't sure of how to go about such a reunion. Should he just knock on the door and hope to be welcomed? Should he send a letter requesting to call? That seemed a little pretentious but might save everyone the uncomfortable surprise of an unannounced, and unwelcome, visit. Perhaps he could just hang around and hope to meet Lillie on her own, find out how she felt and how Benjamin had taken his unexpected departure. What if he ran into one of the others instead? He hadn't quite worked out what he would say to Lillie let alone Sam or one of her sisters or, heaven forbid, old Mister Tolver.

Perhaps he shouldn't go at all. He really didn't know Lillie Tolver all that well. When he thought of her now, he remembered only a kind, honest, and sympathetic woman who had the unnerving ability to read his mind, or maybe it was his heart she saw so clearly. He tried to recall her faults and couldn't bring to mind any except an unwillingness to let him hide his feelings from her. He hadn't seen any evidence of the acrimony or deceitfulness he had come to expect from women. Could she have hidden those qualities from him somehow?

Or perhaps he had been mistaken in those beliefs. His father had certainly thought him so. Portia had seemed an honest creature, as had his father's wife. Viola would be a flirt, he could discern that well enough, but she, too, seemed essentially earnest and trustworthy. Perhaps he had just been unlucky for so long, he had mistaken the truth of things. His mother he could not yet bring himself to forgive, but she was only one woman. His London ladies, when he reconsidered his experiences with them, had each acted according to their known characters. Rosalind Pettygrew had led a life of privilege. If she was spoiled and selfish, that was more attributable to her upbringing than her gender. Madge Whitcomb's betrayal of her friend should also not have surprised him, nor her randy willingness to couple with him. She had never really pretended to any loftiness of moral character and if she had, well, she *was* an actress after all.

And what of the judgment he had placed upon poor little Bess? The thought of her pained him afresh and he bowed his head and pinched his brow with one hand to stave off the heaviness in his eyes that threatened to develop into tears. Yes, she had chosen him over Mott, but if he wasn't being too arrogant, any woman would have. Tim Mott was an ill-kempt and mean-spirited dolt whose mistreatment of horses might well have foretold his inclination to mistreat the people in his life, including a wife or any children he might have had. Bess had surely been intelligent enough to see that. How could he have ever faulted her for choosing him over a worthless creature such as Mott? Had he been so hurt by the rediscovery of his mother's lack of sentiment that he had been willing to attribute that same callousness to even poor Bess. *She died to save you, you ungrateful bastard*, he scolded himself, his eyes misty with tears of self-loathing. *Does a person have to die before you'll believe they might actually love you?*

Jeremy took a swig of his drink and wiped impatiently at his eyes. All right, he was finally willing to rethink his former position. Women in general were not like his mother. Nor were they angels of perfection, he reminded himself, though the Lillie Tolver of his memories seemed nearly so. He thought he might actually love that woman, but was she real? How trustworthy were his memories?

He had known her for nearly six weeks last fall and for another two in March. Both times he had been recovering from a near-mortal wound, so *any* kindness would have been appreciated. Had his natural gratitude exaggerated her good qualities? She had also seemed to have the ability to see through his elusiveness, to understand how he was feeling despite his attempts to remain detached. He had not always appreciated that, but he had admired her intuitiveness and even welcomed the realization that she liked him— even loved him—despite his reserve.

She also was one of the few people who knew who he had been. A betrayal by her could do more than break his heart. It could get him hanged. Did he trust her enough to place his life in her hands?

Another thought troubled him more than any other. What had *he* to offer *her*? His ill-gotten wealth would not last forever. He had only vague notions of possible future endeavors. He had enjoyed working with wood and Mr. Tolver *had* told him he had some innate skill for the task. Was he too old to apprentice as a furniture maker? He had the advantage of having seen many examples of fine furnishings and thought he might even enjoy designing his own pieces and then carrying out their construction. He did not know, and could not know until he tried, whether he had the skill or the patience for such an occupation.

He knew he could do smithing again, though he was still far from being his former able self. But he balked at the idea of himself forever a smithy. It was satisfying work, and useful, but it was also hot, dirty—and here his conceit showed clearly—rather demeaning, for all its worthiness. His hands would never be clean again. His face would show the soot marks even after a thorough bath. It might serve as a profession for a time, but he could never abandon himself to it forever.

Working with horses appealed to him though. He seemed to have a natural comfort around them and a knack for dealing with their varying personalities. He had an eye for quality horse flesh, too, and thought he would do well as a breeder or the overseer at the stables on an estate. He had the capital to invest in a good stallion and few mares, but where to settle? Would his father, perhaps, give him a recommendation with some fellow aristocrat in need of a groom? Perhaps he would be allowed to see to his own horses on the side.

None of it was certain. Was it fair to reenter Lillie's life with so little certainty? But if he waited, would she be there when he had more to offer her?

It might be too late already, he reminded himself, and maybe that was for the best.

An image of Lillie seated with her head bowed over Missus Stone's mending—busy but not too busy to glance up occasionally to check on him and talk of small things—came into his mind and lingered pleasantly. The memory was like a visit with an old friend, but not entirely. For even in his debilitated state her simple beauty had moved him. He had studied her when she had not been looking, having little else to do while flat on his back, and had found himself wishing he could indulge his impulse to loosen her pale hair from its cap and see how far it fell along her trim back. How soft would that velvety-looking cheek feel beneath his fingers? He already knew the sweetness of her bow-shaped lips. During his convalescence they had looked even fuller and sweeter than he remembered them, especially when she smiled encouragingly at him. Even those soul-seeing crystalline eyes had stirred him. As much as he longed to stay removed from the world, he found himself longing to reveal everything about himself to this woman. He imagined how satisfying it would be to have done that and *still* be loved.

"Your supper's ready, sir," the thin, middle-aged cook, Missus Beale, called from the door of the parlor, interrupting his vision of Lillie. That both she and her thirteen year old son were remarkably thin probably did not speak well for her cooking, but she had been available to begin immediately and her boy, Thomas, had been willing to learn butlering and to run odd errands, all of which had suited Jeremy's spontaneous plans well.

He nodded and rose wearily to his feet. Perhaps after dinner he would be able to decide what his course should be.

Sir,

I am glad to hear you're not dead as we had all feared and have so well recovered from your injury that you are now setting up a residence of your own. Our prayers were answered on that score, which is always a gratifying occurrence.

*I regret I cannot offer you the hospitality of our home at this time but have a request to put forward from a certain young man as to whether **he** may come to visit you at your apartments instead. If this is agreeable, please inform Benjamin Harwood, for so he still calls himself, of a time that is convenient and we will send him along.*

Thank you for alleviating our worries by your correspondence. I wish you continued good health.

Jonathan Tolver

Jeremy read the reply Mr. Tolver's with mixed feelings. He was gratified that the old gentleman did not sound antagonistic toward him and even wished him well, and he felt an odd thrill of anticipation at being reunited with Benjamin, though he knew he was probably in for a scolding at having ducked out as he had. He did not mind enduring that, for he deserved it, and more.

But Lillie did not want to see him, that was certain. Her father would surely have shared the news of Jeremy's return with the family, and he also would have honored his daughter's wishes not to have "that man" —he could almost hear her saying it—come to call. She might even have cried. Jeremy could well understand why Mister Tolver would not want to see his little girl grieved further by the stranger who kept coming into their lives bringing nothing but sorrow and hurt feelings.

He thought of going to see her anyway. Would the old man bar the door to him? He thought not. He could stand before them, face to face, and beg their indulgence and their forgiveness for the shabby way he had treated them all, especially Lillie. Perhaps when presented with him in person, she would reconsider her feelings. Perhaps if he looked her in the eye and vowed to…

What? He only thought he *might* love her. He wanted another chance to talk with her and to know her better before making such a vow. All she would see in his eyes at this point was his continued uncertainty, and that wasn't likely to inspire her trust.

Better to leave it be. Better to go about his life and just resolve to do better by the next woman he might love. *It will be easier that way*, he told himself. *Easier for us all.*

But first there was Benjamin to see. He smiled at the thought and sat down to write an invitation. Tomorrow. At the boy's convenience. He would plan to be in all day. He sent the response off to the Tolver's via young Thomas, then set about discussing the next day's meals with Missus Beale.

Jeremy could not get over the change in the lad. It had been only two months since they had seen each other, but Benjamin was taller by nearly two inches it seemed and he had taken to tying back his wayward hair in a neat queue. His face, too, had matured. Jeremy had almost thrown his arms around the boy when he arrived, then thought better of it and settled for offering a heart-felt handshake.

Benjamin's response was none too warm. His former affability had transmuted into wariness, and Jeremy did not blame him. He showed the stiff-backed boy into the parlor and sat down opposite him.

"Aren't you going to rage at me for running off as I did?" he began with a grimace. "I'll not take it unkindly if you do. You have a right to be angry."

"It wasn't right," Benjamin agreed solemnly. "And we were as worried as could be, that's for sure. Why'd you do such a mean thing? We were only tryin' to help you."

Jeremy nodded. "It *was* mean, especially to you. You were no part of why I left. And though it's really no excuse, I think now the fever had my thinking confused. If my father hadn't sought me out, I'm not sure I'd be alive today."

"I thought it was something like that," Benjamin said, smiling for the first time.

Jeremy could see he had nearly been forgiven. Could it be so easy? Were young people so eager to forgive the adults in their lives? He remembered the many times he had done the same with his mother.

"You didn't seem quite yourself when you were givin' me all that money to hand about. I told Lillie that." His face looked suddenly embarrassed. "Sorry. I promised I wouldn't go bringin' her up and there I went and done it."

"Promised who?"

"Why, Lillie, of course. She was terrible hurt by your goin'. I promised I wouldn't tell you *that* either, but it's in me to say it. I can't see why I shouldn't, do you? Since she's so important to both of us?"

"No, but don't tell her I said so." He hesitated a minute before asking, "How do you know she was hurt?"

"Why, she cried when we first learned you was gone, of course. I even felt a bit like bawlin' myself. Mister Oaks was sore at you, too, when he found out you'd no one's leave to go 'cuz he said you told him it was all right. When Reggie got back he said you seemed fit enough when he dropped you off, if a bit tired. I wanted to come after you but Lillie said no, you had reasons to go so there was an end to it. Then she cried some more, but that weren't the worst of it." He bowed his head, looking sheepish again. "The worst of it was she didn't talk nor smile much for weeks afterward. Real mournful like. It was almost like you took part of her with you when you left. It was like she weren't Lillie anymore. Everyone noticed and you won't be too surprised they blamed *you* for it. It's just been lately she's seemed happy again. 'Til your letter came, that is."

"I'd supposed as much or I'd be taking tea with you and the rest of Tolvers right now."

"Right. Mister Tolver seemed willing to have you visit until Lillie ran upstairs crying and Rose told him he mustn't consider having 'that horrible man back in this house.' Those were her words, and when Martha agreed and Lillie kept crying, then wouldn't come down from her room for a time and then came down all quiet like, well, he figured you'd be too great a hurt to her."

187

Jeremy rested his forehead in his hand and let out an involuntary groan. Ah, he hadn't wanted to hurt her again. He shouldn't have come back.

"I shouldn't have come back," he said dully, giving his thoughts voice. "I should have left you all in peace."

"*I* wasn't in peace," Benjamin said, finally beginning his scolding. "I was always a-wonderin' where you was, alive somewheres or in some church yard moldin' away. It woulda troubled me all my life, that wonderin'. You're lucky you came back when you did, Jeremy, cause I can forgive you for the few months I been worried but I might not a been able to forgive years of it."

Jeremy tried to smile. "I'm glad, then, for your sake. You've been a true friend, Benjamin, and I haven't been even a fair one. But for Lillie's sake, I wish I'd have just found you out and left her alone. She didn't need to be hurt again."

"Why's she so upset anyway?"

"Maybe she worries more than you do," Jeremy offered lamely. "Women take things to heart more than we men do."

"It's more than that. It's like you spit on her or offended her honor or something."

Jeremy looked at the boy, now nearing manhood, and decided it wouldn't be out-of-place to confide in him. Perhaps it would save Benjamin from such similar foolishness when he was older.

"She told me she loved me and I told her I didn't love her, that's what. And I didn't say it very nicely either, as I recall. I didn't believe her, I guess, or I might have done better."

Benjamin looked down, seemingly embarrassed by the revelation, but when his eyes came up, there was more anger than embarrassment in them. "How could you do that to Lillie? She's the kindest soul I've ever met, *and* the most honest. If she told you she loved you, then you can take it for truth. Didn't you know that?"

He's still trying to find a way to respect me, Jeremy thought. *Go ahead. Admit you're a simpleton.*

"I didn't. I should have, for she was always forthright with me, but I didn't trust her. I don't trust many people. Never have. It'll get you killed."

"Or saved," the boy said sagely. "You just have to figure out who to trust and who not to."

Jeremy sighed heavily and leaned back in his chair. "I guess I've never trusted myself to be wise enough to figure out which was which. Easier to just distrust everyone."

Benjamin nodded and looked down to his hands again. "I figured out something while you was away the first time," he said quietly. "You been takin' the easy way for a long while. Robbin' was easier than workin'. Keepin' to yourself is easier than being sociable. Leavin' is easier than stayin'. But Jeremy, easier ain't always better. Fact is, most times it ain't."

Jeremy let Benjamin's words sink in and suddenly felt more ashamed of himself than he ever had before. *The boy's right! The easy way. I've always taken the easy way. What a poor excuse for a man I am!*

"You're not angry at me, are you?" Benjamin asked in alarm.

"At myself only," he admitted fiercely. "I don't know why you've put up with me from the start, nor why you came to help me like you did. Nor even why you're here now. I'm not worth your time, Benjamin, let alone worth your friendship. And I'm not worth the love of a woman like our Lillie. She's well rid of me."

"That ain't so. You're a fine gent in lots a ways. Or maybe it's something we sees in you that's there but waitin' to be better, you know? Like waitin' for an apple to grow on an old tree."

Jeremy couldn't help but smile at the analogy. "So now I'm an old apple tree? I'm not sure if that's a good thing to be or not."

Benjamin grinned. "Old apple trees are fine things. They may be a bit gnarly, but they're great to climb, to sit under, and, like I said, sometimes they ain't past givin' you an apple or two."

Jeremy wanted to rise and hug the boy for his faith in him but again it seemed too awkward. Instead he offered to take him riding. Benjamin frowned and shook his head. "Don't know much about riding horses. I'd prove myself a fool."

"Then it's well past time you learned. It's something I can give you, to make up for some of your worrying over me. I'd like to do that for you."

"Well, if you put it that way," Benjamin said warily. "Does it hurt much to fall?"

* * *

Jeremy had never been so nervous in his life. Not before his first sexual experience. Not before robbing a coach. Not even before killing Philip Bramhearst. It felt as if he might stop breathing if he didn't consciously force himself to keep doing so. How embarrassing it would be if he fainted! *Perhaps it would endear me to her*, he thought wryly, but forced himself to breathe nonetheless.

It seemed an interminable wait, though in truth the Tolver's little maid had only been gone from the front parlor a minute or two to tell the household of his arrival. To tell *Lillie* of his arrival, he cared not just now for the others. Would she send him on his way? Well, if she did, he would return again. And again. And again until she saw him, for during the last week of being with Benjamin on their daily riding lessons, he had had numerous glimpses of her through Benjamin's words—little snippets of conversation, stories about family doings, casually dropped information that made him hunger for her all the more—and he could finally honor her privacy no longer.

He would beg her to forgive him for hurting her with not only his words but his deeds. She would know that he cared for her, too. He would be honest and say he didn't know if it was true love but that he would like the chance to see if it were.

It was not Lillie's face that appeared in the archway, but Rose's. And she did not look pleased to see him.

"My sister sends her regrets, Mister Harwood, but she cannot see you now."

"When would be a more convenient time, Miss Rose?" he returned evenly.

"I don't think there will *ever* be a more convenient time," Rose replied.

"Then please inform your sister that I will be back to beg her forgiveness at some *in*convenient time and apologize for that inconvenience when I do."

Rose pursed her lips. "We're trying to be polite to you, Mister Harwood, but you will not have it so. Lillie doesn't want to see you...ever."

"Why?"

"Why?"

"Yes, has she told you why she will not see me? I understand only part of it, or thought I did. Now I am not so certain. Is it that she no longer cares for me or that she still does?"

Rose looked at him in astonishment. "This is most improper. It is not a question a gentleman should ask."

"I've few claims to that title," he said simply, "and at this moment, it serves me not at all. If being a gentleman means I must leave here bewildered and disappointed, then I don't want to be a gentleman."

Rose finally seemed moved to something like her old sympathy for him. "I don't know, Mister Harwood. I only know your presence here upsets her."

"Tell Lillie I'll keep coming back until I see her. If she truly wants me gone, it would be in her best interest to see me *now*, for then I will be gone from her life all the sooner. Please, Miss Tolver. Will you tell her that for me?"

Rose thought a moment then nodded. "I'll tell her—"

"I heard."

Lillie stood in the doorway, her back straight. To Jeremy she looked again like an angel, only this angel was the avenging sort. Her crystal-blue eyes met his with seeming coldness, but he saw the uncertainty behind them, too, and it gave him hope.

"May we speak privately," he said gently, glancing only momentarily at Rose.

Lillie nodded, then proceeded into the room, choosing the farthest chair from where he stood.

"You look well," he said, thinking she looked so wonderful he wanted to take her in his arms and hold her forever.

"And you. Much better than when last I saw you." Her voice was polite but humorless.

"I must ask your forgiveness for that. It was cruel of me to leave so suddenly after all your care of me. I have no good excuses, only poor ones."

"Then they shall have to do," she said. "You shall tell them and I shall listen, then I shall do my Christian best to forgive you and you can go away feeling less guilty than you do now."

Jeremy frowned. "Nothing you can say will make me feel less blameworthy. I ran away as I've always run away from the hard

191

things in my life. It's easier to do so but, as Benjamin so wisely informed me, it is usually not the best course to follow. I didn't want to believe you truly loved me. I told myself that you were just another in a string of witless women who fancied me only. When I reconsider that time—a difficult undertaking, I assure you, for much of it is unclear—but when I look back on it, I realize I may have been more afraid that you *did* truly love me than that you were just another mistaken chit from whom I must disentangle myself. It frightened me that you had given your heart to me."

"Because you didn't want it," she said simply, but he thought he heard a catch in her voice.

"Because I don't deserve it," he corrected her gently, finally crossing the room to sit near her. More than anything he wanted to take one of her hands in his, but he feared her withdrawal. "I still don't."

She looked at him then and the earnestness he saw on her face made him draw in a breath of expectancy. "Jeremy, none of us 'deserve' love. It is a gift we give each other."

"I cannot believe that. Surely we earn each other's love or enmity by our daily conduct. Look how I have lost the love you once offered by my actions."

"You have not lost my love," she confided with a smile, "only my trust for a time. *That* must be earned, I fear."

Now he took her hand without even thinking. He did not know what to say, only was glad that she was offering him one of the smiles he had treasured remembering all these months. "I love you," he heard himself saying, and realized he meant it to the core of his being. Her smile broadened. "I swear I'll never hurt you again."

Lillie laughed a little and touched the side of his face with her free hand. "You can't keep that promise, Jeremy. None of us could. But you *can* swear never to leave again without a good-bye, for that is my greatest fear."

"I swear it on my life," he said gravely. "'Twas poorly done both times."

"And promise me you'll start thinking yourself worthy of loving, for you are. To think otherwise makes me a fool for loving you."

He looked baffled. He had never thought of it that way. Benjamin had tried to tell him much the same thing. "I'm an old apple tree," he said reflectively.

"What?"

He smiled. "Even an ugly old apple tree has some worth—to climb, to sit under. I don't know if I've any apples to give, but I'll try. I'll try as hard as I'm able, Lillie."

"'Tis all anyone can ask of another," she replied.

Epilogue

The moon danced upon the wind-chased clouds like a ship in a stormy sea. He hoped it was late enough to avoid seeing any familiar faces except Hobbs' for he would hate to stir up any speculation concerning his existence now that his new life was going so well. It was a risk he had to take, though Lillie hadn't fully agreed.

"You could send it to him," she had urged. "Jeremy, it's too dangerous. The world thinks you're dead."

"Why would Hobbs renounce me? He profited by my thievin' as much as I did."

"His daughter's also dead because of you. He might shoot you on the spot, forget about turning you in."

Jeremy had shaken his head. "I don't think so. And it's too precious to send by mail. Only half of anything gets through."

And so he had said good-bye, as he had vowed he would, with a promise to return in a few days, and had ridden off to Howden to return the locket Bess had once given him.

He had found it when he'd cleared his bank box in Scotland, had forgotten even that he had put it there nearly a year before. She had wanted him to wear it around his neck beneath his shirt but he had declined at once. He might lose it, he argued. It would tie them together if he were captured, he said, for she had installed a crude portrait done by some passing artist within it. It had been her mother's, didn't she want to keep it? He didn't tell her the real reason, that it would unnecessarily hamper any other dalliances he might enter into along his way. But she had insisted he take it and keep it somewhere to remember her by. So he had taken it to Scotland when next he'd gone and absentmindedly stashed it there with the other trinkets he'd brought.

When he had seen it again, he had recognized its worth, not in coin but in sentiment. It rightfully belonged to Mister Hobbs, who

194

had lost his only daughter that terrible night, not just a sometime lover as he had.

The inn was dark, just as Jeremy had expected it to be at this hour, but he reined in Pat and looked down the hill for a minute, fear tingling his spine. It looked so much like that other night, the one when a sudden flash and explosion had echoed in the silence and unalterably changed his life and ended Bess'. It was foolish to think it could happen again, yet the fear was there. He took a few deep breaths to calm his racing heart, then nudged Pat forward cautiously.

There was no quieting the horse's hooves in the cobbled yard, but a sleeping guest would likely think it just a late-arriving traveler. He went to the window of the room he knew Hobbs usually occupied and tapped tentatively on it with his riding crop. All was quiet. Not even Hobbs' snoring sounded behind the shutters. But somewhere…

He guided Pat around to the other corner of the inn and looked up at Bess' window. He almost expected that she would open it if he whistled that tune she had liked so well. The first few notes came to his lips, then he stopped himself and listened again. Someone was snoring behind the closed shutters, but whether it was Hobbs or some guest using Bess' room, he didn't know.

I'll leave the locket in the cubby next to the lamp post, he thought, *then write to Hobbs of its whereabouts. Anonymously, of course, or Lillie will worry.*

He smiled at the thought of her, waiting for him back in Leeds. He worked at Lord Haverston's stables on his estate outside Leeds— had been lately given charge of it as the old head groom was getting too old to continue—but he had managed to see her each Sunday for nearly three months. They were to wed come the next spring and she would be living with him in a little cottage behind the gate house. His secret aspirations still included raising his own horses but he was content for the time being. More than content. He was actually happy.

He pulled a loose notch of wood from the side of the inn revealing a little hole big enough for a sack of gold to fit into. The locket, wrapped in a little handkerchief, was nowhere near that big and he pushed it as far back as he could so that a casual searcher might miss it altogether. Then he fit the notch back into place.

Deborah Ballou

He wasn't sure why he went back to the window and looked up. Maybe it was because he hadn't ever gotten a chance to say good-bye to Bess. The last time he'd seen her, she'd been leaning down as far as she could to touch his hand in farewell. The smell of roses from her loosened hair had washed over him in a sweet wave of enchantment. He could almost smell them again as he remembered kissing her hair in some grandiose show of affection. What a thoughtless ass he'd been. She had loved him and he had treated it all like a game.

"I'm sorry, Bess," he said quietly to the shuttered window.

Then he turned his horse and rode away, looking back once more before the brow of the hill hid the Running Lion from his view.

He did not see the wide-eyed Joan, the little kitchen maid he had often teased about her red hair being spun of gold worth stealing, peering out the side door of the inn, nor the sleepy eyes of the new stable boy who'd thought he'd heard a late-night traveler to tend to. The boy, of course, had never seen the strange rider before, but Joan had not forgotten him, and the boy's confirmation of the mysterious visitor loaned credence to the excited tale she would tell for years.

"I seen him myself! Poor Jeremy Knox's ghost it was, big as life, though pale as the grave, of course. Rode right over to her window and looked up, whistled for her, then waited for little Bess Hobbs to open it like she used to do. I almost cried when I saw him, for I never seen such a sad look on a face in my life. Then he just rode away over that hill yonder, and I hope I never see the likes o' him again, though I 'spect I will. He's been doomed for his sins, that's certain, an' won't find no rest 'til he finds his lady love."

196

...And still of a winter's night, they say, when the wind is in the trees,
When the moon is a ghostly galleon tossed upon cloudy seas,
When the road is a ribbon of moonlight over the purple moor,
A highwayman comes riding—riding, riding—
A highwayman comes riding up to the old inn-door.

Over the cobbles he clatters and clangs in the dark inn-yard;
He taps with his whip on the shutters, but all is locked and barred;
He whistles a tune to the window, and who should be waiting there
But the landlord's black-eyed daughter—Bess, the landlord's daughter—
Plaiting a dark red love-knot into her long black hair.

The Highwayman,
by Alfred Noyes, 1880-1958

About the Author

"*The Highwayman* is quite a departure from my first novel, *Yeshua Wept*, but for me, variety is what keeps writing fun," says Deborah Ballou, a former technical writer and high school English teacher. "It's especially wonderful to find a subject that *compels* me to write, and even more wonderful when my readers enjoy what I've written." Mrs. Ballou lives in northern California with her husband, son, and daughter.

Printed in the United States
34048LVS00003B/76

9 781403 305930